F
H78   Horbach, Michael.
                Out of the night.

OUT OF THE NIGHT

OUT
of the
NIGHT

by

Michael Horbach

Translated from the German by Nina Watkins

A World of Books That Fill a Need

FREDERICK FELL, INC.   NEW YORK

CONTENTS

" Out of the night that covers me,
Black as the pit from pole to pole,
I thank whatever gods might be
For my unconquerable soul."

INVICTUS, by W. E. Henley.

Foreword

This is a book of uneven fragments; but they are worth taking trouble over, because they are fragments of vital episodes. Moreover, they come from a situation—Nazi Germany in wartime—that, although quite recent, is so strange that nobody who did not experience it at first hand can find it easy to understand. Even fragments of information of how people actually behaved then may be of value in helping us to understand what happened.

The author has gone to great trouble to collect and tell imaginatively the stories of a few individuals who acted with exceptional courage and humanity in those circumstances. The book is based on interviews with survivors of Nazi persecution and with those who helped them. These brief accounts do not tell us as much as one would like to know about these individuals. But, at least, we meet these exceptional people and gain a glimpse of their personalities.

To me, the most moving of these stories are those about apparently ordinary people. The Berlin hairdresser who hides his old client behind a wardrobe for several years—and then takes in another man on the run, who is a stranger to him, as well. The school-teacher, who happens to be Jewish, and his wife and child, who survive in Berlin throughout the entire war, moving from house to house and earning his living by private tuition : part of his technique of survival was learning always to look his enemy in the eye and never to seem afraid.

Although it is numbing and deeply disturbing to read what happened to individuals in this Dark Age of yesterday, it is inspiring to learn how people you would never pick out in a crowd as unusual behaved superbly. Nobody can, of course, tell what he himself would have done under such circumstances : but everyone must have serious doubts that he could have done what so few proved able to do.

It is the *sanity* of those who remained unfrightened and humane in a vicious society that comes through so strikingly in these short stories. Everyone around them was either hectoring or terrified : they managed to go on behaving ordinarily. If they were Jews and treated as outcasts fit only for extinction, they nevertheless managed to behave with the composure and judgement of people who were still masters of their fate. If they were non-Jewish and threatened with fiendish punishments should they depart from the Nazi code, they managed to continue behaving towards their fellow human beings as they would have done in non-Nazi circumstances.

Some day we may know more about what makes people enjoy persecuting and what gives others the sanity to resist playing this deadly game. We may also know more about the epic qualities of those who can stand insane treatment without becoming demoralised.

These stories do not indicate the answers ; but they enable us to exchange glances with these heroes of sanity. It is a privilege to meet them.

July, 1967   DAVID ASTOR

" *If international Jewry, the controlling power behind finance in Europe and elsewhere, succeeds in precipitating the nations into another world war, the outcome will not be the world-wide triumph of Bolshevism and, thereby, of Jewry, but the extermination of the Jewish race in Europe.*"

Adolf Hitler to the Reichstag, January 30, 1939.

1

Winter, 1944-45. The Red Army was pressing forward into East Prussia. The Reich Security Head Office issued an order: all concentration camp inmates in the area to be assembled *en masse* near Königsberg. No prisoner was to fall into Russian hands as a living witness.

Celina Manielewitz was 23 then. She was a prisoner in the Jessau camp, about 33 miles from Königsberg, with 700 other young Polish Jewesses; before that she had been in the notorious Stutthof camp, near Elbing.

The Jessau women had to fell trees in the surrounding woods, to clear a plot of land where the Luftwaffe, it seemed, wanted to build another front-line aerodrome. They never got round to it.

The Jessau conditions were the usual ones: watery soup, mouldy bread, hunger, spotted typhus, ill-treatment and shootings.

It was a foggy January day in 1945 when the camp was evacuated. The 700 Jewesses were driven on a forced march in the direction of Königsburg. Meanwhile, 10,000 prisoners from other camps had been rounded up in the snow-laden fields near the East Prussian capital; they just stood there, under the open sky. When the Jessau group arrived they pressed on, this time towards the north-east.

The enormous column dragged itself through knee-deep snow—men, women, old people, children. They marched five abreast, guarded by Lithuanian S.S. under German command. They wore their scanty camp uniforms—nothing else. One or two were lucky enough to possess rugs to wrap around themselves. Occasionally somebody would collapse with exhaustion; the other prisoners would fling themselves on him and tear the rug off. Crazy fights ensued with the skinny fists flying madly around and the broken stumps of teeth grinning in distorted faces. Eyes blazed insanely, beast-fashion. During such "incidents" the S.S. fired ruth-lessly into the ranks. If a prisoner stooped to quench his thirst with a handful of snow, the Lithuanians shot him out of hand.

Celina Manielewitz marched in that column, too. She had nothing on her but her so-called working outfit, a creation of prison grey, and her heavy wooden clogs made every step a torture.

Celina had fever. She mumbled disjointedly to herself, without knowing what she was saying; she staggered behind the person in front, putting one foot before the other without knowing what she was doing. The hoarse shrieking of the crows that encircled the column ravaged her eardrums.

The S.S. marched alongside the main column, but only for a short distance. Within the hour, some sledges arrived; they took their seats and rested. Other guards sprang from the sledges and set about the walking corpses with renewed vigour—cursing, flogging, shooting.

After three days and nights of continuous marching the column finally reached Palmnicken. Seven hundred of the 10,000 marchers had died of exhaustion, or been shot, in the meantime.

At Palmnicken the prisoners were housed in a large factory building, the Burstin works. The mayor of the place, who obviously had some human sensibilities, organised a share-out of potatoes when he heard of their arrival. It worked out at three potatoes a head. In the process the prisoners, half demented with hunger, rushed at the crates, fought desper-ately for every potato and trampled one another underfoot. Celina went away hungry. She did not have the strength to fight for her food.

They stayed in the factory for days. It was cold; they had nothing to eat or drink; and again countless people died. Suddenly, one evening, soon after dark, they were called out. They had to line up outside five abreast. In a few minutes they were on the march, flanked to right and left by heavily-armed S.S. There must have been at least a thousand of them; and they had sub-machine guns. Even the accom-panying sledges were mounted with machine-guns. They were heading for the Baltic Sea. It was the evening of January 31, 1945.

So far, Celina had told her story without faltering. But now she was silent; and I could see the tortured memories in her eyes.

I waited. For a while there was silence in the room. As I gazed out of the window I could see, in the yellow haze of noon, the hills girding the city of Jerusalem; the tawny brown sand like the fur of a scruffy jaguar, flecked with the patchy vegetation of the region; and above it all the tenuous glimmer of a transparent layer of mist, a trembling aura of heat. . . . The night was radiant over Jerusalem when I arrived the day before to hear her story; of her escape, and the people who helped.

I scrutinised Celina's face: chubby, yet delicate, and crowned with thick, black hair. Neither the years nor the horror of the past had etched their pattern in this face. Only the shade of eternal sadness lay across it, indicating that she had experienced something frightful.

She tried to pull herself together. She murmured desperately, " I've forgotten, I've forgotten."

Her husband laid a comforting hand on her arm. He was a customs official at the Mandelbaum Gate, the Israel-Jordan crossing point; a slim, sunburned Polish Jew who, with bitter tenacity, had built a new life here for himself and his family.

" Go on," he said protectively. " Tell him everything. I'm here—remember."

She nodded slowly. Her black eyes wandered from her husband to me. Then she told it.

" We were still marching in fives. In my row there were Genia Weinberg, Manja Zweig, Fela Lewcowicz and another girl I didn't know. The Germans had started a rumour that at the coast we'd be put on board ship for Hamburg; we didn't believe it. We believed the Germans meant to kill us. We saw the pickets; a guard every five yards with submachine guns pointed at us; and the heavily armed sledges, travelling constantly up and down the column. We didn't believe the evacuation story; we were too exhausted to build

5

up such hopes. We'd stopped thinking. We didn't give a damn.

Suddenly we heard a terrific shooting coming from up front, where the men were marching. Flares flew up and illuminated the whole landscape. It was only later that I heard that, at that moment, a group of 300 prisoners had gone for the S.S. with their bare hands. They were all shot. We saw their bodies lying in the snow when we passed the spot where they had tried, in their desperation, to get rid of their tormentors.

Then, the rumour: the S.S. are driving us into the sea!

This was true, we knew it at once.

Where were the ships that were waiting for us, then? We were making for a steep headland with dangerous rocks. There was no harbour anywhere, no kind of bay where a big ship could anchor. Besides, there were still over 8,000 of us. What ship could carry these 8,000—here on this desolate coast?

'We've had it,' Genia whispered to me. I could only nod. I was so worn out that I was quite indifferent. I didn't even have the strength to bend down for the guard to shoot me. I just stumbled along in my row without looking left or right. I'd lost my clogs long ago; I was just staggering barefoot in the snow.

Again we heard shooting—quite near this time—from up front. This time it didn't stop.

We were getting nearer. Again the flares flew up and we could see it: the coast, lying before us. Great, steep cliffs sloping down to the sea. S.S. men with machine-guns stood on the rocks to the left and right of us. They drove the prisoners to the edge of the precipice and shot them down mercilessly. If anyone tried to turn back he was soon grabbed by the armed guards before he could manage a step.

We said our goodbyes.

Those in front of us shrank back horrified from the frightful abyss opening out at their feet; their shrieks ripped the night open. I was so numbed, mentally, that it didn't affect me.

'Get going!' the S.S. chief in charge of the operation shouted. I knew him—Sergeant Stock, a great blond hulk, and a pitiless bully. When he saw us young girls he bounded over to us.

6

'Get down,' he yelled, 'down, you Jew bitches.' He swung his gun and hit Genia with the butt in the small of the back. She staggered and fell over; an S.S. man pushed her over the cliff edge. Then I was knocked with the butt, too—in the back of my neck—and I reeled. I saw the abyss before me and hurtled over. Then I felt nothing.

When I came to again I was lying half in water and half on an ice-block. There were the great slopes above me, the open sea behind me. People were still falling over the cliff, the machine-guns still barking. All around, in that grey-green sea, corpses were floating, half hanging on the ice blocks. The wounded were moaning; some prayed to God to let them die.

Suddenly it was quiet up there; the last salvoes from the machine-guns died away.

Then: dark figures on the beach, S.S. men who'd climbed down.

'If you're still alive lift up your head!' they screamed. And those poor creatures who were still living lifted their heads in one final, lethargic movement; the sentries sprang from one iceberg to another and finished them off.

Fela Lewcowicz lay at my feet. I heard her moan. I wanted to crawl over to her, but then she raised her arm, shouting:

'I'm still alive, Mr. Guard!'

One of the S.S. turned and shot her in the temple, a few inches from my feet.

'Don't move,' a voice behind me whispered. Genia.

I don't know how long we lay there, like that. Icy water gnawed away at our skin and bones. I knew we'd never survive if we had to lie there much longer. Why shouldn't I lift my head, too, and let them shoot me? There was no escape, anyway.

Then, suddenly, I started. Genia had been shaking me, waking me up. 'They've gone,' she whispered.

I propped myself up on my elbows. Far as the eye could reach, in that misty dawn, we saw a welter of swirling corpses, washed by the current to the open sea or slowly sinking.

The S.S. had vanished. We gazed at the cliff top: no trace of the murderers.

Genia got up. As she stood there, Manja's figure raised itself not far from me. She, too, had survived the massacre. A miracle.

Genia jumped from the ice block ; the water was up to her hips. Slowly, she waded ashore. While she tore pieces of clothing and rugs from the corpses floating around us, Manja and I slipped into the water, too, and followed. On the beach she gave us the rugs, and we wrapped them round us. All our limbs were trembling and our teeth chattering. I was shaking with cold and fever. I'd swallowed sea water, and was pretty sick. Laboriously, we clambered to the top of the cliff ; there wasn't the slightest trace of S.S.

I could hardly put one foot before the other. Manja was very weak, too ; but Genia kept driving us on.

'We can't let up,' she said. 'If we hold out now, we're saved.'

In the distance we heard a rumble, like thunder.

'The front line,' whispered Genia, 'the Russians. If we can hang on just a few days—if we can hide somewhere—we're all right.'

But where could we hide ?

After struggling up that cliff we looked around : over the flat, pale landscape. Only the misty twilight shielded us.

Our ragged clothes froze solidly to our bodies, and we were soon covered with a white layer of ice. I simply couldn't go on. I wanted to sit down for just a moment, just to rest ; but Genia hurried me on.

'If we sit down now we're done for,' she insisted. 'We must go on.'

She kept saying that as we staggered through the snow, the three of us. We must go on. We must go on.

We'd been stumbling along like that for about an hour, I suppose, when we saw the dark outline of a small village before us. Smoke rose from the chimneys, forming blue curls in the cold air.

It was very quiet ; it was still early in the morning. We approached the houses and knew we had to stake everything on one throw. We couldn't go any further ; in bright daylight they'd find us anyway.

But which door to knock at ? Germans lived in every

house. We were Polish Jewesses who'd escaped the massacre; how could we pick out, instinctively, the home of a German who wouldn't betray us to the murderers right away?

But Genia had made up her mind; she went up to the very first house, a farmhouse with a number of outhouses.

Genia banged on the door.

Dumbly we stood and waited. At last, approaching footsteps; the door opened.

A woman stood in the doorway. She was frightened to death when she saw us. All the colour left her face. Without a word, she whirled round and went quickly back into the house. Then a man appeared—a big, uncouth-looking type.

'What d'you want here?' he asked. Pity and fear, repulsion and horror mingled in that face.

'Hide us, please,' said Genia. 'We're the sole survivors from last night. Don't send us away—please.'

The man's face twitched.

'I'll get shot if they find you,' he said.

'Please, give us something to eat,' whispered Manja.

The man hesitated. His wife shouted something from the kitchen.

'Come on, then.' He glanced quickly in all directions. 'Did anybody see you?'

We shook our heads.

He pushed the door open and we entered the house. We were conducted to a flight of stairs leading up to the first floor and from there up to the attic.

'Get a move on—and keep quiet!' the farmer ordered.

We scrambled upstairs. There was a pile of straw in one corner; we threw ourselves down, pulled our rugs over our heads and had dropped off to sleep before the farmer could shut the trapdoor again. We were saved."

Saved—but for how long? The Russian advance, which they had hoped would bring them liberty, had got bogged down. For eight whole days the girls squatted up in the farm's dark granary. They heard the rumble of big guns from the front; but they also heard it subside. They knew what that meant.

The place where they had found shelter was called

Sorginau. Every evening Voss, the farmer who was hiding them, came with a small bucket full of warm soup and a couple of slices of bread. Sometimes he brought hot tea as well—in an old tin pot.

He never spoke to the girls, and they were too terrified to start a conversation. They accepted the food shyly, without a word.

Voss was a heavy man, dark, rather uncanny. He was probably in his late forties. Sometimes his probing eyes moved over the girls, taking in every detail, when he stood at the head of the stairs and waited for them to finish eating. There was no kindness in those eyes.

They were afraid of Voss, but obviously they didn't dare show it openly—he had saved them, after all.

The noise from the front grew fainter and with it the girls' hopes. Their spirits sank from day to day; and when the distant rumble ceased altogether they knew that they were done for, barring a miracle.

On the eighth day Voss came up to the attic room at noon. His manner was, if anything, more morose than usual. He ordered the girls downstairs.

They tottered out into the yard, blinking in the harsh sunlight mirrored in the trodden brightness of the snow. They hadn't had any fresh air for over a week.

"I can't hide you any longer," Voss said without looking at them. "Our boys have beaten the Russians back again. You've got to go."

"You can't do that to us!" Genia cried.

"Get going."

"We can't go any further. Where could we go? Better if you shot us!"

"Let the others do that!"

Horrified, unbelieving, the three girls stared into the farmer's face.

At this point, I interrupted Mrs. Manielewitz's story.

"Did that fellow Voss really say that?"

She nodded. "Yes. That I can swear to. My two friends, Genia and Manja, live in the States today. They're witnesses. You can ask them."

It is perhaps appropriate to state here that all Celina

Manielewitz's statements have been confirmed by eyewitness accounts, given under oath to the Yad Washem Institute, Jerusalem. The Institute is exclusively concerned with the history of the persecution of the Jews, but particularly with the investigation of actions which saved Jews.

It is hard, almost impossible, to project one's self back into that era ; to fathom, after twenty years, the thoughts and emotions of a man like Voss.

Imagine; this dour East Prussian farmer goes and conceals three Jewish girls for eight days ; young things, wild with terror, who had cheated death by a fraction of an inch. He conceals them, only to drive them out to certain doom a week later.

Did he hope to get into the Russians' good books when they marched in, for having hidden three Jewesses ? Was it a sudden impulse that made him act like that eight days previously ? Did he regret it later ? Did he start getting cold feet because the Russians hadn't arrived and the Germans were still around ?

" That man, who had hidden us for eight whole days, now wanted to send us out to be murdered.

' Get going, or I'll hand you over to the Gestapo,' he threatened. We just stood there. The thin rags we'd worn ever since the night of the massacre didn't help much against the cold. We'd left our rugs up in the attic, because we'd had no idea what Voss meant to do with us. We stood barefoot in the snow, freezing.

' All right,' Voss snarled when we showed no sign of shifting. He wheeled round and strode out of the yard.

We looked at Genia, helpless.

' Come on—quick, quick,' she whispered when Voss was out of sight. She hustled us to a shed which served as a storage place for coal and firewood. We slipped inside and burrowed under the coal and logs till we could hardly breathe. Nobody would find us here. After a while we heard footsteps, then voices, and finally a dog panting heavily. They had come back with a police dog!"

On Voss's land, in an adjoining building, another family

11

lived. Both man and wife were in their early fifties. The woman had noticed that Voss had been sheltering refugees. She had also noticed that on that particular afternoon he'd tried to send the girls away again—in clothes which hung off them in tatters and with no shoes on.

" I was standing by the kitchen window, listening to them talking outside," Mrs. Harder reported later. " I peeped out and saw Voss disappearing out of the yard gate. I knew him. I could well imagine what he was up to : betraying the girls to save his own skin. His own courage had scared him. No doubt he thought that if he now gave the girls away, the authorities would turn a blind eye to his having harboured them a few days. He could always say he'd taken them for ordinary refugees, and only found out later they were Jews. Who can tell what went on inside his thick skull ? Anyway, I could see at once that the blighter was actually making for the local police depot where the S.S. were quartered, too. The three girls, poor dears, stood rooted to the ground at first ; then the tall one hustled the other two to our wood-shed. They vanished inside in no time.

I went out. When I got to the yard gate—it was open—I could see Voss coming back with a couple of S.S. They had a police dog on lead.

One of them spoke to me. ' Heil Hitler. Seen a couple of girls drifting around these parts ? It's a case of escaped Jewesses.'

' Oh ? Yes, I did see something. Three gypsies, I thought. They were making for that wood.' I pointed to a copse nearby.

The dog was tugging at the lead ; he wanted to get to the yard. Where we were standing the snow was all trodden down—you couldn't distinguish individual tracks any more.

' Are you sure they went to the wood ? '

' Yes, I tell you. Surely Mr. Voss must have seen them, too.' Voss turned purple. ' I didn't see anything,' he snarled.

' Okay, we'll take a closer look at the wood,' said one of the S.S. He pulled the dog away ; it was still dragging on the lead and snuffling with its nose in the air.

I went back indoors ; I was pretty agitated. I'd seen those three girls distinctly ; they were just skin and bone and looked as if they'd had a ghastly experience. I made up my mind to help them."

From their hideout the three girls listened to the conversation out in the yard, hardly daring to breathe. They heard a woman talk to a couple of men; they also heard the woman say she thought the three " gypsies " had fled to the wood. They were choked with fear when they heard the dog snuffling and snarling; but eventually the men's crunching footsteps in the snow died away, and everything was quiet again.

Trembling with cold, Celina and the others waited for the night. Then they could slink out; where to they had no idea. Prostrate under heaps of coal and firewood, they listened to the farmyard noises, felt hunger burn their entrails and sensed, too, the ghastly recurrence of fear. Fear is something you can't get used to. It is always new and always horrible.

Eventually darkness fell. After a while they heard timorous footsteps outside. Someone was at the door of the shed. He entered. The man whispered: " I'm Albert Harder. Remember the woman who didn't give you away this afternoon ? I'm her husband. We want to help you. Come out."

The girls did not answer. They feared a trap.

" I wonder if they are still alive ? " the man whispered. And behind him, the voice of the woman: " They're probably just frightened."

Harder began clearing the bundles of wood away. That was how he found them; frozen stiff with cold and numbed by their cramped immobility in the dark shed. They couldn't move their limbs any more; Harder had to get them across the yard one at a time. He carried them on his back to a pigsty; under its roof was a little recess, a kind of dovecote, then they were taken up a ladder. They couldn't stretch themselves properly up there—they could only squat—but at least they were over the worst.

"The cold up there was awful," Celina reported. "We were still wet through and half frozen; our clothes were sticking to us. Once every twenty-four hours Harder brought us food. The atmosphere above the sty was suffocating; we had lice; we had no water and no means of washing. Once we begged

13

Mr. Harder to bring us some water, but he said: 'If you wash yourselves now you'll all die of pneumonia.'

In about a week he came to the sty and said we should come down. We didn't trust him; not after our experiences with Voss. Harder wanted to give us away, too—that's what we suspected. We were like terrified, hunted animals, no longer capable of logical reasoning; and we simply refused to get down that ladder. So he had to come up to us and pull us, by force, out of our niche. We couldn't resist; we were still too weak. Our half-paralysed limbs were of no use to us.

It was pitch dark outside. Harder carried us, separately, into the house. Wooden troughs with hot water, and some clean towels and soap, were waiting for us in the kitchen. There were some linen nightdresses on a chair; Mrs. Harder had laid them there all ready for us. She immediately got us out of the rags we were still wearing and took them out to her husband, who burnt them in the stove.

When I caught a glimpse of myself in the mirror on the kitchen wall I nearly fainted. I looked like an old woman, not like a young girl of twenty-three.

Mrs. Harder washed us as if we were small children. The tears were pouring down our faces—with pleasure, excitement and exhaustion. Finally, she took us to her bedroom and tucked us in the big double bed. There were three hot-water bottles in it. . . ."

Celina Manielewitz's voice began to tremble. She gazed past me at her husband and he nodded encouragingly at her. She went on, her voice oddly broken. "You can't imagine what that meant to us. It was almost too much. It was like a dream—having a proper bed again, for the first time after long years of concentration camp! We couldn't really grasp it. Before we were fully conscious that this was reality, not a dream, we'd fallen asleep.

We had a long, deep sleep; then Mrs. Harder appeared in the bedroom about nine next morning and woke us. She carried an enormous breakfast tray.

We cried all over again, the three of us, like children; but then we attacked that breakfast. There was a big food shortage just then, even for the German population, but what Mrs.

Harder dished up appeared to us like a heavenly banquet. Eggs, marvellous farmhouse bread, butter, marmalade, cheese. And steaming hot coffee—black coffee made from real beans.

"We ate and laughed and cried; and meanwhile had to tell Mrs. Harder—quietly, keeping our voices down so that no one could hear—what we had gone through. She nodded to everything we said, murmuring all the time—my poor children. Here, in the midst of our enemies, the Germans, we three Polish girls—and Jewish, too—had suddenly found a mother!"

One has to form a mental picture of the situation at that time. The Russians were making concentrated attacks on the German front in East Prussia. Behind the front there was constant fear of Soviet spies and Polish partisans. Every suspicious character was arrested on the spot; every soldier who couldn't produce papers was strung up on the nearest tree as a "deserter." S.S. contingents reconnoitred the area; police observation was stringent; the party big boys equipped the populace with old guns and drove the Hitler Youth to the front.

In these circumstances, the help which the Harder family gave the Jewish girls involved a gamble with death. People harbouring escaped prisoners-of-war or concentration camp inmates were, if caught, invariably propped up against a wall within twenty-four hours.

This didn't worry the Harders, however. "The children stay here—to the bitter end, if need be!" Mrs. Harder said. Her husband said nothing, just nodded. After a while, he remarked: "You know, mother, I'm glad we can do this; so many bad things have happened. . . ."

After a magnificent breakfast the girls immediately fell asleep again. They slept the whole day through, waking only at evening. Mrs Harder came to their room and clapped her hands above her head in surprise. "Heavens, you're young girls after all! This morning you still looked like old women!"

Then they got their briefing.

"We can't keep you buried here for ever. You have to

come out of hiding some time. You've got to be legalised.
We'll say you're refugees from Memel, German nationals."

After that, Celina Manielewitz was called Elsa, Genia was
transformed into Gerda and Manja got the name of Maria.

" Naturally you had to leave everything at home ; you took
off overnight, and didn't even manage to bring your hand-
bags with your private papers. You were only too glad to
get away from the Russians."

Mrs. Harder impressed on them that their heads had been
shaved because they had caught typhus.

The girls listened obediently. They gazed, hypnotised, at
Mrs. Harder's square-featured, kindly face with the healthy,
glowing cheeks and the delicate golden down on the upper
lip. They hung on every word from her full, pretty lips. For
the first time in years they were in the presence of someone
who wished them well.

Left alone again, they cried themselves to sleep with
emotion, weakness and helpless joy.

Next morning Mrs. Harder got hold of a Memel telephone
book. The girls had to learn all sorts of addresses by heart,
so that they could corroborate their story in the event of a
stiff cross-examination.

When Mrs. Harder had gone, Manja asked, doubtfully :
" Do you really think people will fall for *that* ? They're sure
to recognise us. Take Voss—he actually lives here, on this
estate. . . ."

Genia cut her short. " Be thankful we've got this far. What
more can we expect ? With a bit of luck, we'll make it.
Cheer up !"

They cheered up. And they could feel secure, even ;
because the Harders, simple, decent farming people, radiated
a confidence and serenity which was soon communicated to
the girls.

Harder was a tall, thick-set man ; his round skull sat
squarely on broad shoulders ; when the girls looked at him
he smiled kindly. Then his eyes gleamed, little wrinkles
played over his weather-beaten, yet still unravaged, cheeks,
and he'd smooth his bristling hair with a rapid, somewhat
embarrassed gesture.

" Everything will be all right again," he'd say in his vibrant, sympathetic bass, " you'll see!"

At the end of three days Mrs. Harder took the girls, as if it were the only natural thing to do, to the Nazi Welfare Office, to sign them in. Nobody doubted their story there. There were too many refugees from Memel and the northern part of East Prussia ; one couldn't keep too close a watch on them all.

From then onwards, the daring Genia and Mrs. Harder went every day to fetch the girls' welfare rations—a real help, because it was the sixth year of war and the Harders weren't exactly living in luxury.

Celina and Manja stayed at home most of the time. They hardly trusted themselves beyond the front door. If they went out at all, they wore headscarves pulled low over their foreheads.

One day Celina went to fetch some firewood from the shed. She ran straight into Voss's arms out in the yard.

She stood immobile with terror.

Voss screwed up his eyes, staring at her.

" We know each other, don't we ? " His voice was subdued.

" Elsa! " Mrs. Harder called from the kitchen.

Suddenly Voss smiled, a little embarrassed, a little conspiratorial. " Aren't you one of the girls I hid ? You must know me! I always looked after you nicely, didn't I ? "

Fear, disgust and anger made Celina forget, momentarily, who she was and where she was.

She raised her hand quickly and struck Voss a terrific blow across the face. Then she turned and ran into the kitchen.

Mrs. Harder was puzzled. " What's wrong with you ? "

Weeping, Celina fell into a chair.

" Voss . . . he recognised me. . . ."

Mrs. Harder did not speak for a minute. Then she said : " So what ? He'll be careful not to say anything. One word, and he's finished. He knows that. He'll keep his mouth shut."

Voss kept his mouth shut. He dared not report the Harders.

Once a Wehrmacht reconnaissance party appeared on the estate. Apparently they were still hunting for Russian spies.

" Why haven't those three girls got proper identity cards

yet ? " their commander demanded of Mrs. Harder.

" We applied for them long ago," she replied ; " but you know what these bureaucrats are! "

In the end she presented him with the Nazi Welfare Board's refugee cards, and he seemed satisfied.

" I'll get hold of the new cards at once, at the town hall," Mrs. Harder promised. " But remember, those girls had to run from the Russians without a thing! "

All of them, the Harders and the girls, were tiptoeing on a fragile layer of ice which could crack at any moment. But now the girls didn't brood on catastrophes of that sort. They had regained hope.

Then something happened which was so unexpected, so shattering and so fraught with danger that they were all caught off guard ; a conflict of fear, amazement and resignation forced them just to let things take their course. A young German officer fell in love with one of the Jewish girls.

German soldiers were quartered near the estate where the Harders lived. In the evenings, the reservists loitered round the streets, or sat in the village pub drinking beer. Others hung around the farm in the hope that one of the three girls might show herself. The Germans found their shyness particularly attractive, it seemed.

There was one officer in particular, a handsome young lieutenant, who was interested in Celina. He had asked Mrs. Harder more than once if he could go out with " the pretty refugee girl," but she had refused each time. The lieutenant's unshakeable determination to continue his wooing soon threw the whole house into a panic. Up to now, their scheme had worked ; but now luck seemed to be running out on them, and in a most peculiar way. All the girls could concentrate on was the horrid thought that the lieutenant might find out who they really were.

One fine winter's evening which augured of coming spring, the lieutenant appeared again at the Harders'. He knocked at the front door and was standing in the kitchen before anyone could stop him. Mrs. Harder and Celina were busy sewing.

The young man approached Celina at once.

"It's so nice out tonight! Could you perhaps—I mean—" he blushed. He was easy to look at, this one; big, blond, blue-eyed.

"Look, I'd love to go for a walk with you," he said at last.

Mrs. Harder was on top of this situation, too. She knew that if they went on snubbing the young soldiers they would get suspicious. The other refugees on the estate—two families called Zander and Mayer—were already muttering that the three girls weren't German nationals at all, but decidedly Polish.

"All right," she said. Celina was horrified. "You can go out with Elsa. But not alone! The other two must go as well. And mind you bring the children back here within the hour!"

"Of course!" The young officer was appealing and self-assured as he stood there with his peak cap under one arm, his boots radiating polish, his beautifully fitting jacket and his powerful chest muscles flexing bravely beneath it.

The sight of him aroused in Celina only fear, revulsion and loathing.

The lieutenant took them along the coast road. There was still snow on the ground; but the thaw was already setting in. Icy water, rosy and glistening, trickled beneath their feet. A coppery, evening sun hung low over the horizon. The landscape stretched wide and bleak; they could see the stumpy blue of shadowy houses and the wood, a sinister, menacing wall of black palisades; and the north-west road led directly to the sea.

Genia and Manja walked behind the others. The lieutenant chattered away, gaily, thoughtlessly.

"So you're from Memel? That's what I heard—and you got away from the Russians on foot? How awful. Look, isn't that a gorgeous sunset?"

Celina nodded. She was alternately hot and cold with fright. But she knew Mrs. Harder had done the right thing. They couldn't keep burying themselves—they would only make themselves more conspicuous that way. Death still encircled them—in the shape of the S.S., who were still combing the area for "spies," "traitors," escaped concentration camp prisoners and, above all, hidden Jews.

They walked for quite a while. Suddenly Celina was appalled—she noticed that they were approaching that part of the coast where her friends had been massacred.

"Please," she said, "I'd like to turn back."

The lieutenant grasped her by the hand and led her to the edge of the cliff. Beneath her, the sea lay tranquil in the sun's departing glow. There was nothing to indicate the ghastly tragedy of six weeks before.

The young man lowered his voice. "Do you know what the folks around here say? They're supposed to have killed ten thousand Jews here in January! Just imagine—that many people! Murdered by Germans. The thought of it is just horrible." His ingenuous face clearly registered disgust; indignation made his eyes sparkle and his cheeks were flushed. "I'll tell you straight, Elsa; when the Russians march in they'll do just the same to us as we did to the Jews. There'll be a German hanging from every tree!"

Celina felt her stomach contract.

"Please, let's go," she whispered. Her legs were buckling under. The lieutenant kept a ruthless hold on her.

"Sorry," he mumbled. "I didn't want to—but isn't it frightful, that Germans should be capable of *that*?"

She would have liked to cry out, scream it into his face, yes, yes, I know all too well what Germans are capable of; but then she looked at him as he stood beside her, an expression of genuine passion and disgust on that youthful and still so naïve face; and she knew she couldn't.

"Please, take me back," she implored.

It was only later that she realised how close she had been to betraying herself and her friends in that moment of recollection at the sea's edge.

He escorted her home. It was the first and last date. A couple of nights later there was a persistent rapping at the front door; eventually Mrs. Harder opened up. It was the young officer; he insisted on speaking to Elsa.

When Celina finally confronted him in nightdress and dressing-gown, he produced a box of foodstuffs and handed it over to Mrs. Harder. "That's for you and your family." And to Celina: "Elsa get dressed right now. The Russians have broken through. You've got to get away. I've reserved a seat in a car for you—we're leaving immediately. I'll get you safely into Germany."

Celina had only grasped one fact properly; the Russians had made a breakthrough. Rescue was near, tangibly so. She would have liked to shout and sing for joy.

"Why do you hesitate, Elsa?"

She glanced at the young officer. Suddenly she felt sorry for him. All at once she was conscious of the suffering of a whole generation, of her sorrow and his sorrow, her destiny and his destiny; saw the abyss sprawling between them, and the tears shot into her eyes.

"Go ahead," she said. "I can't come with you."

"Why on earth not?"

She shook her head, mutely.

He insisted, pleaded with her, swore that he loved her, but she was determined. How could he know what was going on in her mind?

In the end she advised him to stay in Sorginau. "Take your uniform off. Stay here. You can say you're a farmer, when the Russians come. No one will give you away."

He looked at her for a long time. He had some idea now—surely.

"I can't do that," he said after some thought. "I'm an officer. I've got to play the game, or my part of it, to the end."

He left the house shortly afterwards. The last Celina saw of him was his hand waving as he crossed the yard.

During the night they heard distinctly the explosion of tank guns and the rattle of machine-guns. The sky was lit up with red, green and white flares. Quickly drifting clouds reflected the glare of the rockets, mirrored in turn on the surface of the snow.

They all sat in the cellar: the Harders, the girls, German refugees. Some prayed and felt frightened; others awaited the new day with a quiver of hope.

Towards morning the noise of combat died down. They heard the roar of engines, tramping boots, strange, throaty voices. The Russians had arrived.

At this point Celina Manielewitz hesitated. She looked at her husband and lowered her eyes.

He made a vague gesture. In his harsh, guttural accent, he said: "You know what war is like; soldiers come looking for schnaps and girls. The Russians didn't believe the three girls were Jewish. You can imagine what happened?"

Not even the Harders, who had saved their lives, could help the girls now. The Red Army men laughed in their faces when they tried to impress on them that the girls were Jewish. "The Jewesses have all been killed," they said, pointing to the Baltic coastline.

It was only next day, after another twenty-four hours of horror, that the girls managed to be brought before a Jewish officer of the Red Army. They were subjected to a gruelling cross-examination during which, granted, they made their Polish Jewish identity sound plausible; but it took an age to dispel the suspicions against them. The Russians maintained that every Jew who had survived the Nazi holocaust must be a German spy; how else *could* he have survived?

Eventually, ten other survivors of the Baltic slaughter showed up in the Sorginau area; they, too, had managed to keep under cover right up to the Russian advance. They confirmed the girls' statements. The thirteen survivors were immediately interned in a Russian refugee camp. The girls had to say goodbye to the Harders, a heartrending moment.

Celina Manielewitz's story should actually have ended here; but it had a moving sequel.

In February, 1946, Celina met the man she married. It was in Friedland, in Polish-occupied Lower Silesia. Manielewitz had been in German concentration camps himself and was then, as he says now, "radically anti-German." But his wife's story moved him deeply. "We must get the Harders out of the Soviet zone," he said.

He wrote to Sorginau; no reply. In the meantime he emigrated, with his wife, to the U.S. zone. Their aim: Israel.

In the Wetzler D.P. camp Manielewitz renewed his exertions to find the Harders. Again he wrote to Sorginau, without results. Then, in 1947, he got a letter from a Mrs. Schroeder in West Berlin. This woman, Mrs. Harder's sister-in-law, had escaped from East Germany; she told Manielewitz that the Harders had received his letter but could not reply. Meanwhile Harder had died in a Russian internment camp. His last words to his wife were: "Any news of our girls?"

Almost all Germans in East Prussia who had not joined the exodus to the West had either been deported to the Soviet Union for forced labour or, if they were physically unfit, shut up in internment camps. The Harders fell into the latter category. The Russians did not seem to care that they had hidden three concentration camp inmates in their home for weeks, at the risk of their own lives. What happened to farmer Voss was never ascertained.

Mrs. Harder was finally taken to a camp on the outskirts of East Berlin. Manielewitz tried to make contact with her through people who crossed the border illegally; no luck here, either.

But Manielewitz was simply determined to help this woman, who had done so much for Celina, in her own time of need. He scurried from one organisation to another, from the Allies to the Germans and back again. In 1947, people thought he was a bit crazy. Here was a Polish Jew, who had been in concentration camps, looking for a German woman to give her a home; he even wanted to take her to Palestine, he said. Something wrong there.

Then, one day in 1948, one of the guards at the D.P. camp entrance approached Manielewitz. "German woman wants to speak to you."

Manielewitz went. An old woman waited at the fence; tired, spent, pale.

"I'd never seen her before—but I recognised her from all Celina's descriptions. It was Mrs. Harder."

Manielewitz smiled. He was a little melancholy, a little nostalgic.

"We let her move in with us, in our room," he continued, "all quite illegal, of course. She was the only German woman who ever lived in a D.P. camp, as far as I know. She had no one in the West, so she stayed with us. You can imagine that it wasn't easy for us. We only had the one room; we were newly wed; and yet we put up the old lady as well. But you've no idea what she was like; goodness itself, an angel in human form. I adored her. What she did for the three girls, out of sheer humanity, just couldn't be recompensed."

Manielewitz went on pressing for his emigration to Palestine. When Israel gained independence in 1948, he got his permit—and a visa for Mrs. Harder.

"She was the first German non-Jew who was allowed to emigrate legally to Israel," he said proudly.

But things did not turn out that way. Mrs. Harder did not want to go with them.

"I can't," she said. "Look—you're emigrating to a new country, you want to build a new life for yourselves. I'm an old woman. I'd only be in your way ; unnecessary ballast for a young couple like you. You'd have to think of me, all the time. And that I don't want."

They pleaded with her. It did not help. She had made up her mind, and she stayed in Germany.

Mrs. Harder lives in the small farming village of Chieming in Upper Bavaria. They exchange letters every week. Now that the Manielewitzes have established themselves in Israel, Mrs. Harder would like to visit them ; but the doctor will not let her make the journey. She is an old woman ; and she is ill.

As I left the Manielewitz dwelling, a modern terrace house on the outskirts of Jerusalem, they said to me in parting : "Please go and see Mrs. Harder in Germany. Give her our regards ; tell her we miss her."

I promised.

"Shalom. Peace be with you." This was Manielewitz's farewell to me.

Celina Manielewitz is one of the few who survived the dissolution of the concentration camps in East Prussia. At the beginning of 1945 there were about sixty thousand prisoners in the East Prussian camps ; according to the records of the Yad Vashem Institute only 1,500 were saved —500 from the Preust camp near Danzig, which was liberated by the Red Army on March 23, 1945, and about a thousand through the action of a German naval officer, of whom more later. All other prisoners perished during the death marches to the west, in the Palmnicken massacre or during the Baltic Sea " evacuation."

" Shooting is too good for you!" That is what S.S. Sergeant Stock screamed at the Jewish girls before he battered them over the precipice into the foaming sea. Celina was one of those Jewish girls.

And her husband said to me : "Shalom. Peace be with you."

" Now, in all frankness, I want to bring a very difficult topic to your attention. I mean the extermination of the Jewish race. . . . Most of you will know what it means when a hundred corpses lie side by side; when there are five hundred, or a thousand. To have stuck this out, and still—apart from exceptions caused by human weakness—to have remained decent, this is what has made us tough. This is a glorious chapter in our history, which has never been written and never shall be."

Heinrich Himmler to S.S. leaders
in Posen, October 4, 1943.

2

The man standing at the open door of the hotel room smiled shyly at me.

"I'm Tannenzapf. Have I come to the right place ? "

It was just four o'clock. He was dead on time.

We shook hands ; I offered him a seat. The room was not very large, and not too comfortable, either. But it was the week of Passover, the most important Jewish festival. All Israel was overflowing with tourists, with Jews from Europe and the United States who wished to celebrate in the land of their forefathers the exodus of the children of Israel from the land of the Pharaohs. The hotels were crowded, and I was lucky to get this room at all—in the clean little *pension* off the Ben Yehuda Street in Tel Aviv.

We sat at the round table near the window. From there we could look at the houses opposite with their white and yellow stuccoed frontages, and into a green garden where palms grew.

Tannenzapf gave me a long look. "You're a German Jew ? " he asked.

I shook my head.

"I'm not Jewish," I said.

He smiled again, a bit embarrassed. He rested his crutch against the window-ledge. He limped ; a legacy from the concentration camp he won't lose.

"Alfred Grube was a German, too," said Tannenzapf. "Grube and good old grandpa Heinrich Puhl. Then, there were two other good men—Paul Flieger and Schweisser. I can't remember his first name. Those Germans were like friends." For a whole minute the lids closed over the bright blue eyes. His expression became thoughtful; sharp wrinkles encircled his mouth.

Then he sighed. "Well, what do you want to know ? "

"It would be best if you told me exactly what happened."

" Everything ? "

" Everything."

He hesitated ; and after looking at me a long time, " All right."

" At that time, when it all began, in 1941, I was 29. I had a young, pretty wife—Esther was just 21—and I was running a small but successful jeweller's business in Czernowitz with one partner. That was the capital of the Rumanian province Bukovina.

In 1940 this territory had been ceded to the Soviet Union. It was a time when men and provinces were shoved backwards and forwards by the great Powers like pieces in a chess game The Russians left us Jews alone. It was only after the beginning of the Russian campaign that our misery started; when the Rumanians and the Germans got Bukovina back again. The Rumanians set up ghettoes for the Jews post-haste, to oblige the Germans. The Czernowitz Jews, about 58,000 of them, were allocated a ghetto in the poorest part of the town. They were mainly of German descent and spoke only German amongst themselves.

Immediately after that the deportations started. We didn't know where people were taken to. It was rumoured that they were sent to forced labour camps in the territory captured from the Russians between the Dniester and the Bug— Transnistria, as it was called. This was Rumanian-occupied. We were well aware that under the Rumanians in Transnistria one could just about survive. It's true that there were a lot of antisemites amongst them, too, but the Rumanians never dreamed of the extermination of the Jews in the way the Germans planned it.

It was at dawn on October 12, 1941, that our turn came. They practically battered down the door with the butt-ends of their guns—we were living cooped up in that house with several other families. There were Rumanian military police standing outside. They gave us fifteen minutes to pack a few necessities, the things we most needed. Everyone was allowed to carry one rucksack, no more.

We were herded on to a football stadium just outside Czernowitz. There were thousands of people: men, women, children, old and young, healthy and sick, strong and weak. It got hot quickly and the sun blazed down on us. Rumours circulated. Finally, round about noon, we were taken to a goods station outside the city—constantly badgered through dusty streets by the shrieking Rumanian police. On the station we each got half a loaf, then we were loaded on to cattle trucks. We stood squashed tightly together ; sitting or lying down was out of the question. They gave us a bucket of water for drinking and another bucket to relieve ourselves in. Then the truck was bolted and barred.

Esther nestled up against me. She was scared. But she had faith, too, that I would protect her, that nothing could happen to her as long as we were together.

We spent four whole days travelling in that train. By day the heat inside the carriages was stifling. It wasn't much better at night, either. People tore their clothes off and cried aloud for air. The water bucket was empty by the first evening. An old man died. We called the gendarmes, who were travelling with us in the brake vans. No one took any notice.

Finally, the train came to a halt, and they threw the doors open. We staggered out, collapsed, and pulled ourselves to our feet again.

Greedily, I gulped draughts of fresh air, and held Esther up. She smiled. 'Good,' she whispered. 'We've arrived.'

We had, indeed. At crack of dawn, in a dew-soaked patch of meadow. Nearby was a village and a stream. They let us fetch water from there. We rushed at it, almost crazy with thirst. Then we had to form rows and everybody got half a loaf. After a little rest we were on our way, on foot this time ; the march lasted all day. Soon the rumour spread along the column that we were in Transnistria, but still in Rumanian territory ; not amongst the Germans, whom we dreaded.

Towards evening we came to a barrack camp surrounded by barbed wire. It was on the shores of the Bug—a wide, greyish-yellow river on a shallow bed. On the other side of the river was Russia ; wide, gigantic, infinite.

We were quartered in the barracks, 35 people to a building. Families were allowed to remain together.

It soon turned out that it was a transit camp. Five weeks, we were there. Then we were put on a truck to Tulczin, where there was a big Rumanian concentration camp. Esther and I were lucky ; we were housed with some other people in a solid-looking building, which used to be a school."

The Tannenzapfs remained there over six months. The Rumanians hardly bothered about them. Their lives were those of prisoners ; but nobody ill-treated them and nobody forced them to work. The food was bad but just about adequate. And so it went on ; till that fateful day in June, 1942, when they were suddenly summoned to a special roll-call first thing in the morning.

"We had to line up in the playground in front of the school. I was terrified when I saw the men sitting at the table which they'd set up in the middle of the yard. They wore S.S. uniforms.

They called our names and we had to step forward ; then they asked questions about our occupations. I said I was a mechanic, so I was assigned to the manual workers' group. Esther announced herself as a dressmaker. We were allowed to stay together.

We crossed the Bug in a ferry ; now we were at the mercy of the Germans. The very same day we were transferred to Krassnopolka camp, about 40 miles from the Bug. Here, and in two other camps in the area, there were about 14,000 Jews from Czernowitz, whom the Germans had taken over from the Rumanians for slave labour.

Krassnopolka was a former Soviet collective farm where they bred cattle. The camp personnel was decently housed ; the prisoners lived in the former outhouses, built in square formation round a big courtyard. They had erected a barbed-wire fence, three yards high, round the whole setup.

They drove us into the barracks ; families could stay together. We were given straw to sleep on ; those who had rugs were lucky, and those who hadn't just had to sleep on the hard floor.

In the evening an S.S. sergeant appeared and elected one of us block elder.

'Tomorrow, you lot will start work,' he said. 'If you work you get fed. If you're too lazy to work, you starve.' And off he went.

The next day was very hot. Even the morning, before the

sun was at its zenith, was pretty close. We all had to assemble in the yard, men and women. Then they called out our names, counted us and took us to work.

We had to dig ditches for a road-building operation. It was then I first saw the Todt organisation fellows, who were supervising on the technical side.

But it was the S.S. who decided what we should do. Each of us was allocated a stretch of ditch which we had to finish by the evening.

I can't remember how big the stretch was. We got spades and began work.

I remember quite well, though, how the first man was shot. It was an old man, and he didn't work fast enough for the S.S. guard. It was about ten in the morning ; we were sweating and feeling the hard labour in our stiff joints. The S.S. guard walked over to the old boy and said something to him ; he didn't understand. The guard just lifted his gun, aimed, and shot him right in the temple.

He was the first. But there were others, too. The S.S. shot them haphazardly ; while they worked, during the march to work, or on the way back to camp in the evening. Whoever didn't finish his allotted job died.

Esther was delicate, and the long period of imprisonment had weakened her. I tried to manage her quota as well. It was almost beyond me, but I did it. I prayed. I prayed as I slaved away, and I looked at Esther and knew I had to go through with it for her sake.

We've got to live, I thought. We were young ; I was just thirty, she twenty-two. We couldn't let up; we had to make it.

Esther was a good-looking girl. One day an S.S. man noticed her. He gave her a long look, weighing her up.

'Can you do anything apart from shovelling muck ? ' he asked.

' I'm a dressmaker.'

' My coat needs altering. You can do it,' he said.

In the evening he brought the coat to our barracks and Esther altered it. Two days later she was transferred to the so-called " base " in Iwangorod village ; from then on she worked in the tailoring department there.

The " base " comprised the administrative department for

33

road-building operations, a few workshops for the require-
ments of the three labour camps in the area, and a supplies
depot. A number of prisoners were taken every morning by
truck from Krassnopolka to Iwangorod. They were the lucky
ones, the élite, since they had lighter duties and better food.
Our camp food consisted of one chunk of bread in the mornings and a drop of watery soup in the evenings. People were
dying of hunger all the time.

Esther picked up very quickly after her transfer. Soon she
managed to get me a transfer, too—to the smithy.

That's when I met Heinrich Puhl.

He was about 55 then ; a tall, emaciated man with kindly
eyes. He wore a moustache, which he stroked reflectively
when he talked ; his hair was close-cropped and already
pretty grey.

When I reported to him for the first day he said : ' Have
something to eat.'

He gave me his own rations. When he saw how I gulped
down the bread, butter and cheese he turned away.

' Things are pretty bad for you people, aren't they ? ' he
asked.

I could only nod.

' Poor devil,' he murmured.

' I've got a wife,' I said slowly. ' Esther. She's 22. She
works here, too.'

Puhl nodded. ' I've seen her. Good-looking girl.'

In the afternoon he fetched me a double ration of soup,
in a bowl, from the canteen. When an S.S. man appeared—
I didn't know him—he cursed me and drove me to work.
But I knew he was putting on an act. At a time like that
people couldn't show their feelings openly.

The time I spent with Puhl was like heaven. He stole bread
and potatoes for me from the canteen ; he scrounged bits of
clothing for me and my wife ; he called me pig Jew, and
often cried as he did so. He was one of those people who
hide their sympathetic natures under a brusque front."

Puhl was not the only German who helped the Jews. There
was a man called Schweisser, too. One morning Tannenzapf
saw him taking away half-a-dozen Jewish children, who had

been brought to base to tend the milch cows, on a truck. He handed them over to some Russian farmers in the neighbourhood. The children were little orphans who had been picked up in Czernowitz and their lives were saved; Schweisser was risking his own life ; Tannenzapf knew that.

And finally, Alfred Grube. He was chief engineer at Iwangorod base. He worked in the office, mainly. Tannenzapf had the job of washing his car.

One day Tannenzapf was leaning over the bonnet of the open car, polishing the windscreen. Grube sat inside fumbling about with the dashboard.

Then he suddenly shot out a muffled question: "Why don't you beat it, you dumb idiot ? "

Tannenzapf, taken aback, stopped working.

" Carry on working," Grube snarled.

Then: " Those S.S. bastards are going to do you all in ; surely you know that ? "

Tannenzapf gulped. " I can't get out. I don't understand Russian."

" Learn it, then ! "

Grube kept smuggling provisions to Tannenzapf, too—plus something quite unusual, German newspapers. Newspapers for prisoners were strictly taboo. But they craved for the printed word, for news from the outside world—even such distorted news as the German press provided.

Tannenzapf found the solicitude, so hazardous to themselves, of the German civilian officials at the base a spiritual balm. Later, when the S.S. committed their atrocities in camp, he was to fall back on such memories, time and time again.

Things could have drifted on in the same way ; but then something dreadful happened.

Esther had been pregnant since July. At first she'd hidden it from Tannenzapf, but later she came out with it. They felt helpless and despairing. Newly-born babies were taken away by the S.S., they knew. No one knew exactly what happened but they guessed that the children were murdered.

There were a few children in camp, aged between two and ten, who stayed hidden in the straw whenever there was a roll-call or (a rare occurrence) a barrack inspection. The older children reported for work as "adults." That enabled them to draw the miserable ration allotted to prisoners.

Tannenzapf and Esther decided that the child had to be born. Then, they would hide it.

Esther gave birth to a boy—on March 24, 1943. She was attended by a Jewish doctor and a woman from the barrack. They had gagged her so that nobody would hear her screams ; everything went according to plan.

Tannenzapf had been reproaching himself dreadfully but now, holding his child in his arms, amid all the wretchedness of the camp, he forgot everything : their suffering, their grim future, their pitiless fate. He wept, stirred with ecstasy.

In accordance with the regulations, Esther was given official "leave" from the tailoring shop at base. She did not have to go to work for three weeks, but she still drew her rations.

The head of the tailoring department was a good-natured German whose name Tannenzapf could not remember.

Tannenzapf and the other prisoners from his barrack succeeded, for three weeks, in hushing up Esther's absence from roll-call ; they also kept the child out of the way of the S.S.

Those were nerve-racking weeks.

"When I got back from my job in Iwangorod in the evenings, my first question was : 'How's Esther ?' Usually a couple of old women from our barrack would come and meet me and give me a crafty smile. Then I'd know everything was all right.

Esther lay on a palliasse in the half-dark, in the cheerless room where we lived ; squashed right into the furthest corner, to evade the curiosity of the S.S. if by any chance one of them should come in. They hardly ever did ; it was as if they were afraid to go inside. Anyway, they had sufficient opportunity to torment us during roll-call or working parties. The S.S. would never have dreamed that anyone could have the nerve not to show up at roll-call, like Esther. She was very weak after the birth. The prisoners scrounged food for her and brought her some of their pathetic scraps that they so badly needed themselves. Puhl gave me some eggs on the quiet, and occasionally some sausages and cheese

—things that he risked his neck to steal from the canteen or the base kitchen. But Esther couldn't eat. She would look at me, eyes all feverish and blazing, just whispering: ' Hermann, nothing must happen to the baby.'

I comforted her. ' Nothing will happen to the child.' I took the little bundle of humanity into my arms. The infant regarded me gravely with his big, black eyes. He had tiny fat cheeks, quite firm, and powerful little fists ; he'd wind his fingers round mine when I spoke to him. I never heard him cry. It was as if this tiny child, barely three weeks old, guessed that he wasn't allowed to bawl and cry like other babies.

At night I would lie sleepless beside Esther and pray: ' Lord, let him live, Lord, give him a better life than we've got. Lord, save him, at least save *him*.' "

On the evening of April 9, Tannenzapf was returning, as usual, with the other base workers on the truck from Iwangorod to Krassnopolka. They jumped off at the camp gate, got counted again by the guard on duty, and were allowed to go. Tannenzapf made for his barrack.

A couple of women ran towards him, crying.

" Hermann . . . Hermann!" they cried.

He stood stock still. A fiery wave sent the blood rushing to his brain.

" What is it ? "

" The child! He wants to take your wife's baby away!"

Tannenzapf began to run.

At that moment the barrack door was flung open from the inside. An S.S. sergeant appeared with a white bundle on his arm.

" Stop!" cried Tannenzapf. Then the two women were at his side, clinging to his arms.

" Keep quiet," they sobbed, " or they'll shoot you!"

The three of them stood there, unable to move.

The S.S. man walked away with the child on his arm. He was heading for the refuse dump near the camp fence.

Tannenzapf wanted to scream, but his throat emitted no sound.

The S.S. man lifted up the child and snapped it in two across his knee, just as one breaks a twig. They could hear distinctly, in the clear evening air, the cracking of the spine. Then the German threw the corpse of the three-week-old baby on to the rubbish heap. He wiped his hands and gazed perfunctorily over at the people who, dumb and frozen with horror, had gathered at the entrance of Barrack No. 3. Then he turned round and walked to the washroom. His footsteps were sure and steady.

" Those criminals," Puhl whispered. " Those bastards." He grabbed the bottle and took a swig. His eyes were bloodshot and his hands trembled.

" I've applied for retirement,' he said after a while. " I'll get myself invalided out. Because of illness. Because of my gallstones. Do you think I could stand this another day ? I've lost a son in this war ; my son has been butchered for the sake of this mob, he's thrown his life away for these gangsters, for these swine, who are torturing and murdering people here behind the front line."

" Please, Mr. Puhl, don't talk so loud," implored Tannenzapf.

Puhl, the master blacksmith, banged his fist down on the table.

" Why not ? What have I got to lose ? My son is dead— your son is dead. My wife is still alive, that's all. It's only for her sake that I don't shout it right into their faces. Just because of her."

He was silent for a while. Then he raised his head.

" You know something ? " His voice was bewildered. " You know—these blackguards can only do all this because each of us has a wife or mother at home that he's got to think of . . . a fiancée, or a daughter. . . ." He wiped his face with his hand. " That's it—people have too many things to consider. After all, you're not alone in this world. And these S.S. devils exploit the fact." Bitterly, he added : " Because we've all got to keep our mouths shut—because we all—." He broke off. He got up clumsily, wavering a bit. " Well, get to work!" he yelled suddenly. " Go on—move!"

Tannenzapf turned aside quickly, to avoid looking Puhl in the face.

A couple of weeks later Puhl approached Tannenzapf in

the afternoon and held out his hand. " All the best, lad. I'm off in half an hour. Home. They've authorised my retirement."

Tannenzapf felt a searing wave rise in his throat.

" Listen to me. Beat it, go to the Russians. Get out as fast as you can."

Tannenzapf nodded.

" Will you promise me that ? "

Tannenzapf looked at him without speaking. Impulsively, the older man took him in his arms and embraced him. " Goodbye," he whispered. Then he tore himself away and rushed outside. " Where's the car ? " he yelled, till the square re-echoed.

A dilapidated Russian horse-drawn cart ambled into view ; Puhl swung himself up next to the driver's seat. It was the last that Tannenzapf saw of him ; he listened to the sharp crack of hooves as the horses trotted away ; he heard the lash of the whip and the voice of the driver, a Russian *hiwi* : " Dawai . . . dawai. . . ." Then all was quiet.

Beat it, Puhl had said, promise me you will.

But Tannenzapf hesitated. Too long.

" Sometimes, in the past, I used to reproach myself," said Tannenzapf, polishing his glasses. " I used to think sometimes that perhaps I should have tried to escape with Esther, that summer."

I glanced down at my desk, at the sheets of paper covered with writing.

" Shall we leave the rest for another day ? " I asked. " It's Passover eve, after all."

He shook his head. " No, I want to tell you everything. Now."

His head sank to his chest, he closed his eyes ; and he was part of the past again, 1943, twenty years ago.

" One morning in December—on the tenth—I drove as usual to Iwangorod by truck. Esther was ill and stayed in camp. That particular morning Josef Hermann—a German administrative clerk—got me to compile lists of equipment. I was sitting in the office by myself—Hermann had gone off somewhere. Round about eleven the Polish blacksmith who had replaced Puhl burst noisily in.

'Base being attacked!' he whispered, pointing towards the window.

I jumped up and looked out.

The whole base was surrounded by S.S. They stood there in full battledress, weapons at the ready. Armoured personnel-carriers and radio vans roared round the camp.

The Pole shuffled out again, banging the door behind him.

I had to sit down ; my legs were too weak to support me.

Then I heard heavy footsteps outside. The crunch of boots in the snow. The door swung open ; there stood an S.S. man, automatic poised.

'What are you doing there ?' he shouted at me.

'Working,' I said with raised eyebrows.

'And what's all this here ?'

'The office,' I said, 'and shut the door, please, it's cold.'

That sentence saved my life. Obviously he took me for a German, not a Jew. He gave me a curt nod and shut the door behind him.

I leapt up and ran to the back door, rushing along the narrow gangway between the barracks till I got to the storehouse where the barrels of dynamite were kept. There were Jews running towards me, faces white as chalk.

'A raid!' they said. 'They're arresting all the Jews!'

'Jews, come out! All out on the camp square!' boomed a voice from the base entrance.

I hurried into the dynamite shed, jumping clean over the barrels and making for a corner where there was a pile of empty crates and casks.

'Jews, come out!' yelled the voice again, quite far away this time. I heard the roar of engines, voices, screams, blows ; someone walked through the warehouse but went out again.

I crept into an empty barrel. I was scared to breathe. All I could hear in the silence was my own heart hammering."

Tannenzapf doesn't know how long he was hunched up in there. His limbs became stiff from squatting in the barrel and his thin suit let the cold in. His fingers were numb and bloodless ; only the tips burned, as if he'd held a lighted match a little too long. The temptation to move, to stand upright and stretch his limbs, became almost irresistible.

"I gritted my teeth and counted the breaths I took. Twenty breaths—one minute. Sixty minutes one hour. Gradually it got dark, and the warehouse got dark, too. Then something rustled in a corner. I jumped. There was a great rat staring at me. Its fur was grey, flecked with mud. It drew back its lips and showed its sharp, pointed teeth.

I cursed at it. The creature sprang back and disappeared again between the barrels.

The evening shadows grew denser. It must have been four o'clock; the early Russian winter's night had set in.

My head was sinking on to my chest. I felt a flush rise to my cheeks and then a cold shudder. I drew my ragged clothes tighter about me and tried to burrow into the skimpy stuff.

I must have fallen asleep, because suddenly I was jerked awake by the sounds of knocking-off time. You couldn't mistake them. Voices outside the shed; doors banging; footsteps, which died away.

I glanced round me, but I couldn't see anything in the dark. Quite a way behind me I could make out a faint glimmer; the door, probably. After a while I heard solitary footsteps; that was all. The light above the door vanished; he'd switched it off. His footsteps died away. Then silence. I was all alone at the base. The most critical phase was over.

I crawled out of my hiding place and stood upright, but with a mighty effort. Everything was spinning. My knees gave way and I fell flat on my face, knocking my head on a sharp ledge so that the blood ran down my face.

I lay there for some time, trying to move my paralysed limbs. Gradually my circulation got back to normal. I staggered to my feet and groped my way along the wall to the door. It was a long, exhausting journey. I knocked my knees against sharp corners and scratched my hands on jagged bits of wood. Eventually I made it. I pressed down the latch; it wasn't locked.

I took a deep breath, then gritted my teeth and opened the door, very slowly, chink by chink. There outside was the night, palely glowing in the snow. I slipped cautiously outside and stayed with my back against the warehouse wall, not moving.

I was used to the dark inside the storehouse and so I could soon make out the unlit courtyard and the base buildings, all black in that bright, winter's night.

The snow drizzled down on to my face. There wasn't a soul around. Quickly I moved along the storehouse wall, got to the gangway between the storehouse and the carpenter's barrack and reached the outer wall. I jumped, managed to clutch on to the top, pulled myself up and stayed squatting there for a bit. I could see the houses in the village; there wasn't a single chink of light from the windows. Darkness everywhere.

I jumped down from the wall and fell flat, but soon picked myself up again.

I ran round the corner and stood on the Krassnopolka road. Where to now?

To camp, of course. Where else could I go? Where else could I run to, all alone in a snowy waste, somewhere in Russia?

Esther, my wife, was waiting in camp. The camp was my home, however insane that may sound now. It was the hole I wanted to hide myself in like a hunted beast. When I look back, after all these years, I know that my mental processes weren't working properly at the time. It just didn't occur to me that something could have happened in camp, too; that maybe I would never find Esther again. . . .

I began to run, then; I'd soon left the houses of Iwangorod behind me. I was out in open country now. The wind had come up, driving the snow over the flat Ukrainian plain.

I leaned against the wind, trudging through the snow, and orientated myself by means of the stakes with bits of straw tied to them which the Germans had put up to mark out the route. I made pretty slow progress although I was running.

In front of me were the houses of Krassnopolka, still far away and barely visible in the twilight. I stopped.

The camp was to my left. I couldn't see it from where I was. If I wanted to get there without being seen I'd have to go across the fields.

I turned off the road. The wind had dropped; the driving

snow had settled. The sky was clearing and the grey haze sharpening into blue. Suddenly the moon cast a pallid gleam over the landscape. I moved on more quickly, wading through the snow and panting.

I could see a hazy something in front of me, which seemed to sprout from the ground ; a black shadow in the moonlight.

I ducked. I thought: they can see me. I thought of the guards making their routine inspections round the camp. I had plenty of time ; but something told me I hadn't. I tried to force myself to keep calm, but impatience drove me on.

I was crawling through the snow on all fours now. Suddenly my hand hit something ; grasped something cold, which was neither hard nor soft. I instinctively pulled my fingers back. It was a human body. I was holding a dead man's leg.

My throat was dry. I wanted to swallow but my tongue clove to the roof of my mouth.

I stood upright and ran towards the camp. I stumbled over a foot, all frozen stiff, which was projecting from the snow ; over an arm and a wizened hand.

A spray of snow blew up. That must be the fence.

But there wasn't a fence any more. The stakes were broken down, the barbed wire all hanging loose in a disorderly tangle.

The barracks were behind the wire. But they hadn't any walls. Only a few corner posts were left standing, protruding from the charred ruins.

Not a soul breathed in that place.

I bent down, groped aimlessly around, found nothing. I turned back and fell over frozen arms, severed legs and torsos flung indiscriminately in all directions ; all locked in the torpor of death, mangled by bullet wounds, hacked to pieces—rendered unrecognisable, faceless.

Up there in Heaven, how could they approach their God ? How would He recognise them as His children ?

I collapsed and fell into the snow, buried my face in my hands and wept. I wept for the first time since they had captured us. I wept for the first time since they dragged us to our prison, to our new Babylon.

I heard the rabbi singing in the synagogue of Czernowitz ; I heard Esther's voice in the darkness, they can't kill us, they won't kill us. I saw the S.S. man with my child, saw the little tender body with its head jerking, saw the little life ebbing away, second by second. I heard again the words of Puhl : ' Jew, make yourself scarce, Jew, run away and hide, Jew, beat it.' I saw his rough face again, his oh so kindly eyes.

I heard the rabbi singing, I heard my father's voice, I was in the garden at home again, playing under the apple tree ; I saw them all, the companions of my childhood, and I knew I was a Jew.

I was a Jew and bore within me the destiny of my people ; and here, in the snowy waters of Krassnopolka, the end had come. The end of everything.

Eventually I got up. I would never see Esther again. I knew that now.

I walked round the camp ; round the ruins which were all that was left of it. Finally I clambered over the demolished fence into the square. Once there had been a thousand people there ; vegetating like the animals before them, but still remaining human beings because they had retained that vital spark of life : hope. Now hope was dead.

I ran out through the camp gate, which was wide open, rushing through the snow without turning round once. I reeled and staggered but my legs carried me. I was running towards the houses of Krassnopolka. I heard nothing ; I saw nothing ; I knew nothing. I knew only that my wife was dead."

Tannenzapf was silent. He hung his head and did not look at me. He wiped his hands on a pocket handkerchief.

"But all that isn't very important, perhaps," he said abruptly. His voice was subdued ; his words had an apologetic ring.

He tucked his handkerchief away and glanced at me through his glasses. It was a bewildered, tentative glance. He opened his lips, then pressed them tightly together again.

Outside the window of my hotel room the hamsin, the desert wind, whirled the dust skywards and dashed it against the panes. The palms in the garden opposite us bowed in the breeze. My throat was dry, though I hadn't spoken a word for the past hour.

"Would you like a coffee ? " I asked Tannenzapf.

He shook his head. The shy smile flitted over his face again.

"Tea, maybe ? "

"I don't want to cause any trouble. . . ."

I got up and rang the bell.

When I sat down again Tannenzapf had removed his glasses and was polishing the lenses. I saw, for the first time, how tired his eyes were.

We drank some hot tea with lemon and a lot of sugar. Tannenzapf studied his hands. Clearing his throat, he went on. As I began to take notes I could see my own hand trembling.

"That's not very important, actually," said Tannenzapf again. "It was about the Germans I wanted to tell you.

I was approaching the village, Krassnopolka.

The houses lay stumpy and black in the snow, the roofs glistening in the moonlight. I walked right in the middle of the road ; now, I wasn't scared any more. Nothing else could happen to me now. My child was dead. My wife was dead. I was alone. Was it worth going on living ?

Then I stopped dead.

Then I knew I had to go on living. Then I knew what I had to do. I knew I had to avenge them, those who lay out there in the snow. I had to live ; every single individual who could escape those beasts had to live. The mere fact of my survival would be our vengeance. The Germans, the Nazis, had said: 'There won't be a single sign that Jews ever existed, only the gravestones in the old cemeteries.' So, I had to go on living. Even if only a handful remained, one here, one there. Something would testify to our existence apart from the gravestones.

Now I was in the village. Suddenly, I felt far stronger than I had done for many months. My footsteps were firm and confident ; and my hand didn't shake as I knocked at the door of the first little farmhouse.

After a while I heard a voice asking in Ukrainian : 'Who is it ? '

'A good friend,' I said.

The bolt was shot back and the door opened. An old farmer with a wrinkled face blinked sleepily at me. His eyes narrowed as they peered out into the night, from a room lit by a paraffin lamp.

I went in, pulling the door shut behind me.

'What do you want?' he asked. He held his trousers up with one hand; his shirt gaped open, revealing a hairy chest. I could see the eyes of an old woman, who lay motionless under a pile of rugs in the chimney corner staring, at me.

'When did it happen?' I enquired.

The old man raised his hand to his chin and rubbed his bristly beard.

'This morning,' he said.

He shuffled over to the table and got a bottle and a glass, which he filled and handed to me. It was vodka. Home distilled. I drained it at one gulp. I've never drunk much alcohol and couldn't take much, and this was my first drink for years. A whole tumbler full of vodka. But I didn't feel any effects; I kept a clear head.

'This morning,' said the old man, 'a big S.S. troop came with cars and sledges. They and the camp guards got together and shot the prisoners. The whole lot. On the spot. They rounded them up, and mowed them down with machine-guns. Some of them wouldn't come out of the barracks, but they were killed when the S.S. threw hand-grenades in there. Then there was an enormous blaze. It burned the whole day. Until evening.'

I looked at the old boy. 'Give me another glass,' I said in my broken Ukrainian.

He poured me out another. 'You've got to go,' he said. 'They mustn't find you here. You're one of them, aren't you? Aren't you a Jew?'

'Yes, I'm a Jew,' I said, draining the glass.

He slammed the door behind me and I was alone again with the night. But it wasn't cold, or terrible, any more; everything was different now.

I walked along the road in the direction of Iwangorod. I knew exactly where to go; to Alfred Grube. He was the only one who could help me. Without him I was done for.

I could not survive. And all at once survival was vital."

The engineer, Alfred Grube, lived in a farm outside Iwangorod. It was almost midnight when Tannenzapf knocked him up.

"Who is that?" Grube's voice.

"Open the door, please. It's me, Tannenzapf."

Grube opened. He had a revolver at the ready.

He looked at Tannenzapf as if he were a being from another planet.

"You're still alive? And you're not out of the wood yet?"

"Shoot," said Tannenzapf, "shoot if you like."

Grube looked down at his revolver in amazement, as if he'd long forgotten that he had it. Hastily, he shoved it into his trousers pocket.

"Well, come in!" He pulled Tannenzapf into the house.

His wife was in the room; a pretty, dark-haired Ukrainian.

"Give him something to eat," Grube ordered. She went off to the adjoining room without a word.

Grube's eyes were like slits as he regarded Tannenzapf.

"Well," he asked, "what now?"

Tannenzapf was silent.

"You'll have to cross the Bug," Grube said quietly; "once you're over there you're safe."

"I've no idea where the Bug lies," said Tannenzapf; "I've no food, I don't even know how to get there. . . ."

Suddenly Grube came to life. "You must get away. You must escape from these . . . people. Listen, Tannenzapf. . . ." He pulled him aside, towards a map fastened to the wall with drawing pins.

"Look, this is where we are now. Here's Iwangorod and there's the Bug." His fingers glided over the map. "Here's a pencil—just copy the map, the most important landmarks. . . ." He shoved paper and pencil into his hands.

The woman appeared with a bowl of hot soup. After he had eaten, Tannenzapf made some notes from the map. Grube stood watching.

"If we had been caught," said Tannenzapf in my hotel room in Tel Aviv, "Grube's life wouldn't have been worth a light. He risked his neck that night. He risked his life to

47

help a Jew who had witnessed the Krassnopolka massacre. He, a German, even provided that witness with a means of escape. He let me copy a military district map—that was quite unheard of. I don't know if you can understand that today ? "

After Tannenzapf had finished his copying and stuffed his pockets with hard-boiled eggs and chunks of bread, Grube sent him to another German in Iwangorod, Paul Flieger, from Hanover. He was a friend of Grube. Without wasting words Flieger took Tannenzapf to an old Ukrainian woman in the village who had been hiding a Jewish family, a married couple, in her home. That same night the three of them set out for the Bug.

" What happened that night is a bit hazy in my mind," said Tannenzapf, shutting his eyes to concentrate better. " It had grown dark outside. It was the eve of the Passover, one of the most important Jewish festivals. There were lighted candles in the windows of the houses opposite. The Orthodox Jews were preparing for the Seder, the evening meal.

The first shock I had—when I found the camp in ruins —had stupefied me. I know that. During the night the shock began to wear off and instead I felt a kind of numb pain. Suddenly all my strength—which came from my will to survive—deserted me. I became very weak ; the hardships of the last few months and the terror and the worries of the past eighteen hours took their toll."

The three fugitives made pretty slow progress. The other man tried in vain to get Tannenzapf to move faster.

After a couple of hours they hit on a railway line, which according to Tannenzapf's plan led directly to the Bug. They decided to proceed in a southerly direction along the track. In the early morning they came to a signal box ; the signalman, a Ukrainian, let them hide there during the day without troubling himself much about them. He was travelling almost all day and only returned in the evenings.

The next night the married couple left Tannenzapf ; his weakness was holding them up.

Tannenzapf dragged himself alongside the railway line, alone. At dawn, he hid in some bushes and devoured his last piece of bread and last hard-boiled egg. He had difficulty in keeping awake that day, but he knew he would freeze to death if he fell asleep.

In the evening he pressed on. On the morning of the third day he staggered into a village ; he was beyond caring now. His legs would hardly support him ; his feet were numb and his fingers cramped, like talons. Watchdogs in the village began to bark, but he paid no attention. He stumbled to the nearest barn, crept into the warm hay and fell asleep at once.

That evening he woke up and groped his way outside. In the fading light he consulted his crumpled map ; it couldn't be far to the Bug now.

He pulled himself together again. In the dead of night he made it to the river, which was frozen over. A Russian saw him over safely. On the far side the Rumanians arrested him and for a whole year he drifted from one prison camp to another. But his life had been saved. In the summer of 1944 the Russians liberated him. Returning to Czernowitz at the end of the war, he found that 35,000 of the city's former 58,000 Jews had been deported ; of these, only a few survived. Tannenzapf was one of them.

"I was one of them, thanks to the men of the Emmerich firm in Coblenz," Tannenzapf says today. "Particularly the engineer, Alfred Grube."

The horrors of the past are never really past. Neither can they be entirely forgotten. Even Tannenzapf thinks about them sometimes.

"When I go on my inspection trips alone in the Negev, memories come crowding in on me," he said. "Then I've got to pull myself together by sheer force so as not to shriek out loud and remonstrate with my God. But then I think of my wife and children, and I'm glad that life has given me a second chance."

The second chance: his wife, Rita, whom he married in Bucharest in 1947, and his two children, Joseph and Esther, 15 and 13 years old. Tannenzapf lives in a little bungalow on the outskirts of Tel Aviv. He is only at home during weekends, since he works as inspector of water installations in the Negev desert, which the Israelis hope to turn into a Garden of Eden.

Will it come off ? Will they manage it, Tannenzapf and all the others who have fled to this country, to this antique land, the cradle of man's history, the Holy Land of Jews, Christians and Moslems ?

That is what we believe, Tannenzapf said simply. He has maintained his faith and his hope. All the bitterness of his life and all the disillusionment have not crushed his spirit.

" Gentlemen, if later a generation should follow us too soft and gutless to comprehend our tremendous achievement, then Nazism will have been completely in vain. I think that tablets of bronze should be sunk into the earth, proclaiming that we had the courage to carry out this great and so vital task."

S.S. Lieutenant - General Odilo Globocnik, on a visit to the gassing installations in the Lublin area, August 17, 1942.

3

The settlement of Givat Aviv lies on the road from Tel Aviv to the south. The houses straggled, flat and white, over the silver-grey hill glowing in the haze of noon. Hedges of cypress and oleander bushes obstructed our view as we approached.

" We've got to turn right," said Chaim Mass, my colleague from Jerusalem.

" I think it's left," I replied.

A couple of children were playing by the roadside.

" Shikun Givat Aviv ? " Chaim Mass yelled at them. They shrugged and made some reply in Hebrew.

" Nobody knows a bloody thing here," Mass growled. He started up again with a jerk. The dry, hard heat of Israel blazed down on the roof of the car.

We made a left turn into a bumpy road. Clouds of dust swallowed us up.

A woman with a gaudy blue headscarf, standing behind the flowering crimsons and yellows of her garden hedge, shouted in German : " Where d'you want to go ? "

We explained. She indicated the house just opposite. Mass and I looked at each other and started to laugh. We got out and walked over to the house ; a woman came to meet us. She had a friendly, pretty face. She smiled. She showed us upstairs to her flat. Flowers and evergreen plants everywhere ; a pleasant living-room with tasteful, light-coloured furniture ; dimmed lighting which filtered through half-drawn venetian blinds.

" You're from Germany ? " she asked with a soft, central German intonation. She came from Tiefenort in Thuringia, a little place on the Werra, near Bad Salzungen. This was the home she had to leave—twenty-four years ago.

It had stopped raining. Outside everything was quiet.

Quiet except for the wind sweeping over the surrounding countryside. It was the evening of November 9, 1938.

They slept badly; they always did. They were scared.

At first it was just a splintering sound, like glass breaking. But they heard it at once.

Then it was more distinct: hurried footsteps, the tramp of heavy boots. A stifled scream somewhere.

"There's something going on," Emil Rothschild whispered.

Charlotte felt him stir by her side; the mattress was giving and she was aware of his breath on her neck.

She threw back the bedcover and sat up. Even before she could put her slippers on, the footsteps seemed much nearer.

"They're coming," she whispered.

"They're coming!" she repeated, so loudly that the room echoed. Just then there was a thunderous knocking at the front door.

Charlotte jumped up, grabbed her dressing-gown, snatched her clothes and flung the door open.

"Emil!" He was at her side.

"Open up!" a voice bawled from outside the front door.

They dashed out into the hall in the darkness. Then a door opened on the first floor and the landing was lit up.

"Quick—come up here!"

They stood there paralysed, gazing up. Then the face of their neighbour, Hans Hüter, appeared over the bannister rail.

"Come on!" he insisted.

They dashed up the stairs with bare feet and half dressed; Charlotte just had her flimsy nightgown on.

"Thanks," she stammered as Hans Hüter hustled her into the flat. His wife stood at the table; she was tall, with a big frame and a back like a ramrod. She had her hands on her hips and her face glowed like a lobster.

"Just let that mob come in here!" she cried. Two swift strides and she was by Charlotte's side. "Come on—you can get dressed in the bedroom."

Suddenly they could hear it all quite distinctly: a piercing scream out in the street somewhere, raucous laughter, the front door being broken to splinters and footsteps down in the hall. They had broken in.

Charlotte began to tremble. "God," she murmured.

Hans Hüter was pale and his lips twitched; but his eyes were hard. "Don't be scared," he reassured her, "this is my flat and nobody's going to come in here."

Emil Rothschild was leaning against the wall, white-faced. He was holding his trousers by the waistband, all bunched up; his hand was steady, but the knuckles stood out, protruding whitely.

"Come on," said Lisa Hüter again, leading Charlotte to the bedroom where she hurriedly dressed.

The noise of the rowdy mob downstairs stormed up at them.

Suppose they came upstairs . . . just suppose they broke in here. . . .

They'd kill Emil; they'd drag her off with them to one of their guard rooms, to a Nazi den; they'd beat her up, use force on her, they'd. . . .

Wild images raced through her brain.

She was a good-looking girl of twenty-four; she had only been married a year. She knew that men gazed after her in the street; she also knew that mob downstairs were drunk.

I beg you, let this cup of sorrow pass us by, she thought. I beg you, spare my husband. Spare me. Just another month, or maybe three—we'll be all right then. Spare me this time.

Fully dressed now, she went over to the kitchen. The mob were still creating an unholy racket in the Rothschilds' flat; there was a lot of noise in the street again, too.

Then Lisa Hüter ran to the window, pulled it up and leaned out.

"Stop it!" she yelled. "Quiet, down there!" And then: "Well, well, his worship the Mayor's son is with you too, I see!"

For a moment they all stood there numbed, the Rothschilds and Hans Hüter. Then Lisa banged the window shut, turned to the others and announced with deep satisfaction: "Just had to get that off my chest!"

"Are you mad?" her husband asked. "If those scoundrels—" then he started to laugh. A liberating kind of laugh. "She's right. Why should we put up with all this?"

C

In their initial terror they had all thought: now the S.A. will burst into the Hüters' flat as well, smash everything to pieces and drag Lisa, at least, away with them. But nothing happened to the Hüters—not even later, in the days after the *Kristallnacht.* Their fearless intervention on the Roth-schilds' behalf had apparently daunted the Nazis.

But at that time, in that flat, nobody knew what might happen.

"Please—somebody got a cigarette ? " Charlotte muttered.

Her husband passed her one. She smoked feverishly, puffing out wild gusts of smoke.

Eventually, the frightening noises ceased ; the shattering of glass, the stamping, people wandering about the down-stairs flat. Quiet at last. The last they heard was the sound of hobnailed boots dying away, a couple of shouts, then nothing.

And yet it was not like the silence of any other night, any more. It was as if something had come alive that night ; something which would never find rest again.

They sat together till morning, smoked, drank coffee, didn't speak much, knowing only that they were four human beings. Two were the persecuted and two the protectors.

There was murder in the air—they knew that. Murder and despoiling and rape and misery. But as they sat upstairs with that unsophisticated working-class pair they felt secure.

Finally, they went downstairs, thinking the whole thing was a hallucination which daylight would have dispelled. The flat was in complete chaos. They began clearing up ; but before they were through four uniformed S.S. came to arrest them.

There was a long silence in the cool house, out in the torrid settlements of Givat Aviv. Chaim Mass was leaning back in his chair, regarding Mrs. Rothschild with narrowed eyes.

Mass came to Israel all alone while he was still a young man. His family originated from Brno, in Czechoslovakia. He himself had had no direct physical experience of the horrors of Nazism ; but he was all the more intensely interested in the Nazi persecution of the Jews because his parents were victims of the " final solution."

" We thought it was all up with us," said Charlotte Rothschild. " We'd already applied—months ago—for legal emigration at the Palestine office in Berlin. Our passports were there ; and we'd deposited £2,000 there, to cover us both. We knew that staying in Germany was out of the question ; though the prospect of giving up everything connected with the life we knew, and starting from scratch in a foreign country, was not exactly encouraging. We knew we'd find life hard in Palestine. My husband was a merchant. He'd been working in a Jewish clothing business in Tiefenort till the owners shut up shop and emigrated. We were in for a difficult time in Palestine ; they couldn't do much with business people there. They were looking for pioneers, men and women who could handle a pick and shovel—and a gun. But we had no choice.

The morning after the *Kristallnacht* the S.S. took us to the police station in Tiefenort, where they'd already dragged other Jews. We were in despair. We'd sent our money to Berlin and packed our belongings, all ready to emigrate— and now this. After some argument the S.S. released me that afternoon ; I hurried over to the Katzes in Tiefenort, for somewhere to stay ; I was terribly worried about my husband, who was still under arrest. But that evening he got out, too. The Katzes—they were Jews, too—let us have an attic room. We didn't dare go back to our place. My husband and I lay sleepless till the small hours in the narrow bed in the tiny attic. Finally we decided not to wait for a legal emigration permit. We'd try to leave Germany illegally."

At that time the solution of the Jewish problem meant, to the Nazi hierarchy, the expulsion from Germany of as many Jews as possible. Therefore, the Gestapo tended to turn a blind eye to Jews who emigrated illegally. This happened mainly because the emigration quota of Jews to Palestine— and this is where most of the persecuted wanted to go—was kept very low by the British Mandate. So the Gestapo usually ignored illegal Jewish transports over the border to foreign countries. However, the whole situation was quite unpredictable and it could happen, too, that a transport was suddenly stopped, the secret emigrants arrested and put in concentration camps and all their belongings stolen. Crossing the border in this way, then, was a life-and-death gamble. The Rothschilds were aware of this ; but they took the risk.

During that month — November — Mrs. Rothschild travelled to Leipzig, where there was a Jewish office for illegal emigration run by a man called Bernd Bergmann. He promised to help the Rothschilds. The young woman returned to Tiefenort with fresh hope.

In all the weeks that followed the Rothschilds found countless Germans who helped them without concern for their own safety.

There was shorthand typist Elly Häusler, a woman in her early thirties, who rushed around from one organisation to another on the Rothschilds' behalf, did their correspondence and cheered them during those trying weeks.

There was the Hüter family, who had sheltered them in their own home that dreadful night.

There was Christine Hill, who often slipped them something to eat when times were hard.

And all these people showed their eagerness to help in the small town of Tiefenort, where everybody knew everybody else, and where an " Aryan " could expect serious consequences if he aided Jews.

The help and understanding of these people mitigated their hardship. But in December, when rumours piled up about the deportations to concentration camps, and about arrests and further indignities, their nerves gave way. They decided to escape to the countryside till it was actually time to emigrate—to a small village in the Hessian mountains, where an aunt, Johanna Richheimer, lived.

"Again a Gentile neighbour helped us—Otto Schlechtweg, a taxi proprietor," said Charlotte. " He took us in his car to Aschenhausen, where my aunt lived. It was snowing that night. Even as we left Tiefenort we had a vague feeling that we weren't doing the right thing. Schlechtweg dropped us at auntie's door and the neighbours saw us arriving. My aunt was upset, and obviously frightened ; we knew, right away, that we couldn't stay. After a little while we decided to go back on foot, the way we'd come—a distance of over 25 miles. It was dark and cold and the snow lashed our faces. My husband and I were carrying a suitcase each, and found it hard going. After about an hour's trudge, two men in long leather coats loomed up out of the dark, just outside Kaltennordheim. They demanded our idenity cards and arrested us—then took us to the Stag Hotel in the town."

This time, the Rothschilds refused to be intimidated. They were in a state of nervous agitation, but their consciences were clear. Charlotte Rothschild absolutely insisted that the men telephone the police station in Tiefenort for information about them. When they were reproached with " wandering about all over the place " (against the rules, for Jews) they explained that they only wanted to visit their aunt in Aschenhausen. The Gestapo were suspicious and didn't believe them ; there must be a shady motive, they thought, behind this sudden departure from Tiefenort. But after a long telephone conversation with the police there, they decided to release them. Once again they were out of danger.

Back in Tiefenort they felt lucky to have survived their ' outing ' so well. It had proved to them that they were obviously under constant observation, and that they had no alternative but to wait helplessly till the secret cue for their illegal emigration reached them—or till they were sent to a concentration camp.

Weeks and months passed. Nothing happened. Mrs. Rothschild reported once more at the liaison office for illegal emigration in Leipzig, but they just told her to be patient.

One day the Gestapo organised a lightning house-to-house search. Uniformed and plain-clothes officials burst into the Katz flat and ransacked cupboards and suitcases. They terrified the women with their threats ; but they found nothing. A few days earlier Charlotte had burnt all her private correspondence—innocent letters from friends and acquaintances. One never knew.

Shortly afterwards the Rothschilds started up from the table in alarm. Window panes were being smashed and stones hurtled into the room.

When they ventured near enough to see into the street,

there was a gang of twelve or fifteen children, booing and screaming and bombarding the house. Their faces were distorted with hate.

" That was one of the most terrible hours of my life," said Charlotte Rothschild, " the hate of those children . . . those poor kids with their poisoned minds. . . .

' Jewish pigs!' they yelled up at the windows, sticking their fingers in their mouths, whistling shrilly, laughing, shouting obscenities. A few of them wore Hitler Youth uniforms.

' Perish Judah!'

Then they sang in a raucous chorus:

' Die Juden zieh'n dahin, daher, sie zieh'n durchs Rote Meer, die Wellen schlagen zu, die Welt hat Ruh'!"*

Charlotte Rothschild pressed her hands over her face. She couldn't look or listen any more.

But this passed, too.

In May, 1939, the Rothschilds received news which could have proved pretty disastrous to them. They had already asked, some time ago, for their passports to be sent back from the Palestine office where they had applied for legal emigration ; now it transpired that Charlotte's passport had got lost.

" We were staying with my mother-in-law in Grunsfeld in Baden at the time. I travelled home immediately. It was Saturday ; I got photos taken and dashed to the passport office with the photos still wet—hoping against hope that they'd issue me with a new passport."

The unlikely happened. The director of the official passport office in Eisenach, a man called Hagedorn, presented Mrs. Rothschild with a new passport without any fuss.

"I probably owe my life to that man," she says today. "Even illegal emigrants need passports. One was lost without papers, then."

At the beginning of July, 1939, a few weeks before war broke out, the Rothschilds got a telegram from Cologne urging them to get moving. They arrived at the cathedral city at two in the morning.

* " The Jews march hither and thither ; they march through the Red Sea. The waves swallow them up and the world has peace."

Some Jewish helpers from the illegal emigration organisation took them to a suburban house. They were not allowed to leave the premises. All the rooms were crammed with camp-beds and the house was packed to the attic with illegal emigrants, most of them young people. After a couple of days there was a sudden panic ; a Gestapo check-up was in the offing, apparently. Then the emigrants had to leave the house and stay out till evening. The Rothschilds spent the day on the Rhine.

" We lay on the grass near the river ; the summer sky above us was cloudless. Everything was green and fragrant around us. The wind rustled in the poplars ; the ships passed up river ; and on the farther side the cathedral rose gracefully to the sky from a sea of houses. We lay there the whole day, drinking it all in, this last image of Germany ; and we realised then, for the first time, how beautiful our homeland was." Suddenly there were tears in Mrs. Rothschild's eyes. As she spoke I could see it all, too, the river and the city and the cathedral ; I felt guilty, almost, that I can sit there on the banks of the Rhine whenever I want to ; and that others can sit there, too, in the evening, when the heat abates and the sun is sinking and the mountains cast long shadows on the water. I felt guilty because we are allowed to keep all this ; and yet it was taken away from those who loved it as much as we do.

Two days after this final trip they were told that everything was ready. That evening, after dark, lorries covered with tarpaulins drove up to the emigrants' shelter—right up to the front door, so that the fugitives could jump on straight from the entrance hall. They sat tightly squashed together inside the trucks, on narrow wooden benches. All they could hear was the engine running in neutral ; then they felt a sudden jerk as the vehicle started up.

No one spoke. Everyone was wrapped up in himself.

It was a warm evening and the air under the low tarpaulin was stifling ; they found it hard to breathe. You could hear their gasping for breath in the dark ; otherwise, everything was quiet.

Charlotte Rothschild snuggled up close to her husband.

She was conscious of his nearness and needed his support, now that the decisive step had been taken. Now they were heading for a dark, mysterious future ; a new life from which they could expect nothing except worry, toil and the primitive conditions of a land in the process of development, and menaced by enemies.

Charlotte tried to distinguish the faces of the others in the gloom, to establish, from their expressions, what they were thinking of. But she could hardly see anything in the dim, ghostly light filtering in from the street or flashing spasmodically through a gap in the tarpaulin whenever they drove under an arc lamp.

She would have liked to know whether they all shared her emotions : fear, hopelessness, apprehension, dread of the menace of the unknown, and mourning. Mourning for the lost homeland that they would never see again.

Each mile the vehicle covered took her further from home ; with each passing minute the years of her youth passed into nothingness.

They were going to a land where Arabs fought Jews and Jews fought Arabs and both fought the English together. They were going to a land where people still lived in huts, under the merciless glare of a blazing sun.

Where there was no water and not much bread. Where people didn't wear ties, but open-necked khaki shirts, and women learned how to handle a gun better than their kitchen tools.

But that wasn't what she was thinking about. She was thinking of the past. Childhood days. Her aunt's back garden ; the rose trees in bloom ; the broom a golden blaze ; the aroma of pines in the sun ; the silvery rustle of birch leaves as the wind hummed through. The cows lying in the shade, in the dark-green luscious valleys of her Thuringian home ; the quiet villages, and the young lads singing in the evenings ; the flickering glow of the fires in the fields, every autumn, during the potato harvest. She thought of the peaceful days before Christmas, and the snow, and the ice cracking when the spring sun thawed the river. She thought of the cosy rooms in the old panelled houses, and the long evenings at home ; of her father and mother, and of the peace they had lost.

"You shouldn't cry," said Emil, squeezing her hand.

Charlotte shook her head mutely.

"We're starting from scratch. What are you crying for ? Because we've got to leave Germany ? There's nothing left for us here." His voice was bitter.

He was a male. It was different for him. She was leaving something behind ; her girlhood years, her youth. A man couldn't understand that.

"Will it be over quickly ? " a voice near her asked. "At the border, I mean."

"I'm sure it'll be over quickly," Emil replied.

They were travelling along the main road now ; the driver was accelerating.

"Won't be long now," Emil said.

"I wish we were there now," said Charlotte.

"Where ? " with a light laugh.

"In our old homeland," she answered ; this time *her* voice was bitter.

"Our old homeland is where we're going," said Emil.

"You really believe that ? "

"What else *can* I believe ? "

"Do you really think that this Middle Eastern country is our country—not Germany, where our ancestors were born, where they've lived for countless generations—far longer than lots of people who call themselves Germans today ? "

Emil laid his hand on hers. "It must be our home, this land in the East. We must believe in that, if we want to build up a new life. For ourselves—and for our children."

She hung her head.

For our children.

Would they have any children, anyway ? Was it right to have children at all at a time like this, in a world like this ?

The truck was travelling more slowly. The noise of traffic surged up.

"We're in Aachen," said someone who was sitting in front, peeping through a gap in the tarpaulin.

Suddenly the vehicle stopped with a jerk.

They heard voices singing lustily and heavy boots stamping on the roadway.

" The S.A. on the march," said the man who was in front looking out. Then he let the awning drop suddenly and leaned back.

Suddenly, fear returned. My God, I hope nothing happens to us now ; not now, when we're so near the border and safety.

All of a sudden Charlotte knew that she didn't want to go back any more ; that her nostalgia for the past had melted away ; all at once she knew that she was glad to leave it all behind, that she was longing for the new life beyond the sea, and that her yearning was for the Jordan and not the Rhine. She knew it, listening to the S.A. bawling their raucous battle song as they marched past.

No, this isn't our world any more, she thought. Our world is waiting for us in another land.

On they went. They passed through the town, the last German town, the ancient imperial city. They saw nothing of it ; they heard nothing of it but the noise of traffic and the S.A. singing.

At last, a couple of miles beyond Aachen, the vehicle pulled up. Someone came up to the tailboard and opened it ; the tarpaulin was pulled up and a muffled voice commanded : " Get out, all of you—quick ! "

They jumped down. Everybody had his item of luggage— each person was allowed to take just over 40 lb.

It was dark outside.

A dark figure, massive against a pale background of sky, indicated right.

" Up the hill ! "

They clambered up a slope overgrown with bushes. On the road before them they could see, quite distinctly, the light from the German and Belgian customs offices and the brightly lit turnpike.

They were marched into the wood.

" Single file ! "

They formed a column.

The leader had a big sheepdog with him, running up

and down the column of silent marchers as if he were guarding a flock of sheep. He was trained for the job, obviously.

They got to the top of the hill, took a transverse route through the wood and then marched along a road.

Suddenly the sheepdog came running noiselessly up to them, nuzzling them with his nose into the bushes. A man on a bike passed; the light from his lamp flickered grotesquely in front of him.

When he had gone the German leader drove them onwards again. Soon they heard somebody hooting like an owl. The leader returned the call; they were in Belgium.

They marched for five solid hours, first along a road and then along a railway track. In the morning they rested in a damp field; and when the sun rose they knew they were safe.

On their arrival in Belgium the Rothschilds shared the fate of all illegal Jewish emigrants at that time.

The refugees slept three to a berth on a chartered Greek ship, the Dora, the women port side and the men starboard. There wasn't much to eat, hardly any drinking water and still less for washing. It was hot and the boat stank of sweaty bodies, refuse and stagnant salt water. Days and weeks passed.

Finally, one night, they disembarked off the coast of Palestine. Drifting clouds hid the moon; the voyagers waded the last few yards to the shore. We've arrived, Charlotte thought dully, as she set her feet firmly on the sand. We've arrived—to start a new life.

They made it, the Rothschilds, virtually at the eleventh hour. In spite of all the trouble and hardship that awaited them in a strange land, they were among the lucky ones; they escaped from Hitler's Germany before the trap snapped shut, before war made all emigration impossible and delivered the helpless Jews to their murderers.

The Rothschilds were among the 310,000 German Jews who emigrated before 1939. Five hundred thousand Jews lived in Germany before Hitler seized power; of these, 190,000 still remained in their native land when war broke out. A mere 10,000 survived the end of the war ; over 180,000 died in concentration camps and the gas chambers.

As Chaim Mass and I made our way back to the car Charlotte stood in the garden of her house at Givat Aviv, waving goodbye. I waved back. She was smiling. She had two grown-up sons, one of whom was serving in the Israeli Army ; her husband was director of a flourishing shipping agency. Charlotte had adapted herself to Israel. It was 25 years since she first arrived. But she had not forgotten her old home, Thuringia.

" Give my regards to Germany," she called after us.

" I'll remember," I called back from the open car window.

When we got to the wide Jerusalem road and drove into the blue-washed hills of Judæa, Chaim Mass said: " She'll never forget where she comes from." And after a pause:

" She'll want to go back some day, like so many of her generation. But—can she ? Would you advise her to go back ? "

What could I answer to that ?

. . . . I observed, too, that women with the fear of death in their eyes, suspecting, or knowing, what lay before them, still mustered up the courage to chatter gaily to their children. Once, a woman on her way to the gas chambers came up to me and pointed to her four children, who were courageously supporting each other to get the smallest one over the rough ground, and whispered : " How can you bear to kill these dear, lovely children ? Have you no heart at all ? " . . . I remember, too, that once when the door of the chamber was being shut, a woman tried to push her children out. She was crying and shouting : " At least let my little children live." There were many moving individual incidents like that which affected everybody present. In the spring of 1942 hundreds of people in the prime of life went to the gas chambers, through the orchards with their flowering fruit trees, unsuspecting, to their deaths.

From the Autobiography of Rudolf Höss, Commandant at Auschwitz.

4

Evening sets in swiftly in Israel. The sun sinks abruptly below the horizon, and within a single minute the darkness has dispelled the shimmering light of this land.

The wind had come up from the sea, sweeping over the level coastline. After the languorous heat of the day people were crowding on to the dusty streets of Tel Aviv to get some fresh air. The babel of numerous foreign tongues throbbed in my ears as I was jostled, in that colourful crowd, towards Dizengoff Square. Hebrew and German; Yiddish, Polish, Russian, Arabic and Ladino, the dialect of the Spanish Jews. The languages of the ancestors of those Jews who had returned home, to Palestine.

Adolescent boys with their lively child's eyes shrilled forth the evening papers. Rabbis with long beards and black hats strode past, sunk deep in introspection. Then a young couple in uniform came towards me. He was a parachutist, with a red beret; the girl wore the khaki uniform of a signals unit. She and the young soldier laughed together. Their eyes were shining. Israel's young people are beautiful; they are a living refutation of the Nazi hate slogan about "Jewish sub-humans."

I turned into Dizengoff Street. It is a wide boulevard with rows of modern stores and cafés. It was easy to see that the strolling passers-by were Europeans. The elegant tables on the sidewalk retained some of the atmosphere of their old home. You could imagine yourself in Paris, or Berlin in the 'twenties, or Vienna, or Budapest.

I walked more quickly. I had a date with Eisenberg at eight. After walking smartly for twenty minutes I got to number 262, a four-storied block of flats.

Eisenberg was waiting down in the street. He smiled and held his hand out genially.

"Glad to see you," he said. "Shalom."

He led me through a narrow passageway to the front door—narrow because of the thick partition, built as a protection against possible Arab raids during the Sinai campaign of 1956. Nearly all the houses in Tel Aviv have these anti-air-raid walls in front of their doors.

We went upstairs. Eisenberg's flat was on the first floor. I expected to find a typical bachelor's den, but stepped into a small, comfortable two-roomed flat where everything was in scrupulous order, just as if the man who lived there was waiting, day after day, for the return of those dearest to him.

I sat down on the settee near the bamboo frame with its green climbing plants.

It wasn't hard to make conversation. I watched Eisenberg as he talked; tall and slim, his shoulders a little bowed; sleek hair, combed back, blond with a few streaks of grey; and very large, intelligent eyes behind gleaming spectacles. His clothes were casual but by no means sloppy; he wore a blue pullover with a grey, open-necked sports shirt underneath.

"After the war, I kept trying to contact the people who helped me at that time; but I got nowhere," said Eisenberg.

"They'll come forward, perhaps, when this report appears," I replied.

Eisenberg leaned over torwards me. "I'd so like to get in touch with them. I'm very grateful to them, even though they couldn't save my wife."

This was the first I heard of his having been married. I looked at him enquiringly.

"My wife was killed," he said. "My wife Olga and little daughter, Erika."

He hesitated. "They were deported and never came back. They ended up in Belzec death camp. Nobody ever came back from there. They're dead."

He said it as if he were trying to convince himself. But somehow there was a doubt in his voice. His last sentence sounded less like a statement than a question.

For twenty years this question had secretly haunted his brain. For twenty years he had known that these people were dead, but for twenty years he had been tortured by uncertainty and doubt because the final proof was lacking.

Before the war Eisenberg had an electrical business in Kattowicz. When German troops occupied Poland in 1939 Eisenberg escaped from Kattowicz, which was re-annexed to Germany as a former Upper Silesian town, and made for the so-called newly established " General Government," because he believed that he would not be subject to the German anti-Jewish laws there and would therefore be safer from persecution than in German territory.

His wanderings through occupied and divided Poland were pretty exciting, but he eventually, in the autumn of 1940, reached Rzeszow, now called Reichshof. In the meantime anti-Jewish laws had been issued for the General Government, too. Eisenberg, like all his co-religionists, had to wear a white armband with a blue Magen David (Star of David). When he arrived at Reichshof he reported at the local labour office, where the chief was a German Nazi called Pfeifer. Pfeifer despatched Eisenberg as a radio mechanic and electrician to the local Wehrmacht headquarters. At that time the Germans were urgently seeking skilled labour and technicians for the maintenance of their equipment.

Wehrmacht headquarters were in Reichshof's main thoroughfare, the Herrenstrasse. The enormous building— which used to be a monastery—had a big central courtyard.

Early one morning—it was autumn—Eisenberg presented himself to the ordnance officer, Lieutenant Vinne.

" Eisenberg ? A German name ? "

" Yes, sir."

" Where do you come from ? "

" Bielitz, in Silesia."

" Take that damned thing off as long as you remain in headquarters!" Lieutenant Vinne pointed, with obvious disgust, to the blue and white armband Eisenberg was wearing.

" But I've got to . . ."

" Here you haven't ' got to ' do anything, Eisenberg. Here you're under the local commander. And he doesn't approve of treating a certain group of people like second-class citizens."

Eisenberg felt how moist his palms were. "Yes, sir," he said, hesitantly.

"We can't pay you more than twenty zloty a week, Eisenberg. But, of course, you'll get the same food as the Wehrmacht, from the canteen."

Twenty zloty was equivalent to about ten Reichsmarks. Twenty or two hundred, however, the main thing for Eisenberg was food from the German canteen—and what Vinne had said about second-class citizens.

Later, he was standing in front of the local commander himself, Major Sprockhoff. Sprockhoff was a reserve officer, a grammar school teacher by profession. He hadn't much time for "the brown bosses" as he sometimes expressed himself in front of friends. His landlady was a Jewess.

"I'd like you to feel at home here," said Sprockhoff to Eisenberg. "And, above all, to feel safe with us."

"Thanks," Eisenberg muttered.

"I do expect you to turn out decent work. But that goes without saying."

Later, Eisenberg also met the adjutant, a Captain Zwiener. He seemed just as progressive in outlook as his boss. That day Eisenberg went home feeling—for the first time for ages —that he was a human being.

His home was a little room on a Polish farmer's estate on the outskirts of the town. It was an hour's walk from headquarters. He had to pass several police checkpoints on the way. Since freedom of movement was denied to Jews, unforeseen difficulties arose here. When Major Sprockhoff heard of this he came to the rescue immediately. Eisenberg was given a pass issued by army headquarters.

One day Eisenberg was stopped by a police patrol. They took a dim view of his not having a permit issued, according to regulations, by the civil authorities. The patrol leader reported the matter; Lieutenant Vinne was called to the district commander, who gave him a good dressing down.

"The higher officers of the local army headquarters were constantly getting into trouble for employing a Jew. But the more difficulties they encountered, the more aggressive their reactions to the civilian authorities and to the police. It was obvious that I enjoyed special protection, as very few Jews did at that time."

Eisenberg was extremely lucky. The first deportations of Jews to concentration camps, from which there was no return, had already begun. And—though Eisenberg and the other Jews from Reichshof didn't know it—the mass exterminations had begun, too. Major Sprockhoff and his staff belonged to that group of officers who had no sympathy with "the brown bosses"; but it was by no means easy for them to help Jews. The Jews fell under the jurisdiction of the German civil administration, in which the Gestapo played an all-powerful role. And the Gestapo would soon settle the hash of any officer who dared, by word or deed, to interfere with their powers. A Jewish survivor from Lublin—he, too, lives in Israel now—remembers quite well how a major and a lieutenant (his adjutant, apparently, though unfortunately he does not know their names) were cashiered and sent to a concentration camp overnight without as much as a court martial. This was simply because they had lodged a complaint that Jews doing road-building work in blazing heat got no water to drink, and had arranged for several cans of water to be brought them in an army truck.

But Eisenberg was by no means the Reichshof officers' "conscience Jew." "If they could have helped others they would certainly have done so," he said. But they could only help him; and this they did wholeheartedly.

After a while Eisenberg sent for his wife, Olga, and his little daughter, Erika. He believed they would be safer there with him than on her parents' estate near Triblitz. But were they?

Shortly after the family were reunited all the Reichshof Jews had to move into the ghetto in the northern part of the town. The roads leading to the ghetto were fenced off with barbed wire barricades and partly walled up. There was just one gate one could leave the ghetto by—even then only if one had a valid travel permit. And that was obtainable, then, only by Jews employed in a specialist capacity in German offices or factories and who had settled in or around Reichshof.

With the enclosure of the ghetto the Reichshof Jews' struggle for life began. This is where the story of Fritz Eisenberg really begins.

"We lived in a one-room flat in the ghetto centre. We didn't have much space but, considering the circumstances, we were content. We'd only been married a few years and our little daughter was a great joy to us. We were always consoling ourselves, saying the war couldn't last for ever and that after the war would come better times—even for us Jews.

In the evening, when I came home from work, my child used to come running out in the street to meet me. She'd throw herself into my arms and I used to whirl her round and kiss her hair; she'd laugh and snuggle up to me; then we'd walk the last few yards home together.

I'd always bring them both something to eat—a basinful of thick, nourishing Wehrmacht soup and sometimes a loaf, a bit of cheese or some tinned meat.

Often the soldiers used to come to me as I worked—it was right next to the general office and on the same floor as Major Sprockhoff's room—and brought me their radios. I repaired them on the quiet. I never asked for a thing. But they brought me foodstuffs and I took them home to the family.

Because of my privileged position I was naturally able to help the other poor devils who lived with us in the ghetto. I brought them food, maybe some meat, maybe some bread —everything we got we shared.

'I don't want to be better off if the others aren't,' Olga said.

Most of the military personnel at headquarters had no idea I was a Jew. A few knew but apparently weren't interested. When I met the officers they always greeted me pleasantly. If I had problems I'd always confide in Lieutenant Vinne or Captain Zwiener. They helped.

At home, in the evenings, I'd sit at the window with my wife, looking down on the ghetto street where people traded in old clothes and second-hand crockery. Now and then they'd barter a piece of jewellery, which they'd managed to hide, for a loaf or some butter.

'If only it could go on like this,' said Olga, 'so that

nothing bad should happen to the people down there or to us.'

'Don't worry; nothing will. Major Sprockhoff will look after us.' That was my answer and I really meant it."

Of course the Major would look after them. Hadn't he managed to find them this room all to themselves—through the quartermaster, Captain Becker? Hadn't he provided Olga with an official letter stating that the Eisenberg family was under the protection of Wehrmacht headquarters because the husband, Fritz Eisenberg, was engaged in urgent duties for the Wehrmacht? Then he'd had a second official letter pinned up on their front door, stating that the German civilian authorities weren't allowed entrance to the flat. What else could he do? He would look after them—no doubt about that.

"They've been deporting people," Olga said. "This morning. I didn't want to tell you at first in case it upset you."

"I know, anyway. A few old people."

Olga said: "They'll be taking the young ones away, too, one day." Her head drooped; her voice sounded discouraged.

Eisenberg put his arm round her shoulders. "Nothing will happen to us," he said quietly. "I'm sure."

Eisenberg paused in his narrative. There was a deep furrow across his forehead.

I believed what I said implicitly, then. I told Olga that. I knew that they were taking the old people from the ghettoes. The Germans pretended they were being transferred to special ghettoes, for people who couldn't work—old people's homes, so to speak. We knew better. We found out through the Polish underground that they were murdered. But all we younger Jews clung desperately to the hope that the Germans would leave us alone because they needed our labour. I believed that, too—I particularly, because I felt so secure under the officers' protection. We suffered agonies whenever we heard that another transport had left the ghetto, but we thought we were exempt. The Major would look after us; nothing would happen.

So far Eisenberg had spoken up in a clear voice. He was sitting upright in front of me, arms folded. But his last few sentences were muffled and indistinct. He had turned his face away ; he no longer looked at me ; he was gazing into the past.

"That's what we believed—until that day in August, 1942."

I glanced at my notes and put my biro down. In the silence we could hear the evening traffic in Dizengoff Street, the confusing babble of voices, the dull rumbling of a metropolitan thoroughfare.

Eisenberg cleared his throat.

"It's a long time ago," he said, "you know, so much has happened since. But to me—I can't explain it, really—it isn't a long time ago at all. Sometimes I think it must have been last night.

It's all so sharp in my memory, still. Maybe I've been thinking too much about it. I can remember every word spoken that day, every little detail of what happened."

The day began with General von Unruh's visit to Reichshof.

"Lance-Corporal Kunert, from the office, appeared in my workroom first thing. He told me an inspection was in the offing. So as not to make it embarrassingly obvious to the General that Major Sprockhoff was employing a Jew, I was to make myself scarce somewhere so that the General didn't run into me. I took a copy of a German magazine under one arm and disappeared into the attic. I was able to watch the inspection through the window. Military police and a couple of platoons of soldiers, who were directly under the jurisdiction of the district commander, were on parade in the courtyard. After a while the General appeared to do his inspection. Later I heard him and his escort creating a rumpus indoors. The whole business lasted till 3 p.m. When the coast was clear I came out of my hole and went downstairs. I got something to eat in the canteen and then went on working at my bench till five. When I left a few minutes later I took, as usual, the tureen full of soup for my wife and little daughter.

The minute I reached the street I noticed a general, pervasive atmosphere of disquiet. I couldn't have explained exactly what it was ; but it made me put on speed, without meaning to.

It was half an hour to the ghetto but this time I covered the distance in barely fifteen minutes. As usual, I presented my permit at the ghetto entrance and got through the check-point without trouble.

Inside the ghetto I saw small groups of people standing on the street whispering to each other. The air was peculiarly tense ; there was a strange, uneasy atmosphere, a bad sign. I felt my mouth tighten with tension ; I began to run, and dashed round the corner of our street panting for breath.

My heart was beating wildly when I got to the front door. I rushed into the hall and bumped into a woman who lived in one of the rooms beneath us. She put her hand up to her mouth.

'What happened ? ' I yelled.

'Your wife. . . .'

'What about my wife ? '

'She got taken away . . . the Germans . . . a special operation . . . all young mothers with children. . . .'

I only understood half of the last bit. I flew up the stairs.

Our flat door was open ; I ran into the room, stopped short, saw what had happened

The room was empty. All gone.

Everything was just as usual ; the kitchenette tidied up, the room nice and orderly. Everything in its place. But the sweater. . . .

My wife's sweater lay in the middle of the room, as if she'd been interrupted in her packing. She *had* been packing. Her suitcase, which was usually on top of the wardrobe in the corner, had gone. *She* had gone. They had taken her away from me !

When I saw the sweater I lost control. I screamed till the walls resounded.

Suddenly I saw, too, my daughter's little frock, lying near the settee. A tiny woollen dress. I picked it up, put it on the settee, smoothed it with my hand.

At that moment I knew : I had to get help.

I wheeled round, ran to the door, staggered downstairs and raced along the street. People gazed after me stupefied.

At the ghetto gate I pulled out my permit, held it before the guard's face, pushed it away again and went on running. I reached the headquarters in the Herrenstrasse gasping for breath.

Sprockhoff was standing out in the yard, all ready to leave for his holidays.

'Major!'

He looked up.

'What is it, Eisenberg?'

'My wife . . . they've taken her . . . she's gone. . . . Major, help me! Please help me!'

He laid his hand on my arm.

'Easy now, Eisenberg. What happened? Tell me, from the beginning.'

'There's been a raid in the ghetto, Major. All young women with children have been transported. So has my wife. My wife! And my child!'

I saw how Sprockhoff's lips narrowed. His cheeks were flushed.

'But I wrote you a protection letter!'

I just looked at him, dumb.

'Come on,' he said, pulling me towards the staircase. 'Zwiener!' he called. 'Captain Zwiener!'

The adjutant appeared in the office doorway.

'Yes, Major?'

'They've taken Eisenberg's wife. See to it she's brought back.'

'I'll try.' Helplessness, sympathy and inexorable determination fought for dominance in his expression.

'Captain . . .' I stammered.

'I'll try,' Zwiener said again. 'I'll get on to Pfeifer at once.' The labour office chief was one of the highest party officials in Reichshof.

Major Sprockhoff turned to me. 'My car is waiting downstairs,' he said. 'I'm going to Germany. But you can depend on Captain Zwiener.' He slapped me on the back. 'It'll turn out all right, Eisenberg.'

I gulped. I nodded without speaking. Sprockhoff proceeded downstairs and then shouted for his car; his voice sounded agitated and nervy.

Captain Zwiener went back into his office and glanced at the clock. 'I hope I can still get hold of somebody.'

I waited in the open doorway while Captain Zwiener telephoned. But he couldn't reach anyone who knew about the transport. Pfeifer, the boss, whom Zwiener knew well and who was in touch with the Gestapo, was away.

'I'm sorry,' Zwiener said. 'We'll have to try first thing tomorrow morning.'.

'My wife, captain . . .' I whispered. My voice seemed toneless ; I had to clear my throat.

'I know, Eisenberg, but we can't do a thing at the moment.'

I went home. Don't ask me how I spent that night. It was the most frightful night of my life.

Next morning I was at work by seven ; Zwiener came at eight. He did not look very communicative. He went straight into the office and I heard him telephoning.

I stood near the door, listening. He was speaking to Pfeifer. Headquarters was prepared to fetch Mrs. Eisenberg and the child back in a Wehrmacht car. I heard the fight he put up for us ; but I also heard his voice become gradually less sure, his replies more monosyllabic.

Silence at last.

My heart beat till it echoed in my throat. I felt a fiery wave shoot up from my stomach ; I felt sick.

The office door opened and Captain Zwiener came out.

He didn't need to say anything. I could see it in his face.

'Help me, Captain! Help my wife!'

'I can't,' the Captain said. 'There's nothing I can do, Eisenberg.'

Then something happened I'll never forget. Captain Zwiener sobbed. 'I've got a family, too, Eisenberg,' he said hoarsely.

I saw the tears streaming down his cheeks. He laid a hand on my shoulder. 'Do you think I don't understand, Eisenberg ?'

'I know,' I muttered, 'I know, Captain.' I could no longer bear to see this man, whom I respected so much, crying like that.

I made my way downstairs. I don't know how I got home. I only know that I shut myself in my room, lay on the divan, pulled a rug over my head and closed my eyes. I didn't want to wake up again, ever."

There was silence in the room. I said—just to make it less oppressive—" What about the things you found in the room, belonging to your wife and daughter? A sweater? A dress?"

" Here." Eisenberg got up.

I followed him into the bedroom and he opened the wardrobe door. He had his suits and a couple of coats hanging there—and between the coats two hangers with woollens on. A blue sweater and a tiny, pink, knitted dress.

He took them off the hangers, laying them carefully and lovingly on the bed.

"Souvenirs," he said softly. "I'm one of the lucky ones who at least have a memento of their loved ones."

In spite of all his tribulations he carried the sweater and the dress around with him—through all the ghettoes, camps, hotel rooms, dormitories and lodgings—from that day in August, 1942, to this day, from Reichshof in Poland to Tel Aviv in Israel.

I stood mutely beside him, staring at the clothes.

Eisenberg opened a photograph album and showed me a couple of snapshots of his wife and child. I studied them silently.

" I'm very lucky, really," he said again, " to have been able to save these things and these photos."

Then, I knew it. He was still waiting for the return of his wife and child, in spite of the twenty years between. He had never re-married. He knew his wife was dead; his little daughter, too. But, for him, a gleam of hope still remained —that one day the door would open and his wife would walk in. I could see it in his face as he hung up the dress and the sweater again.

Reason assured him they were dead; but his heart refused to believe it.

After that dreadful day Eisenberg stayed away from work. Nothing mattered to him any more. What had he got to live for?

Two days later Lance-Corporal Kunert appeared at Eisenberg's flat. He wanted to know whether Eisenberg was coming back to work. Eisenberg screamed and yelled at him and cursed all Germans. Kunert made no reply. He heard out Eisenberg's outburst without comment. Finally he went away, mission unaccomplished.

That afternoon the Chairman of the Reichshof Jewish Committee, Dr. Kahane, came. He advised Eisenberg to return to work. If he immured himself in his ghetto room he couldn't possibly do anything for his wife, Kahane explained. Over at headquarters, perhaps, he might still be able to find a way to help her, and maybe find out where she and the other women had been taken. After hours of shilly-shallying he eventually talked Eisenberg round. Next morning he returned to work at headquarters.

He kept his ears open and spoke to Lieutenant Vinne and Captain Zwiener, and eventually to Major Sprockhoff when he returned from holiday, but all in vain. His wife was still missing. At first, Sprockhoff just couldn't believe that Eisenberg's wife would never come back again. Eisenberg is absolutely certain, today, that the officers of Wehrmacht headquarters did all in their power to try to save his family. When, at last, they were forced to concede their helplessness against the Gestapo, they were all the more determined to protect Eisenberg himself.

About four weeks after the young women and children had been taken away the Gestapo telephoned Major Sprockhoff, demanding to know why Eisenberg, as a Jew, was still employed at headquarters. Sprockhoff described him as the best radio technician in the whole of Reichshof ; the Wehrmacht couldn't do without him. The Gestapo then proposed a bargain ; if Eisenberg repaired their radios and made a good job of it he could stay with Sprockhoff.

Eisenberg did—and stayed.

Shortly afterwards, some young Poles sneaked up to the ghetto wall one evening and shouted to the Jews that they had been able to establish contact with the deportees through the Resistance. The women needed food and money to bribe the guards with—then they would be released.

The men in the ghetto frantically collected together several boxes full of provisions and a few thousand zloty, which they handed over to the Poles with hurriedly scribbled letters and makeshift parcels. Eisenberg, too, gave them all the money he had left and all the food he could scrounge. The young Poles disappeared and were never seen again.

Eisenberg was spared deportation. He had nothing to live for, but in the quiet hours of loneliness he asked himself what Olga would have wanted. That he give up ? Or that he live on to cherish her memory ?

Where was she ? Was she still alive, or dead—liquidated, as they put it ?

All around Eisenberg the murderers of Jews reigned supreme. The " final solution " had reached Reichshof. The ghetto diminished day by day. Whole rows of streets were evacuated, in one mighty sweep, through the deportations. The barbed wire fence was drawn in and the vacant flats put at the disposal of " Aryans."

Finally, there were only 60 Jews left of the 30,000 who used to live in the Reichshof ghetto. The S.S. were ordered to " dissolve " the ghetto.

That was in 1944. The front line was drawing nearer the town. It was an open secret that the Jews left in the ghetto were to be sent to extermination camps so that they should not fall into Russian hands as witnesses of German atrocities.

Eisenberg reported to Major Sprockhoff to say goodbye, because he expected to be deported any minute. Once again, Sprockhoff saved him, by getting him transferred as radio technician to an aircraft factory near Reichshof. So Eisenberg escaped deportation and, in all probability, death in the gas chambers. One foggy day in the autumn of 1944 all the factory's machines were packed ready for transport back to the Reich. The atmosphere was that of breaking up camp. Eisenberg and a couple of other Jews—skilled workers— escaped by climbing over the barbed wire round the slave labourers' barracks in the night and making for the woods. They were captured by Polish partisans, who at first treated them as likely spies. Jews who had escaped from the Germans must be suspicious characters, according to their way of thinking. They were beaten up and left to starve. But then the Russians came, who were persuaded that Eisenberg

and his unhappy friends were not collaborators in disguise.
Eisenberg was free; he could go where he wanted. So he
returned to Reichshof where he had lost his wife and child.
He collected information and made enquiries. Finally, the
rumours were confirmed; the transport of men and women
from the Reichshof ghetto in August, 1942, had gone to
Belzec death camp between Lublin and Lemberg.

No one came alive out of Belzec. It was the very first
organised extermination camp in Poland. Here, in March,
1942, the first permanent gas chambers were put into
operation.

There is a macabre eyewitness account about the gassings
in Belzec—dated August, 1942, when Eisenberg's wife and
daughter were taken away. It was written by S.S. Lieutenant
Kurst Gerstein from the S.S. Ministry of Health.

Gerstein had sneaked into the S.S. for his own purposes—
that has been authentically proved since. Originally he was
studying to be a missionary and a doctor and was arrested
twice by the Gestapo—in 1936 and 1938—for distributing
religious pamphlets. After his second release he learned of the
death of a relation in the Hadamar asylum, where the Nazis
had begun murdering the mentally sick. In order to investi-
gate the background of these "euthanasia" murders Gerstein
reported at the S.S. Ministry of Health in 1941 and was
immediately accepted on account of his medical knowledge.
In 1942 he was already head of the section dealing with
poison gas "for disinfection purposes." Among other things,
this section supplied prussic acid for the disinfection of
S.S. uniforms.

On June 8, 1942, Eichmann's deputy in Prague, Hans
Günther, ordered Gerstein to go to Lublin. There he was
received by Globocnik, concentration camp chief in that
area. Hitherto, the extermination camps in southern Poland
had run gas chambers fed with exhaust gases from diesel
engines. This method seemed too circuitous to Eichmann.
Gerstein was now to act as "gas expert" and inspect the
extermination chambers in order to work out a plan whereby
they could be adapted to Zyklon B. Gerstein never did this;
on the contrary, he sabotaged the supply of prussic acid

to concentration camps and actually diverted it to real delousing stations.

Gerstein came, saw—and wrote a horrifying report. On the return journey from the death camps he spent the night in the corridor of a sleeping-car to Berlin, where he happened to meet Baron von Otter, Secretary to the Swedish Embassy. Still completely distraught because of what he had seen, he gave the Baron a detailed account of what was going on in Poland. He entreated him to inform his government immediately and to incite world-wide publicity. He explained to von Otter that he had only joined the S.S. to get a complete picture of the ghastly things going on behind the scenes in the Third Reich.

It seems almost uncanny now; von Otter reported to Stockholm, but the Swedish Government did nothing. It was not until after the war that they sent the British Foreign Office a memorandum about Gerstein's report!

That was not all. Gerstein tried to contact the nunciature of the Holy See in Berlin. They had no interest in the statements of an S.S. officer. He was ordered, politely but firmly, to leave the embassy building. After the war the Americans found Gerstein in a Rottweil hotel. He handed them a memorandum about what he had seen in the extermination camps and about his attempts to awaken the world's conscience. From then onwards we lose track of Gerstein. He is supposed to have been captured by the French, and died in mysterious circumstances in Fresnes prison, near Paris, in July, 1945. He was found hanged in a cell which, apparently, he shared with several hard-boiled S.S. types. In 1949 his wife received a communication saying it was impossible to throw light on the exact circumstances of Gerstein's death. Even his burial place is unknown.

This man's eyewitness report is probably the most horrific ever written about what happened in concentration camps.

" Next day we travelled to Belzec. A small railway station had been specially built for this purpose, on a hill, due north of the Lublin-Lemberg highway, in the left corner of the demarcation line. To the south of the highway were a few houses with the inscription ' Special Command of the Waffen S.S., Belzec.' The actual head of all the lethal installations, police captain Wirth, had not yet arrived, so Globocnik introduced me to S.S. Captain Obermeyer from Pirmasens. Obermeyer showed me only what he was obliged to. I did not see any corpses at that time, but the smell of the whole district in the August heat was pestilential and there were millions of flies everywhere. Near the little two-line station was a large barrack building, the so-called 'cloakrooms,' with a large valuables counter. This was followed by a room with about a hundred chairs, the barber's room. Then a narrow pathway out in the open, under birch trees, with double barbed wire on either side, and notices: To the Baths and Inhalation Rooms. Before us stood a kind of bathing hut with geraniums, then a small staircase, and then three rooms on either side, measuring five metres by five and 1 metre 90 high, with wooden doors like garages. At the far wall, difficult to see in the dark, were great wooden ramp doors. On the roof—as 'an apt little joke'—was the Star of David; and in front of the building a notice saying 'Heckenholt Foundation.' I wasn't able to see any more that afternoon.

Next morning, just before seven, I was informed that the first transport was due to arrive in ten minutes. And, in fact, in a few minutes, the first train from Lemberg arrived. The 45 carriages contained 6,700 people; 1,450 of them were already dead on arrival. Children, their faces terribly pale and fearful and the dread of death in their eyes, peered out through the barred hatches; the adults were farther up. Two hundred Ukrainians tore open the doors and whipped people out with their leather thongs. A large loudspeaker gave out instructions: 'Undress completely, and remove your glasses, artificial limbs, dentures, etc. Surrender your valuables at the counter, no receipt given. Fasten your shoes together carefully, for collection later.' In a pile of about 25 yards high no one could possibly match them up together otherwise. Then the women and girls went to the barber, who cut off their hair in two or three snips and threw it into potato sacks. 'That's for some special purpose, for the U-boats—caulking, or something,' the S.S. man on duty told me.

The column started moving, a beautiful young girl in front; so they walked along the path all naked, men, women and children; without dentures, without anything. I was standing with Captain Wirth up on the ramp between the chambers. Mothers with babies at their breasts walked up hesitantly and stepped into the death chambers. A hefty S.S. man stood in the corner, reassuring the poor people in parsonic tones that 'Nothing at all is going to happen to you! When you get inside, just take a deep breath. This expands your lungs. It is necessary to inhale in this way to avoid illness and infection.' They asked what was to become of them and he replied: 'Of course, the men will have to work, and build houses and roads, but the women don't have to. They can help with the domestic chores or cooking, if they like.' This faint gleam of hope was enough to get some of them—poor devils—to step into the gas chambers without resistance. Most people knew better; the smell was enough for them. So they climbed up the few steps and then saw it all: mothers with tiny children, quite naked, grown-up men and women—they hesitated, but they walked into the gas chambers, pushed on by those behind them or driven by the S.S. with their leather whips. Without a word, most of them. A Jewess of about forty, with blazing eyes, cursed the murderers for the blood they were spilling. She received five or six strokes with a riding crop in the face from Captain Wirth personally, then she disappeared inside, too. Many people prayed. I prayed with them; I cowered in a corner and cried out loud to my God and theirs. I longed to go with them into the gas chambers; I longed to die their death with them. Then they would have found an S.S. man in uniform in the chambers, and the whole matter would have been treated as an unfortunate accident and consigned to oblivion. But I must not do that. First I must tell the world what I have seen here. The chambers are filling up. See that they're well packed—Captain Wirth's orders. People are standing on each other's feet. Seven to eight hundred in 25 square metres—45 cubic metres! The S.S. use physical force to cram them together as tightly as possible. The doors close. Meanwhile the others wait out in the open, naked. 'They do it in winter, too,' I am told. 'But that's enough to kill them,' I said. 'That's just what they're here for,' replied an S.S. man in his north German dialect. Then at last I understood why the whole setup was called the Heckenholt Foundation. Heckenholt was the driver of the diesel engine, a minor technician who also built the plant. The people were to be murdered with the diesel exhaust gas ; but the diesel wouldn't work. Here comes Wirth. It is embarrassing for him, one can see that ; this has to happen today of all days, with me here. Yes, I see everything. I wait. My stop-watch has registered it all accurately—50 minutes, 70 minutes ; and the diesel won't start. They wait in their gas chambers. In vain. They can be heard crying and sobbing. Captain Wirth gives the Ukrainian, who is supposed to be helping Heckenholt with the diesel, thirteen strokes across the face with his riding crop. After 2 hours 49 minutes—my stop-watch registered it accurately—the diesel starts. Right up to this moment, the people in those four chambers—four times 750 people in four times 45 cubic metres—were alive. Another 25 minutes go by. Right: many of them are dead now. I can just see it, through the little window. After 28 minutes there are not many left alive. At last, after 32 minutes, they are all dead !

The men from the working party open the wooden doors from the other side. They—themselves Jews—have been promised their freedom, and a certain percentage of all valuables found, in return for their horrible duties. The dead stand upright in the chambers like columns of basalt, pressed tightly together. There would be no room to fall or even to bend over. Even in death you can recognise the families. Their hands are locked together in a death grip ; it is hard to tear them apart, to make room for the next contingent. They throw out the corpses—wet with sweat and urine, and some defiled with excrement or with menstrual blood on the legs. The corpses of children fly through the air. Time is short ; the Ukrainians rain their whiplashes on the working parties. Two dozen dentists clamp open the mouths, looking for gold. Gold to the left, no gold to the right. Other dentists break off the gold teeth and crowns with forceps and hammers.

Captain Wirth keeps scurrying around. He is in his

element. A few workers look for gold, diamonds and valuables concealed in the anus or the genitals. Wirth calls out to me: 'Try and lift this box of gold teeth—that's only from yesterday and the day before!' And in an incredibly vulgar and ingratiating tone: 'You wouldn't believe how much gold and diamonds we find in one day—and dollars, too. Look for yourself!' Then he took me to the "jeweller" who had to look after all these treasures, and showed me everything. Then they pointed out to me a former director of the 'Western' store in Berlin, and a violinist: 'That is a former captain in the old Austrian Imperial Army, holder of the Iron Cross Class I; he's now a camp elder and member of the Jewish working party!' The naked bodies were taken on wooden stretchers, only a few yards wide, to graves measuring 100 x 20 x 12 metres. After a few days the corpses swelled up, but caved in again shortly afterwards, so that they could throw another layer on top. Then they sprinkled about 10 centimetres of sand over the surface so that just a few solitary arms and heads protruded. I saw some Jews scrambling around on top of the corpses in one of these places, working in the graves. I was told that, through an error, those who had arrived already dead on one of the transports had not been undressed; obviously this had to be rectified to avoid their taking their clothing and valuables with them to the grave. They never took the trouble, either in Belzec or in Treblinka, to register or to count the dead. They just based their estimates on the size of the carriages. . . . Captain Wirth asked me not to put forward any suggestions in Berlin for changing the setup; but to leave everything as it was, just as if all had gone according to plan.

All my statements are literally true. I am well aware of the extraordinary implications of my allegations—and I make them before God and the whole of mankind. I swear on oath that nothing I have recorded here is an invention or an exaggeration—this is exactly what happened."

Olga and Erika Eisenberg were deported from Reichshof at the beginning of August and it has been established that they were taken to Belzec. It is also established that on August 18, 1942, a mass execution took place in Belzec—

5,000 people within a few hours. Kurt Gerstein was an eye-witness of this. It is nearly certain that Olga Eisenberg and her child were among the victims whom he saw go into the gas chambers.

Eisenberg soon left Reichshof. The spectres of the past drove him away from a land so defiled with the blood of those he loved. He turned his back on Europe and went to Israel; he has lived in Tel Aviv since 1949. He runs an electrical business in Dizengoff Street with an old friend he met during his last days in the aeroplane factory.

Israel has become his new home. But it is a lonely home; it cannot dispel the nostalgia of this exile from Europe for the land where he spent his youth and the happiest years of his life—the most terrible years, too.

Later we walked along Yarkonia Street, past the ultra-modern Sheraton Hotel, a gigantic honeycomb radiating light. There the American tourists meet their Israeli relations; there they all stare at each other in amazement, the bankers from Brooklyn and the sunburned kibbutzniks, the Chicago businessmen and the toilers from the Negev or the Huleh marshes. We could see them behind the sparkling glass façade of the Sheraton Hotel, and Eisenberg smiled, as one smiles when one thinks of a dear, kind relative who is totally ignorant of what has been happening in his own family.

We said goodbye outside my hotel.

"Shalom," said Eisenberg, pressing my hand. He waved again as he turned the corner. Then he vanished into the night, a man condemned to solitude.

Early next morning I drove to Lydda Airport. Dew hung on the grass and shimmered on the bushes with their violet blooms. As I looked back I could see the vast, undulating countryside, dotted with blue and red and yellow and streaked with white. The white streak—that was the desert, with the glow of morning sun on it. Mist shrouded from view the hills of Judaea.

We had a smooth take-off. From the air I gazed eastwards and my eyes were blinded. The east was where Jerusalem lay. It vanished. I opened my diary. One word sprawled right across the next page: Berlin.

" Let me make one thing clear: I shouldn't like to be a Jew in Germany. Secondly : if, in the foreseeable future, the Third Reich becomes involved in hostilities with foreign countries, then it goes without saying that we in Germany must give first priority to settling our account with the Jews—and in no uncertain fashion."

Hermann Göring after November 9, 1938.

5

If you stood in the yard of the old house in the Landwehr-strasse in Berlin, you could see, through the bushes and the bright green foliage of the trees, the Home for Aged Jews. And sometimes you could see, in the windows looking out on to the garden, the old peoples' faces ; their white hair and their eyes either half extinguished behind thick glasses or still bright and alert, gazing out over the lawn, as if seeking a path to lead them out swiftly and securely to a new and more pleasant land.

But there was no such land for them. There was Theresien-stadt instead. That was the Nazi " pensioners' concentration camp," where elderly Jews over 65 who were no longer " dangerous " were incarcerated. Theresienstadt was not an extermination setup like Maidenek or Auschwitz, but a sort of geriatric camp. That was how the brown bosses looked at it, anyway. Half Jews, former Jewish bureaucrats and Jewish officers with decorations who had fought for Germany in World War I, were also sent there. The selection was not systematic, however. You either went to Theresienstadt or Auschwitz according to the whim of some S.S. chief or other. And even Theresienstadt did not guarantee your survival ; tens of thousands were gradually " transferred " to the extermination camps in the east.

The Nazis' main aim was to make Theresienstadt a " model " concentration camp to deceive the neutral countries ; this misfired, however. It was a sort of Potemkin village. It is true that there was some " Jewish self-govern-ment " ; but the S.S. were the actual bosses.

In 1942, in Theresienstadt, 87,000 prisoners were crowded into an extremely narrow area, in a small town which normally numbered about 7,000 inhabitants. By the end of the year, however, the number of prisoners, according to a "statistical report" compiled for Himmler as a State secret in 1943, had been "reduced" to 49,000. The reason given by the author for this rapid depopulation: "decease."

33,200 Jews from Germany, 14,200 from Czechoslovakia and 39,700 from Austria arrived at Theresienstadt in huge transports during the course of the year. Many of the deportees had even "bought" their places on the transport; in other words, they had handed over to the S.S. jewellery or currency which they had hitherto managed to conceal, in order to get into this allegedly "privileged" camp. But 38,000 soon continued their journey—to the extermination camps of Poland and Russia.

The total number of people "channelled" through Theresienstadt can no longer be calculated. In October, 1944, there were still 11,000 people there. From that period to the end of the war the number of prisoners increased again to 32,000 because of "admissions" from evacuated Polish camps. On May 11, 1945, the Russians occupied the camp and brought the horror to an end.

The old people from the Jewish home in Gerlachstrasse went to Theresienstadt, too.

It was in the afternoons that the covered trucks drove up to the house. You sensed it was coming, days before; you knew the grey vehicle would appear and that some face or other would disappear from the window and never look out at the garden again. You knew, too, that it would be all quiet over there afterwards, absolutely quiet.

They came in the afternoon.

They pulled up right outside the door. A few uniformed S.S. formed a loose guard on either side of the pavement through which the old people were conducted by Gestapo officials in plain clothes. The old people had been waiting, apparently. The first few began to come out almost as soon as the engine was switched off and the door had closed behind the Gestapo officials who walked into the Home for Aged Jews, their faces expressionless. They came out, these old people, whose faces you could have seen in the windows the night before.

They were all wrapped up in faded coats which had gone out of fashion long ago, and wore felt hats which, for all the care they took of them, had become a little grubby. They carried small suitcases and briefcases and little bundles tied with string.

They came out of the house quickly and stepped up to the lorry ; there was some pushing and shoving but hardly a word was spoken apart from an occasional " come on, move," from the uniformed guards. Then the tailboards at the back of the truck were pulled up and the steel bolts shot into place. You could see the guards' knees, with their rifles laid diagonally across them ; you couldn't see the old people any more. A sudden cloud of greyish gas puffed out of the exhaust and the truck drove off.

The Gestapo men in civvies walked over to a limousine parked unobtrusively near by. Soon they, too, had disappeared.

They sat opposite each other in the kitchen, in the feeble light of an electric bulb. Friedel looked at her mother.

" What's going to happen to the old people ? "

Leon Knychala, who was standing at the window staring out into the garden—the Jewish old people's home was just behind it—turned round slowly. He took his pipe out of his mouth and contemplated the ancient, blackened bowl.

" Are they going to gas them, dad ? "

Leon Knychala was silent.

" The whole town is talking about it," Friedel said.

" I've heard nothing about it."

" What happens to them, dad ? "

" The same as could happen to us if we don't keep our mouths shut."

The girl wouldn't be put off.

" What becomes of them ? "

Leon Knychala's yellowish face, with its sharply etched wrinkles and kindly eyes, darkened.

" It's enough to have to look at it. We don't have to keep talking about it as well."

" Why don't we do something ? "

" Do what ? "

" Something to stop—these crimes."

Gertrud Knychala spoke for the first time. "You don't know what you're talking about, child."

"I know quite well."

"But not enough," said Leon Knychala.

Gertrud was leaning, hands folded on the table ; she looked speculatively at her husband. Then she asked: "Don't you think it's time to tell the child everything ? She'll find out sooner or later."

Leon shrugged. Gertrud turned to Friedel. "You ask what your father is doing. Well, he buys food coupons on the black market for Jews in hiding, for instance. He sees they get something to eat. And letters, newspapers. Is that nothing ? "

Friedel looked at her father. "I didn't know," she said, subdued.

"Why should you ? The fewer there are in the know, the better."

"I'd like to do something, too."

"Your husband's a soldier ; if they catch you he's in for it, too."

"Herbert thinks like we do."

"I haven't asked for help from anyone."

"Dad—I asked you what we were doing in the way of resistance. I asked because I want to do something, too. This afternoon I looked on while those people were taken away, over there in Gerlachstrasse. Old men that you shaved yourself in your barber's shop, your customers. I saw how the S.S. hounded them into the truck. I was just standing there and one of the S.S.—a cheeky young devil—asked me: ' D'you want to get on with them, since you're interested ? ' And he pointed his gun in my direction. The great hulking Gestapo men stared at me and I turned and ran away. I was so ashamed, afterwards. Why do we always buckle under ? Why do we always do everything we're told ? Why the hell don't we stand up to them sometimes ? Do we have to put up with all this ? "

"Do you talk about this at work in your armaments factory ? " Leon asked, appraising her coolly.

"I wouldn't dare," Friedel said. She knew she was blushing. The clock on the kitchen cabinet struck nine.

"Time to go to bed," Leon said.

Friedel went out into the back yard again. Over there, behind the dark bushes in the garden, was the old people's home. But it looked quiet, black, almost dead. Friedel shivered. She pulled her cardigan tighter over her shoulders. She knew there were people still living there ; but the house seemed to her as empty and lifeless as a solitary mussel shell, washed up on the shore by the gale.

From then on, Friedel used to slink out into the garden of the Jewish home every evening. In the dark, under the trees, she used to meet the old people who were left.

"Could you post a letter for me ? Could you do some shopping ? The food's getting worse . . . could you let my daughter know . . . could you. . . ?"

She did it all. She posted letters and bought food. She did what her parents had already done. You had to help ; you couldn't just look on. You couldn't just leave those people to their fate.

Dangerous ? Of course. But then Louis Link arrived, and things became *really* hazardous.

Link was a Jew, a widower around sixty who lived in a furnished room near the Landwehrstrasse. Leon Knychala had shaved him all his life, almost. He knew that Knychala helped "underground" Jews, though he never talked about it. He himself had not yet gone into hiding. He thought the Gestapo would not be interested in him at his age.

He looked much older than he was—small, frail, sickly. He was tougher than he made out, though. After all, sixty is not so ancient, but Link always used to say ". . . at my age. . . ." He talked a lot about death, as if he'd accepted the fact that his life had run out ; but in actual fact he was hanging on tooth and nail to what was left of it.

One afternoon, in the summer of 1940, when he was at the depot collecting his food tokens for the coming month, Link smelt danger. When he showed his identity card the man behind the counter gave him a searching look, then got up and went into another office at the back without a word.

Suddenly, Link was afraid. Something was wrong, he felt. He grabbed his identity card off the desk and fled.

It was only that evening, after closing time, that he ventured to go to the Knychalas.

Leon had been clearing up; he'd washed the last traces of soap from the basins and swept up the last bits of hair, then someone knocked at the door.

"Who is it?" He stood the broom in the corner and went to the front of the shop.

"Please let me in!" It was someone in distress; one could tell from the voice.

Knychala opened up quickly and old Link staggered in. His eyes flickered. He hugged a worn-out briefcase under one arm.

Knychala shut the door behind him without a word and turned the key.

"They're after me," Link gasped.

"Here." Leon took his arm and hustled him into the kitchen at the back of the shop.

Gertrud didn't ask questions. She just set a third place on the table, with a plate and some aluminium cutlery.

Link sagged into a chair. When he was somewhat calmer he told them about the incident in the food-token office; his words were laboured and disconnected.

"I don't know where to go," he said at last.

Leon looked at him, his face expressionless as ever. If you wanted to, you could read his thoughts in his eyes.

"You'll stay here."

"Yes," Link whispered. He had no will of his own.

"You can hide in the cellar till we think of something better."

Link cowered in his chair.

"Well, let's have something to eat," Gertrud Knychala suggested. She brought the casserole to the table and handed Link the bread basket.

"Come on; you must eat something."

She spooned the vegetable stew into Link's plate.

"Thanks, thanks," he murmured.

Gertrud looked askance at him; at his white hair and

weak, rather dreamy face. A man of sixty who was scared.

What would happen to *them* when they were old ? She glanced across at her husband. They weren't exactly young any more. Would they, too, have to run away from someone ? Would they, too, have to ask strangers for shelter, without a thing they could call their own? Would they, too, be haunted by fear in the evening of their lives ; fear threatening and wordless, ever-present as one's own shadow ?

" Eat," she said to Link.

He did. You could see that he had to force every mouthful down. Meanwhile he cast anxious glances at the door leading to the shop.

" What if they come ? " His voice trembled.

" Nobody's going to come," Leon Knychala replied.

" They'll be looking for me."

" Let them. We'll hide you."

" I shouldn't have come here at all."

" Well, you're here now—so eat."

When they had finished Leon got up. " Come on."

A door led right from the bedroom to an adjoining cellar. The Knychalas' rooms, shop and flat, were a kind of semi-basement—not unusual in old houses in Berlin. So the cellar was on a level with the flat, not beneath it. You couldn't see from the street that there was an extra room adjoining the bedroom at all, because it was right underneath the hall leading to the other flats in the house.

It was to this cellar that Knychala took the runaway Link. He took the door between bedroom and cellar off its hinges and put the wardrobe in front of the space ; he loosened the plywood back so that one could lift it up and open it from the bottom. During the next couple of days he secured it, from the cellar, with a narrow wooden bar. When he heard a certain knock—and only then—Link would release the crossbar, then one could lift up the plywood partition and crawl through the wardrobe into the cellar.

It was an ideal hiding-place. No one who didn't know his way about the flat could possibly guess that the wardrobe concealed an opening to a secret cellar. It would fool any layman. But would it fool the " specialists," the Gestapo, if through fate or sheer bad luck they managed to follow Link's trail this far ?

The heat that day was oppressive. Balls of pearly blue clouds over Berlin ; thunder in the air which never broke out. Heavy drops of rain falling occasionally. I was looking for Adalbertstrasse in Kreuzberg, near Neukölln ; a working class area. Here you could still see grey curtains behind grey windows. Stretches of dull asphalt without a single tree or shrub ; haggard frontages ; stones and heat. Kreuzberg, as a residential area, is not pleasant.

The people I was looking for lived in one of these houses. A couple of steps led to a door on the ground floor. Soon I was in a room with two beds, a wardrobe, a couple of trunks and chests, a one-ring electric cooker on a wooden stand and a table in the middle of the room between the beds.

Mrs. Knychala gave me a hand—a white, flaccid hand with trembling fingers. Her lips, all twisted as the result of a stroke, tried to smile.

Her daughter, Friedel, was sitting on one of the beds. She was pale ; she had only recently been operated on. There was a smell of medicine.

They only had this one room facing the street—a scene of poverty and resignation.

The old woman's glance, inquiring and helpless, shifted from me to her daughter. She offered me a chair and I asked for her story. She had forgotten so much, she said, it was so long ago—but with her daughter's help she managed it.

The Berlin Senate had acclaimed her an "unsung heroine." The Senate is the only provincial government which recognises officially the help given by Germans to victims of Nazism. That means 100 marks a month—a small fortune for the Knychalas, because the old woman got an old-age pension of only 135 marks a month and the daughter got 105 as a premature invalid.

Mrs. Knychala sat down with hands folded. They trembled. Her knuckle bones stood out, thick with gout.

An unsung heroine. She was 78 and sometimes she didn't know where the next day's cash was coming from. She was ill and her daughter was unemployable. Yesterday they followed the laws of humanity ; today, in the affluent 'sixties, they lack the necessities of life.

"When I came home that evening I told my father: ' You can't do it. You can't hide Link here. You'll have us all hanged, dad.'

Friedel smoked leisurely. . . . Her eyes were half shut, and the sickly face relaxed as she inhaled.

"That's what I told him, because I was afraid it would all come out. Helping the Jews over at the home, or someone else that came to us on the quiet—that was all right, one had to do it, but to hide someone in our very home—someone they were after—that was another thing. I wasn't afraid myself ; I was thinking of my parents. I knew what they'd do to my father if they caught him. But he just said, quite calmly: ' Friedel, just leave me alone. Link's staying.'

And so he stayed. In the evenings, when my father's assistant had left and all the doors were shut and the blackout curtains drawn, we let Link out.

As soon as it was dark he was allowed out in the street for a walk and a little fresh air.

It was only after dark that the day began for him. You see, you have to project yourself into that time. Some decent people lived in the house above us, but there were plenty of Nazis there, too. Suppose they'd had an inkling that we were harbouring a Jew! We couldn't hope for mercy, then. We were being watched, all the time. Already people were beginning to talk because they knew where my father stood. And I'm quite sure they noticed the various errands that my mother and I ran for the poor people in the old folks' home.

Now, with Link around, we had to be more careful still.

You can imagine how horrified we were one day when Link didn't come back from his walk.

Nine o'clock, ten o'clock—no sign.

There was a rapping at the back door at eleven—the usual signal.

I rushed to the door and opened it. Link was outside —but not alone."

It was some time before the three Knychalas pulled themselves together. Link had brought another runaway Jew with him, a man in his early thirties called Salli Strien. Strien worked at a coal merchant's ; all Jews who were still allowed to work, or forced to, were dustmen or street sweepers or did other heavy manual labour of some kind. That afternoon, he had heard he was to be deported. And so he came, in his dirty, black coal-heaver's uniform, to the Knychalas.

The first thing Leon did was to bolt all the doors and draw all the curtains carefully. Then he got Strien a washbasin with warm water. The attractive features of a young man soon revealed themselves under the layer of grit which had covered Strien's face. He didn't look a bit " Jewish " ; he was big and blond and quick to smile, and though he knew of the danger he was in he didn't seem to give a damn.

They quickly prepared supper for Link and Strien and then debated what to do. Leon Knychala said: " Where there's room for one there's room for another." Of course he meant the cellar where Link lived.

Friedel said: " I can still remember how my heart nearly stopped with fright. Link was a big enough risk for us ; if we were to hide yet another Jew what on earth would happen ? Apart from that, Strien obviously wasn't the man to allow himself to be locked up, all day, for months on end. He'd brought his bike—it was chained up just outside our shop—and he just grinned and informed us he meant to go on using it."

Leon Knychala proceeded to give Strien a lecture on the art of survival when the Gestapo was on one's track. He was a bit less voluble after that.

They crept into the cellar through the wardrobe. They now had a camp bed in there which they'd brought over one night from the Jewish old people's home, and a sofa and an old armchair that one could sleep on at a pinch.

In the few seconds that the glow from Leon's torch slid over the room, Strien looked around him. Naturally they couldn't put the light on because the cellar's air vent led directly on to the pavement.

" Here . . .", he muttered.

Leon Knychala nodded.

Strien turned and grasped Leon's hand.

" Thank you so much. I'm truly grateful. God bless you."

"Nonsense," said Leon Knychala, "it's nothing at all." When he was embarrassed he slipped into the Berlin dialect, though he usually spoke with a rolling intonation which betrayed his East German origin.

When they had closed the wardrobe door behind them, Knychala sighed deeply.

"I don't know," he murmured, "I don't know. . . ."

"What don't you know, dad?"

"This Salli Strien. A nice young fellow—but there's something about him. . . . I can just sense danger."

"Send him away, then."

"What, just send a man away? Drive him away from my door? How can you think of such a thing, girl!"

Friedel shrugged.

"No," said Leon, "I'd never send him away—even if I knew that one day he'd have all the Nazis in the Alexanderplatz after my blood. If they come, they come—Salli Strien or no Salli Strien."

They came—in the autumn. Just before midnight, there was a loud knocking on the shop door. Friedel, who was sleeping on a settee in the shop, started from her sleep.

"Who on earth is it?"

A fist hammered at the door till the shop re-echoed. "Open up at once! Gestapo!"

Friedel jumped up and threw a dressing-gown around her. She had no time to think. She went to the door and turned the key.

The door was flung open from outside and four men burst in. The first two had leather overcoats, wet and gleaming. The other two wore heavy winter overcoats—and the yellow star.

"Where's your lover, Jewish whore?" the first Gestapo man yelled.

Friedel clutched at the collar of her dressing-gown.

"I've got no lover! My husband's at the front!"

"You Jewish sow! You're having it off with Strien! You've hidden him!"

One of them rushed through the open kitchen door to the back entrance. "He's through here!"

Friedel had pulled herself together. " Don't be silly! The key's still on the inside!"

They stormed into the bedroom and got the Knychalas out of bed.

There were blows, screams from Mrs. Knychala and protests from Leon. They staggered into the kitchen in their nightclothes.

The Gestapo: " Where are the Jews ? "

Friedel: " I don't know any Jews."

Leon: " What's all this about ? "

The Gestapo: " You've hidden them here. We know."

One of the Jewish traitors: " The whole world knows."

Leon: " Nonsense!"

One of the Gestapo struck him in the face with his open palm. The taller of the two Jews whispered something to the other.

The Gestapo whispered to one another, then went to the bedroom again and looked under the bed. They flung the wardrobe door open and its dark innards yawned at them.

They rummaged about in the clothes on the hangers.

Leon looked on indifferently. Gertrud had turned her face away, her cheeks fiery red. Friedel's knees felt like water.

Then one of the Gestapo shut the wardrobe again.

" We're coming back," he promised.

Whereupon the four vanished.

Friedel shut the shop door behind them with trembling hands.

From the cellar they could hear the Gestapo's footsteps and their hoarse yells, and the blows and curses as Leon and his wife were driven out of bed.

Strien sat bolt upright on the sofa staring into blackness, his fists clenched round his bicycle pump. If they came in— he'd make them pay dearly for his life.

Link lay motionless on the camp bed ; he didn't even dare to sit up or make the slightest movement. He was shaking with terror.

Stupefied, they heard one of the police say: " They're here."

Footsteps on the floorboards nearby. Silence. Then, a vague crackling sound.

They'd opened the wardrobe.

Strien held his breath. Link closed his eyes.

A rustling, like mice, in a dark corner of the cellar. More crackling sounds. Footsteps dying away.

Strien exhaled slowly and Link's eyes opened ; but he just saw coloured stars and vivid dancing circles. I'm going to be sick, he thought, but it passed.

" We've got to go," said Strien resolutely.

An hour had passed ; the danger was over. They were having a consultation in the kitchen.

" But where will you go ? "

" I'll go out to the country, where my wife is hiding."

" You know perfectly well, Kurt "—that is what they called Salli then—" that it's much too dangerous. Even your wife isn't safe out there, and anyway she comes to town every week-end to hide in the cellar with you. How d'you think the two of you are going to live out there without being noticed ? In a hut out in an open field ? "

" We can't go on risking your lives."

" Then you can give up your excursions on your bike ! "

" I have to get a bit of exercise. But you're right, Leon, I won't make any more trips."

" I honestly don't know. . . ." Link murmured. " I'm an old man. Look, if they catch me it isn't so bad . . . but you . . . it's up with the whole family if they catch you . . . just because you've hidden us ! "

Leon Knychala rummaged around in the kitchen cabinet. He brought out a bottle of schnapps in which there was just a drop left—a small glass for each of the three men.

He poured out ; they drank.

" Now I want to tell you something," Leon growled when he'd had his drink. " So long as nobody finds this hideout, you stay here. If they find it we're all finished. But as long as they fail they can't prove anything and we're living in Abraham's bosom, so to speak. And, as you saw, it just didn't occur to the Gestapo that the wardrobe was a secret door. Okay—now get moving. Go to bed. It's high time."

They came back exactly two weeks later.

They came at dawn, and this time took Leon away with them.

They found nothing, just like the first time. You could see it in their faces as they searched around the bedroom—they knew they were on the right track. They were snuffling around like hounds on the scent but the scent just stopped dead in the Knychalas' bedroom.

It did not occur to them that the wardrobe was a secret entrance to the Jews' hiding place.

Strien and Link crouched in the cellar, not daring to breathe, like the first night, waiting for the thunderous knocking on the back of the wardrobe, the splintering of the wood, the gun barrel gleaming in the light which would suddenly penetrate their dark underworld from outside. But nothing happened.

They just took Leon with them.

That same night Gertrud Knychala suffered the stroke which still leaves her left side paralysed and her face twisted.

In the morning she lay in bed, unable to stir. This time Friedel didn't have the courage to fetch Strien or Link out of the cellar.

At eight o'clock the barber's assistant came as usual; they couldn't tell him anything.

The hours that passed were agonising. Friedel had just signed off sick at that time and did not have to go to her job in the armaments factory. She smoked one cigarette after another. She paced the kitchen restlessly, waiting for the doctor. He came and saw to her mother; then she waited for her father, for a word from him—just for something.

She thought of the Gestapo cellar in the Prinz-Albrecht-Strasse and the interrogations at police headquarters on the Alexanderplatz. She thought of the concentration camp, place of no return.

Did she know of a single one who came back?

What did they do to the Jews?

What did they do to Germans who helped Jews, or who helped anyone who was persecuted?

She could not think coherently. Her head whirled.

Friedel: "Today I don't think I could do it. My nerves would give way, I think. Perhaps they did, even then. I don't know. My mother was lying in bed without moving, just babbling incoherently, her face twitching; the assistant was bustling around in the shop, looking nervously about him and not knowing what to make of it all ; the air was reeking with misery, and Strien and Link were squatting down in the cellar with nothing to eat because I couldn't go to them. They were sitting there shaking while I waited for my father ; perhaps he'd never come back again. Why had we done it ? Why had we risked our own necks to help other people ? Just why ? I didn't know ; I only knew that we had to, no matter what, and that we had to grit our teeth and go on hoping. Hoping for some luck ; just a little, that's all. That was all we could expect really."

In the lunch hour, when the boy was out, Leon came back. He came in by the back door.

He just said " Don't worry." His cheeks were scratched and bloodstained ; both eyes were blackened and swollen and his lips all puffy. His suit looked dirty and torn and his shirt dripped with sweat.

Friedel : " I couldn't take any more. I shouted at him : Look what you got for it, look what we all got. Why do we do it ? But he just looked at me and said, ' Have a good cry, girl, cry your heart out ; it'll be all right, believe me. It's all over ; they won't come again, that's for sure. I've talked them out of it, you'll see. Everything's all right.' ' All right,' I screamed, ' why do you look like that then, just take a look at yourself,' and he said : ' How can I help what those people are like—I'll go and change and in a couple of days you'll see no more black eyes.' ' What about Strien and Link ?' I asked. ' Well, what about them ? They're staying.' "

They stayed. Leon Knychala was right ; the Gestapo didn't come back. Strien and Link were saved.

Mrs. Knychala smiled at me. Her face, so disfigured by shock and the results of the stroke, beamed kindly.

" Yes—they were saved." But immediately her face clouded. " They would have been," she corrected herself.

It was hot in the room. I asked Friedel to open the door to let some fresh air in. The street noises came through to the flat ; lorries rattling past, the shrill tones of women, children screeching as they played on the asphalt—then boxes being banged around in front of the little shop up the road and bottles clinking in the crates in the pub on the corner.

"Yes, they caught them, both of them," said Gertrud Knychala. "We had them with us four years—four years in hiding."

"How come they caught Strien and Link ?"

The Gestapo did not come again. The coast was clear. At first Strien and Link could not believe their luck and would not venture outside ; even Strien's wife, who had visited him occasionally, came seldom now. They were eaten up with fear, all of them.

Months went by ; nothing happened. They got a bit bolder.

Link started his walks again—after dark, certainly, but he went a bit further each time. And one night he did not come back.

Panic seized the inmates of the little ground-floor flat in the Landwehrstrasse. What had happened to Link ?

A week passed ; no trace.

Finally, the rumour reached the Knychalas that Link had been caught.

That should have made Strien more cautious. On the contrary.

He had money. He bought a forged army identity card. With this to fortify him he even ventured on to the street in the daytime and rode about on his bike to see to his business and hunt out friends who, with the same kind of irresponsible courage as his, had managed to procure food tokens and hoard some provisions.

And that is what happened on July 20, 1944.

That afternoon Berlin was seething with excitement. Wild rumours circulated about the attempt on Hitler's life. There was shooting in the Bendlerstrasse. The military were barricading the roads and the S.S. were on the march. Barricades, checkpoints, arrests.

And Strien rode to town on his bike.

"Are you crazy ?" Friedel yelled at him.

He just laughed. "Nothing's going to happen to me, Friedel ; I've got a lucky charm. My army card." He beat his chest and rode off.

He didn't get further than the Strausberger Platz, where

he rode right into a Greater German Watch Battalion checkpoint. They had occupied parts of the town centre after the assassination attempt had failed. The military and S.S. detachments arrested hundreds of people even remotely suspected of opposition to the Nazi régime. Identity card checkups must have been stringent, which was probably why Strien was caught and arrested. A little while later he was sent to a transit camp in the Grosse Hamburger Strasse for deportation to a concentration camp.

That evening a Jewish acquaintance brought the Knychalas a note that Strien had managed to smuggle out. " I've gone away—Salli." They knew what it meant.

Friedel went over there next morning ; just as the prisoners were being walked in the yard. Among them she recognised Salli. The guard at the gate asked her what she wanted ; she said, nothing. She was told to beat it ; and that was the last she saw of Strien.

They had hidden him for four years. But in Salli Strien the urge for freedom was stronger than the desire to survive. He could not bear waiting, in a dingy cellar, for the day of true liberation to dawn. He is missing since July 22, 1944, and presumably ended up in Auschwitz. His wife survived the war ; she hid in her hut till the Russians came.

Link was deported to Theresienstadt. He, however, survived the war. Suddenly, in 1945, he appeared at the Knychalas' house. He was a bent old man, broken by the concentration camp. But his first visit in Berlin was to those who had protected him, for many years, from the persecutors, and thereby saved his life. For hardly anyone who was included in the first batches of deportations from Berlin in 1940-41 came back alive.

" It would have been better if you had killed a couple of hundred Jews and not destroyed such valuable property!"

Reinhard Heydrich on the occasion of the so-called *Kristallnacht* (Night of the Broken Glass) on November 9, 1938.

6

The figures of the bearers oscillated through the semi-darkness of the gloomy hall. They shuffled around with faltering steps, bowed beneath the weight of the timber. The wood was still damp, freshly cut and very heavy.

Had it not been for the creaking of the electric saw—that penetrating, ear-splitting whine, hour after hour and day after day, you might have heard the bearers coughing and groaning as they lifted the timber and swung it on to their shoulders ; you might have heard them gasping as they laid their burden down, over on the ramp.

They did this for thirteen hours a day. Or night. From six in the morning to seven at night or five in the afternoon to six in the morning.

If they were too slow, the sharp-featured Siegfried Anton came and bored his piercing eyes into them, screaming furiously : " A bit of elbow grease, you Jewish swine ! "

But they couldn't work any faster. Men of sixty cannot work like men of forty. And boys of fourteen haven't the strength of men of thirty. And they were precisely those age groups : sixty or seventy or fourteen and fifteen. All the other men had been deported long ago. They had " got their lists "—the current expression.

It was 1942. Lothar Korn was one of the few Jews in the prime of life who had not yet got their lists. He lived " in safety " with his family in a five-room flat in the Hohen-zollernplatz in Berlin.

In safety ?

He was engaged on essential war work in the timber firm of Kolshorn in Pankow, Berlin, suppliers to the Göring Works. For a Jew, " war work " meant at least twelve hours' strenuous manual labour, not much to eat and virtually no medical care.

Korn worked thirteen hours ; he went home completely

exhausted. Even in his sleep, the same images tormented him: the half-lit, gloomy hall, the tottering steps of the bearer in front of him, a flickering, reddish light somewhere in the background, lungs rattling, hearts beating loud and irregularly under the strain, the saw with its shrill whine, the throbbing of the engine.

He went to sleep gasping, fists clenched; he was gnashing his teeth without knowing it. Sweat streamed off him as he slept.

Suddenly he was shaken into wakefulness.

" Lothar ? "

" Yes ? "

He opened his eyes, at once wide awake.

Trudi, his wife, was bending over him, her hand on his wet cheek. The kindly eyes behind the thick glasses shone with affection; but there was pity there, too, and she could not hide it.

" What is it ? " he asked. He had swung his legs out of the bed.

" The lists have come."

He looked at his watch. It was just 10 a.m. He had slept exactly an hour; he had been on night shift.

The lists had arrived. It had come then. . . . Goodbye to security. Goodbye to Kolshorn and his " essential war work."

Suddenly fear gripped his throat.

" Get my coat."

" What are you going to do ? "

" See Anton."

" Anton ? "

Yes. He had to seek out that slavedriver and implore him to let him stay in hell.

Hell in a depressing hall, musty with wood dust, is still better than being deported. After all, this was his own hell. He had to fight it alone. But now others were involved: his family, Trudi and Hanni, his daughter of six.

He ran out of the house, buttoning his coat inside out so that the yellow star could not be seen. He travelled to Pankow by tram. It was October, and cold; the wind whistled through the streets, sweeping the leaves before it. It's going to be a hard winter, Korn thought. They're just

outside Stalingrad ; you can hear it every day on the wireless. But they're not getting any further. Perhaps the war
will be over next year. Peace ; and with it our salvation, the
salvation of the Jews. And yet, maybe not—not if we're
deported now. I've got to speak to Anton.

Anton was sitting in his office. He nodded at Korn.

He had a soft spot for Korn ; apparently he had saved
him from deportation up to now. But now, it had happened ;
and what could Anton, devil that he was, do ?

Anton reached for the 'phone and spoke to someone called
Doberke. It was obvious from the conversation that he was
a Gestapo official.

It was a long conversation. Korn sat on the edge of his
chair trying not to breathe.

Anton fought doggedly for him ; he wanted to have his
way. Korn knew Anton wasn't doing it for him ; he simply
wanted to win the argument. So what ? I don't care, I don't
give a damn ; I'll kiss this swine's hand if he manages to save
Trudi and Hanni from being deported.

Then Anton yelled into the 'phone : " Oh, all right, take
your friend Korn and stick him . . . okay . . . agreed ! But
I'll tell you one thing—if you take Korn from me, one of
my best workers, you can have Bär, too—the lazy sod !
What ? Yes—pronounced like bear in the zoo ! Heil Hitler ! "

Korn clenched his hands ; they were silppery with sweat.

Anton looked at him. " And the best of luck," he said.
" Sorry. But I can't get anywhere with the big boys." He
grinned crookedly. " Give my love to the concentration
camp."

Korn didn't know how he got home. But he knew that one
day, one far distant day when this was all over, he would
settle with Anton.

The man who opened the door was in his early sixties ;
he did not look it. He was of medium height, slim, casually
dressed, and tough. It was this toughness that had saved
the life of Lothar Korn, the teacher.

He took me to his study. The sliding doors leading to the
adjoining drawing-room were open, and there a woman
was busy arranging flowers in a vase. We were introduced ;
she was Korn's wife, a doctor.

"My second wife," he said later. His first wife, Trudi, who spent those agonising years with him, died after the war as a result of her privations and suffering.

Korn expressed one wish which I promised to grant; he did not want his name mentioned in my report. "I have very strong personal reasons," he said. His story is the only one in which we have altered a character's name at his own request. The names of the people who helped Korn are, of course, genuine.

Korn handed me a list of 23 people, all of whom helped him and his family during their "illegal" existence. Dr. Elisabeth Abegg, a retired teacher who was now 84, headed the list. During that time those persecuted by the Nazis moved freely in and out of her flat. Mrs. Abegg was awarded the Federal Republic Cross of Merit for her heroism at that time.

These are the names of others who helped the Korns:

In Berlin: Ewald and Meta Schmidt, Mrs. Berta Meise, Mrs. Anni Nimz, the Mucha couple, Heinz and Gertrud Lewin, the Gräser family, Mrs. Felicitas Dietrich and Mrs. Hilde Reinefeld.

Mrs. Elfriede Einsiedel, Crailsheim; Dr. Helmut von Frankenberg, Düsseldorf; and Mrs. Becker, Lindow in der Mark.

The following were killed during the war, or have since died: Mrs. Elfriede Loeffke, Mrs. Hedwig von der Lanken, Paul Fischer and his wife, Lieschen, Mrs. Frieda Sachisthal, Dr. Hildegard Wegschneider.

"It wasn't just a few that helped us," said Korn. "There were many. Without them I wouldn't be alive today—neither would any of the Jews who hid in Berlin, for years, some of them."

Korn took some documents out of a file—all manuscripts and notes on that period.

"It was awful, of course, For my wife and child it was torture. We just vegetated in dreadful uncertainty, haunted by danger the whole time, and knowing that however desperately careful we were we could fall into the enemy's hands in the end. But we were alive. We were even free—like outlaws are free, if you like, but free nevertheless."

116

Korn was a born storyteller. I could see it all ; I shared his emotions ; I was with his family in their first days of flight from the Gestapo.

The " lists " arrived on October 8. A clerk from the Jewish community had brought them. The Jews lined up for deportation had to make an inventory of their property ; they could take with them only the personal items they needed, clothing, toilet articles and so forth.

The eighth was a Thursday. That evening Korn conferred with his wife. They soon agreed that they must attempt to escape deportation. Korn had heard enough about the sinister destinations of those transports to know there was no return. He had to choose between the certainty of being liquidated and the insecure existence of a man on the run. He was a determined character and his decision—to stand up to the Nazis—was not a difficult one. In the next few days Korn filled in the lists scrupulously to gain time. Meanwhile Trudi distributed clothing, linen and valuables amongst friends. In the evenings, in the dark, Korn dragged along heavy suitcases full of china and cutlery—the sort of thing one likes to save.

On the evening of October 12 Korn took the lists to the Jewish community headquarters in Oranienburg Street. Then he went home and the whole family left the flat, locked up—and went " underground."

At first he lived with a Mrs. Loeffke, an old family friend. Her daughter, Irmgard Müller, managed to get him an original letterhead from the Reich Ministry of Labour, with the aid of which he forged himself a document describing himself as a lecturer at " The Berlin Institute for the Study of Italian and Italian Fascism." He only altered his name slightly : Korn to Kern.

" Naturally I was under no illusions—I knew my real identity would come to light if the Gestapo interrogated me," Korn said, " but the ' institute ' document was sufficient for superficial checkups on the street by the Wehrmacht or the police—I hoped so, anyway.

When we first went into hiding I had 8,000 marks, food tokens for four weeks and potato cards for six months. Our clothing and linen and other portable goods—and, of course, the most important legal family documents—were left with friends in packing cases.

The biggest problem for us was a safe hideout. We moved from one district to another and lived at countless different addresses—we never stayed long anywhere.

I was on the go all day, getting food and visiting friends, people I thought could help me to find accommodation. Just one dull, grey day after another. Our only pleasure, my wife, my daughter and I, was our hurried meals together, cooked on a spirit stove in an attic, or in the kitchen under the surveillance of the people who lived in the house, behind a locked door.

At night we were tormented by bad dreams ; or one slept like a lump of lead, without dreaming, but waking absolutely whacked in the morning. I was an outcast ; even my voice was the voice of a refugee. But I was always careful to look my enemies straight in the eyes ; because one thing I didn't want to be in those days—a coward. But then I wasn't afraid. Of course I was constantly worried about Trudi and Hanni, but I had no fear for myself. I drummed it into myself again and again : If you get frightened, you've had it. They'll smell your fear like a dog smells it when someone's afraid of him.

Upstairs and downstairs, frantic conversations in doorways, meetings with other "underground" Jews in secret places, furtive whispers in the dark. During the first weeks it was all very new to us ; we were used to wearing the Jewish star. But now we went about like "Aryans," without the star, quite unselfconsciously, on the surface at least. Now we used public transport ; we sat confidently on benches marked "Forbidden to Jews" ; and we used restaurants when we had no opportunity to cook for ourselves.

Autumn came. We heard the news from Stalingrad on the radio and suddenly you could see traces of doubt and uncertainty on the faces of the brown bosses.

Bear up—it can't last much longer. We had to endure it all.

We experienced one scare after another. Hours which seemed like nightmares. One day I 'phoned a pharmacist named Kromrei from whom we used to buy cod liver oil for Hanni. I begged him to put a bottle aside for the child. But

I couldn't come into his shop. Perhaps he could. . . .

He hadn't seen me for ages and probably thought I had been deported long ago. He promised to meet me at a certain place that night.

He arrived at the rendezvous on time—in S.S. uniform. The pharmacist had been called up into the Waffen S.S. meanwhile—which I didn't know—and was on leave at the time.

'Don't worry,' he said, pressing my hand warmly. 'I'd let you stay with us, but we're already hiding refugees.'

I looked at him absolutely stupefied. An S.S. man who took in refugees! He had brought the cod liver oil for Hanni, too, and urged me to let him know if there was anything else he could do for me.

One afternoon I looked up an old friend, Meta Schmidt, in Tempelhof. The accommodation problem had again become very serious. Meta Schmidt had been a domestic with us before her marriage. Her husband was a staff sergeant-major employed by the Reich Ministry of Aviation. She had two young sons.

Meta promised to help us at once, and actually took Hanni in for several months. She found some new accommodation for me, too, since my present place was again getting too hot for me. She sent me to friends in Teltow."

It was high time for the runaway Lothar Korn to change his lodgings. He was on the Gestapo's black list; his life had become a gamble. He had to win. If he drew a blank he was lost. And it was a life and death gamble.

He set off for Teltow.

A small, timbered house out in a green belt. An elderly couple who looked suspiciously up at the stranger as he came along the garden path.

"Good morning; my name is Korn. Mrs. Schmidt in Tempelhof sent me to you."

The man was standing near the shed chopping wood. It was cold, and the first flecks of snow whirled in the air. The fields lay flat and fallow with their tipped-up clods of brown earth. The green of the bushes had lost its brightness and the trees their foliage, long since. Bare branches stretched obliquely across the leaden sky.

The woman looked at him, but said nothing.

"Mrs. Schmidt told me that you might have a room for me." He lowered his voice. "I'm . . . in hiding. I'm . . . a Jew."

The man left his axe buried in the log and came over. He tugged at his dark-blue sailor's cap.

"No," the woman said, "we haven't got a room."

"A Jew?" the man asked. "I'm a social democrat." He spoke with pride and confidence.

"Yes," murmured Korn.

"Are you from Berlin?"

Korn nodded.

"You can't stay here in the daytime."

"No, no," Korn assured him hastily, "just somewhere to sleep."

The man nodded. Then he shook Korn's hand. "I'm Fischer," he grunted, "and this is my wife."

Korn gulped. "Can I . . ."

Fischer nodded and took Korn to the back of the house. They reached, through a side entrance, a wood-panelled verandah with a high-pressure furnace in the corner, and a chaise-longue. A gaslight hung from the ceiling. The place was small but easy to heat, and that was the main thing now that winter was approaching.

Korn gazed outside. Fallow countryside, a few gardens; not many neighbours. He was in the safety of a flat landscape. No one would ask complicated questions here.

"Thanks," he muttered.

They soon came to terms about the rent. Korn stuck to the principle that everything had to be done properly. He paid well for his food and lodging. He didn't really know why he did this; perhaps he wanted to perpetuate the illusion that everything was more or less normal. Of course he knew that a hundred-mark note could not compensate for the risk old Fischer was taking; and he knew that a few hours of tutoring Meta's children would not protect their mother from the Gestapo if the help she gave the Korns ever came to light. But he wanted to do something, at least; just a little to help balance the books.

Early in the morning, while it was still dark, he used to travel by bus to town, from the Hindenburgplatz to the

Olivaer Platz. Then he used to go and teach children ; or he would look up Trudi and do some black-market shopping, or meet other " underground " Jews.

Winter passed. Friends prepared a marvellous Christmas dinner for Hanni. On Christmas night—and on New Year's eve, too—Korn lay awake. His responsibilities were playing on his nerves. He lay awake and thought : How much longer ?

Spring came.

One Sunday he did not travel out to town ; he stayed in Teltow all day with the Fischers. As he lay in a deckchair in the sun, it was almost like peacetime. His eyes were closed.

Suddenly he started. Someone was talking to him.

" Well, well, it's you ! What a surprise ! " The cheerful voice of a woman.

Korn wanted to jump up and run away. His second impulse was to deny everything. You don't know her. You've never seen her before.

" Don't you recognise me ? " she asked.

He glanced at her. A girl stood at the fence ; she had mousy hair with a centre parting and a pretty face. She wore a floral smock and it looked as if she lived nearby.

" You were my teacher at school," she laughed. " You tried in vain to knock some history into me."

He laughed ; it sounded strained. " Of course."

" You *are* Lothar the teacher, aren't you ? " There was no guile in her words ; and he knew at once : She has no idea I'm a Jew.

He laughed with relief ; this time it was quite sincere.

" Yes, I'm Lothar the teacher."

" You were always so gallant to us," she said, blushing a little.

Korn smirked coyly.

" Do you live here ? " the young woman asked.

" I come here week-ends sometimes—I've got so much to do and I'm just relaxing a bit."

" Yes—it's become unbearable in town now. . . . Well, I must be getting along. . . . Goodbye. . . ." And she actually took her leave, her basket swinging on her arm. She turned round once and waved. He waved back.

From then on he was " Lothar the teacher " to everyone in Teltow. They stopped looking suspiciously at him. At first they probably thought this stranger, who appeared at the Fischer's from time to time, was a spy or a shady character of some kind. But now they were all quite satisfied: he was only Lothar the teacher.

In November, 1943, a year after his flight from the Gestapo, Lothar Korn experienced one of the most horrific hours of his life.

He had stopped living with the Fischers then and had moved to Oranienburg. He had found new lodgings—with a local Nazi group leader! Korn came across this man through his tutoring job ; he was a Nazi of the rather naïve, harmless kind who never dreamed that anyone—let alone a Jew—could be so daring as to insinuate himself into his home under a false name. It appealed to Korn's sense of humour to pull the wool over the man's eyes; also, he felt safer in the lion's den than elsewhere.

Korn arrived in Berlin on the evening of November 23 ; that night there was a frightful air raid on the city. He spent hours in a shelter listening to the bombs fall. Then some wardens left the shelter ; Korn left with them.

The whole city centre was a mass of flame.

" God," one of the men near Korn whispered. An explosion brought them all to the ground.

They scrambled up again and rushed to the other side of the street, where a woman was rolling on the ground screaming.

Korn helped.

Finally he was standing alone under a hail of incendiaries.

He must get to Trudi and Hanni.

Terror was throttling him.

Trudi was staying in Neukölln and Hanni in Schöneberg —where the fire seemed to be raging most fiercely.

" Damnation!" Korn shrieked out into the night. Furious tears ran down his face.

He ran down the street. " Hey, you there—come here!" someone shouted from an underground shelter entrance.

Korn yelled some rude words at him and carried on.

Two minutes later he had to take cover. Parts of the road were blown up by explosives. Shrapnel lacerated the house fronts, tore bricks from the walls and whirred past over his bowed head.

At last he started running again. The drone of aeroplanes had ceased and the ack-ack guns were silent. Somewhere in the distance a still undamaged siren wailed the all clear.

The roadway was a mountain of debris and burning rafters. Electric cables hung crazily down. He stumbled over piles of rubble ; people hurried past him aimlessly, hither and thither ; older men in soiled anti-aircraft uniforms, their blue, steel helmets all askew on their heads ; Hitler Youth with pale, determined child faces ; women with long slacks under their coats, their hair hidden by headscarves and their cheeks smoke-stained.

" Here !" a patrol leader called. The men rushed over. They heard knocking from a demolished cellar.

" My child—my child !" a woman groaned. But Korn hurried on.

My child, he thought—my Hanni !

He had a stitch in his side.

A telephone booth at last. He tried to get through. He only got a constant engaged signal with crazy crackling sounds on the line.

There was a post office still standing on the corner. People were crowding in ; they wanted to telephone, too.

" The whole network has been destroyed," an official told him ; " no point in waiting."

On he went.

They had been unlucky the previous day ; they had been unable to meet because of patrols on the streets all the way —Gestapo, S.S., military police, Wehrmacht " watchdogs." He dared not show himself. Also, he'd had nothing to eat.

A little group of workmen stood on a corner ; they'd been summoned to clear the cellars. They were passing a bottle round.

" Just a minute," one said. " You can't get through here, mate."

Korn halted ; the street was barricaded off. An unexploded

bomb lay on the other side ; fireworkers were approaching it with great caution.

"Here," said the workman who had spoken. He handed Korn the bottle. Korn drank—schnapps on an empty stomach! He couldn't help coughing. The workmen grinned ; he grinned back.

Now he felt better, much better.

He made for a side street and ran like a young man.

Schöneberg.

He had reached his destination. A miracle—the dark houses still stood, illuminated only by the glow from the blaze. Each house was intact ; the whole street was intact.

He rushed up to the house where Hanni was staying, and hurried up the stairs into his friends' flat.

Then he was holding his child in his arms and pressing her to him. He had to grit his teeth, lest Hanni see his emotion.

"Come on, we've got to look for mummy," he said, taking her with him.

On the street he thumbed a lift from a Wehrmacht car with an officer inside.

He was ice-cool. "Will you give me a lift ? My wife—"

"Of course."

"I don't know where my wife—"

The officer brushed it aside. "After tonight, many a man won't know where his wife is," he said. His jaw was hard and his lips thin and set. Obviously torn between disdain, fury and resignation, he stared at the conflagration as they drove past.

I wonder what he's thinking, Korn mused. What does a German officer feel when he sees the hell into which this war, instigated by his generals and his Führer, has plunged humanity ?

The officer was silent. He just stared at the inferno and did not move.

Christ, Korn thought, I don't care what he's brooding about, I don't care when he's going to die, and where ; I just want my wife to be alive and my child to survive all this, so that we can laugh and be happy again.

He felt no hate. Why should he ? The man was a German like himself.

That afternoon he found his wife. She, too, had survived the terrible night. But Korn was sure of one thing: they wouldn't stay in Berlin. They wouldn't slink away just to perish like rats in liquid phosphorus.

An incident which could have led to their ruin brought his determination to a head.

One day Korn was on his way to a woman whom he was tutoring. This woman's housekeeper—a Mrs. Nimz—had taken Trudi to stay with her for some months. Mrs. Nimz was risking her life, but she just laughed when you mentioned it.

Near the house where Mrs. Nimz worked, Korn was approached by a strange woman who pushed a note into his hand. Korn took it and went his way with his head down. Once round the corner, he began to run; he came to a breathless halt a couple of hundred yards later.

He took the note from his pocket and read:

" The Gestapo is around. Beat it. My flat isn't safe."

Half an hour later he collected his wife from Mrs. Nimz's flat and they hid in Oranienburg overnight. Now they were absolutely certain: they had to leave Berlin.

Where to, though? To leave the city without identity cards was unthinkable.

Then a friend of theirs, Mrs. Mucha, came to the rescue. She managed to get hold of a refugee card, the kind issued to people who were bombed out. It was a blank form which she got from a kindly clerk in some office or other.

At first Korn was reluctant to use the card. Wouldn't they check up on them when they got to the country? Wouldn't they ring up the Berlin authorities? Wouldn't they want to find out a bit more about the bombed-out teacher, Korn?

" Sheer coincidence and the help of a good friend saved me from this dilemma," said Korn.

" Since the beginning of November, 1943, I'd had a lucrative tutorial job; I was taking a few fifteen-year-old girls in English, mathematics and German. One of the mothers was a Mrs. Felicitas Dietrich, who was well known in Berlin society. She was a fencing champion—a marvellous woman.

125

She soon got to know that I was a Jew living "underground" and she helped as much as she could. She saw to it that I got 250 marks a month for the lessons I gave the girls; they all had well-off parents. You can imagine what that kind of money meant to me then.

But now the air raids were getting worse and worse, and the danger of getting found out at check-ups in shelters much graver. Not to go to a shelter was sheer suicide. So Mrs. Dietrich suggested we move to her country house. This was in the tiny village of Horst-Liebelose on the Baltic, near the well-known resort Fischerkathen. Mrs. Dietrich wanted her daughter out of Berlin, anyway; she was constantly scared of something happening to the girl, who was fifteen. So we were to travel with the child to Horst-Liebelose. And now we *could* travel, because we had the refugee card that Mrs. Mucha got us.

I'll be quite honest. At first the thought of leaving the protection which the anonymity of the metropolis afforded really frightened me. I'd become accustomed to my twilight "underground" existence. Out there, in the country, I would have to assume a name and a personality again. There, I would often have to talk and answer questions. But the thought of my wife and child, exposed to the deadly dangers of being found out or killed in air raids, decided the issue.

We left on February 6, 1944, a Sunday. We'd chosen a week-end on purpose because the trains were crammed with holidaymakers and trippers.

On the way I kept a nervous look-out for guards, the Wehrmacht patrols and the police. True, we had a card describing us as the Kern family from Berlin-Schöneberg, am Stadtpark 18, who had been bombed out. This was a demolished building; so was the local police station, as I had been at pains to ascertain. Any official inquiries, therefore, would probably prove abortive. But it was still a weird feeling—travelling by this train from Berlin to an unknown destination, to a future which was both insecure and dangerous.

It was grey and misty, with a heavy snow falling. We reached Horst-Liebelose station early that evening. During the last hours, our fear had dwindled somewhat and curio-

sity and anticipation had taken its place. A full moon
brightened the winter landscape ; snow shimmered white
on the path before us which led to Felicitas's house in the
wood.

There was already a young Rhineland woman living there,
the fiancée of a young lieutenant at the front. She managed
the house for Mrs. Dietrich. We were greeted cordially ;
Mrs. Dietrich's daughter showed us to our rooms and at last
we were alone. The rooms had no heating, not even a stove ;
but at least we were safe, that was the main thing. There
were no alarms, no sirens howling ; nobody would ask us
for our identity cards in an air-raid shelter ; we would no
longer be terrified by exploding bombs or rudely awakened
by a sudden rattle of ack-ack guns.

To me, as a man, it did not matter so much, perhaps ; but
I knew how my child always trembled at the first note of a
siren and just shrivelled up with fear when a stranger talked
to her. I knew the terror in my wife's eyes whenever she
heard strange footsteps on the stairs, in all the houses we
had ever lived in.

At least all that was over.

The next morning I settled all necessary business, since
I was determined to get all the burdensome—and maybe
even dangerous—formalities over and done with as quickly
as possible. I went to Fischerkathen with our refugee card
and immediately got a residential permit for Horst-Liebelose.
Also, I took Hanni to the headmaster at Horst. I said we had
been bombed out ; that Hanni had been ill and had so far
not attended school, but I wanted to make up for this now.
He showed no sign of suspicion. I replied to his various
questions without hesitation : to his routine inquiry,
' Aryan ? ' I answered coolly, ' Naturally.'

I had to be very careful myself, of course. Clearly I could
not wander around idle in the locality when I was obviously
a man of military age. At first I made out I was on holiday.
I limped about on a stick to show all observers why I had
not been called up.

Then I didn't leave the house at all except at week-ends,
when allegedly I came to visit my family from Berlin.

But even in Horst-Liebelose, sometimes, the sword of

Damocles hung above us. This was brought home to us with bewildering suddenness one Saturday, when I was out shopping with my wife. We bumped into a former friend of hers, a schoolteacher from Berlin. This woman could keep her mouth shut and control herself; she would never have given us away. But this meeting showed us how completely we were at the mercy of chance; we could just as easily have met another acquaintance from Berlin who was less kindly disposed.

Months passed. Then winter, 1944-45. Felicitas's house had become a prison for us. How long would the war continue? What was going to happen?

One day a representative from the local authorities in Fischerkathen called on us. Trudi opened. He said he'd come to ask me to join the Home Guard. My wife kept her head; she said I was in Berlin and would report for duty there. But he was persistent; so my wife explained that her husband knew his duty—after all, he was a government official. Then she banged the door in his face. But we spent a sleepless night after that. I didn't shift from my room for days.

Another problem cropped up; Mrs. Dietrich's daughter had to go to Czechoslovakia on a child evacuation scheme, and the Rhineland woman moved out. Officially, therefore, my wife and Hanni were occupying the big house all by themselves. Evacuees appeared with requisition orders; Trudi kept her end up by pretending that the house was booked for other evacuees. But how much longer would we be able to evade our ultimate fate? "

Days and weeks of terror. The end was approaching, though. Korn knew. He had lived " illegally " with his family for years now—hunted, outlawed. Would he be found out and arrested at the eleventh hour? S.S. and army patrols were combing the locality and every man who had two legs to walk on was conscripted into the Home Guard. The area was overrun with refugees; pitiful processions marched past, and soldiers from the broken German front line were on the retreat.

Korn and his wife lay sleepless night after night. They were absolutely trapped. They could not leave the house, nor did they want to now. They hoped, feverish with apprehension, that the Russians would arrive pretty soon. Only then would they be safe; only then would the endless waiting, the torment and the perpetual hounding come to an end.

"You can't imagine how our nerves were torn to shreds, those last few weeks," Korn said. On March 4, 1945, another great stream of refugees passed through, and again we asked ourselves: Will we be spared this misery, or will we be drawn into the vortex, too? Disorganised bands of soldiers marched past from the direction of Kolberg, throwing their weapons and greatcoats away. We saw women with immobile, staring faces and children who didn't know how to cry any more. We saw all this; but for us the hour that was drawing near would bring not horror but joy.

On March 11 bullets splintered the front door and ricocheted off the passage wall. In a few seconds we were standing before our first Russians. Horst-Liebelose was occupied by the Red Army. For us, occupation meant liberation."

Korn shared the experience of many other Jews whom the Russians caught up with; at first no one believed he was Jewish. Days passed before they met a Jewish commissar from Czernowitz who had the job of evacuating civilians from the area. He spoke fluent German. Korn told him his story and produced documents which he had saved on his secret trips to Berlin and smuggled over into the Dietrich household. "Fantastic, quite fantastic," the commissar repeated over and over again. Then: "You are one of the few Jews to escape death under the Nazis." "I know," Korn said; "and I have my German friends to thank for it, mainly. They weren't all Nazis." The commissar shrugged. "So what?" he said. "A few were not, perhaps. But far *too* few."

" The measures I take will not be sicklied over by considerations of legality. Justice is not my aim, but simply destruction and extermination."

Adolf Hitler, on his political opponents; from a public speech delivered at Frankfurt am Main, March 3, 1933.

7

The train was late. That was not unusual in the summer of 1944, when the Allies were carrying out heavy air raids against the German Reich.

They were travelling at speed, to make good the delay. The carriages rattled over the bumpy, damaged tracks, jogging the passengers. The blue lamp on the ceiling of the compartment cast a feeble light on the faces of the three soldiers who sat near a window blacked out by a venetian blind, playing skat. Their faces looked pale and ghostly in the blueish glow.

The other soldiers in the compartment were asleep or gazing drowsily in front of them—apart from the big, fair-haired corporal who was in command of the small troop. He pretended to be very interested in the three near the window ; in actual fact, he was listening to the noise of the train, waiting for it to travel more slowly. He leaned back. It was quite obvious now ; the train was slowing down.

Corporal Robert Milkau stood up, stretched and sauntered nonchalantly out of the compartment. Out in the corridor he looked at his wristwatch.

It was just ten to ten. Any minute now they would get to the long gradient. Soon they would be in Torgau, the dreaded military fortress where condemned members of the Wehrmacht were shot.

Milkau pulled up the blackout blind and peered out. Inpenetrable darkness shrouded the landscape. He could see his own reflection in the window pane, that was all.

He tugged at the brass bar and opened the window, feeling the sharp rush of air in his face. He blinked. Shreds of soot tore past. The dark countryside lay in the background ; in front Milkau saw, as they went round the bend, the fiery shower of sparks from the engine.

Then came the gradient.

The wheels rattled over patched-up points.

Slower, Milkau thought, slower still, or they'll break their necks.

Maybe they wouldn't have the nerve after all?

He leaned out of the window and gazed towards the back of the train, where the two closed rail trucks with the prisoners were joined on. He could just about distinguish their contours as his eyes got gradually used to the darkness.

In another minute the train would have passed the gradient.

Go on, jump, Milkau thought.

He listened, but heard only the wind raging, the wheels clattering, the engine retching and the hoarse, malicious laughter from the compartment behind him where his guards were. Schulz had lost a packet.

Milkau pushed the window up and pulled down the blind. It was pitch black outside.

"You're not supposed to touch the blackout," said an angry voice behind him.

He turned. There was the railway guard, his cap pulled over his eyes, lips pursed, eyes glaring disapprovingly at Milkau.

"Now don't get excited, little man," said Milkau, stretching himself to his full height, "I only wanted some fresh air."

"It's not allowed," the guard spat, "touching the blackout's not allowed!"

"Keep your hair on," said Milkau, with a contemptuous wave of the hand. "Do you realise there are two carriages full of criminals back there, and that I'm responsible for them?" He was silent a whole minute, then put on an officious air. "You don't want to hinder me in the execution of my duty—do you?"

"Well—I only—I don't—" stammered the guard.

Milkau adjusted his 7.65 automatic in its holster and cleared his throat ominously.

"Well, is that clear?" he asked.

The guard gulped, nodded mutely and fled along the corridor, head bowed. He disappeared swiftly behind the swing doors to the platform.

Milkau grinned. But his face soon hardened again.

He walked back into his compartment.

"Get ready," he said. "We're coming into Torgau."

"Grand hand!" yelled the soldier under the window.

"That'll do," Milkau ordered.

The players threw in the cards; the others roused themselves from their slumber, rubbed their eyes, yawned and put their steel helmets on.

Finally they staggered clumsily out.

As the train approached the platform, they were all standing at attention in the corridor. Milkau paraded down the row. "Everything in order?"

The train stopped.

The guards sprang out and took up their various positions. A couple of men ran to the first carriage; the rest, Milkau in the lead, went over to the last one.

Milkau pulled the key out of his pocket and unlocked the padlock.

"Open up!" he commanded.

Two guards opened the door.

"Out you get," he yelled into the carriage.

They tumbled out of the darkness and leapt on to the platform.

"Come on, gentlemen, move!"

Eight figures stood in a row.

"Well, for Christ's sake wake up!" He pushed his head into the dark carriage. No one else appeared.

Milkau turned around quickly, surveying the eight figures. They stared stupidly back at him.

"What's the meaning of all this?" he snarled. "Have those sods gone to sleep?" He jerked his head in Schulz's direction. "Go and have a look."

Schulz scrambled into the carriage.

In the meantime the occupants of carriage number one had fallen in. Private Hartmann marched up to Milkau, announcing officiously: "Prisoners from carriage one present and correct, sir!"

Milkau nodded.

The prisoners stood in silence, their hands manacled behind their backs.

"What's up?" Milkau yelled over to carriage two.

Schulz appeared in the doorway. His mouth was hanging half open.

"What are you staring at me like that for, you dumb clot?"

"The prisoners—gone, sir!"

"Gone? You're joking, surely!"

He jumped up into the carriage.

Emptiness.

He felt his heart thumping. Now just keep up the act, he thought. Just a little longer.

"Now what the bloody hell's happened here?" he screamed. He leapt out of the carriage again and stormed over to the eight figures standing on the platform.

"Well, what happened—where are the others?"

"Scarpered," one growled.

"Scarpered? How the hell. . . ."

"They had a key. To the handcuffs."

"But—there can't have been one."

"Well, they had one. They had a key and then they crept out of the window."

Just under the roof of the carriage were small air vents without bars, just wide enough for a person who was reasonably slim to worm his way through. They'd got out that way.

"Well, this is bloody marvellous," said Milkau. Then— "Quick march!"

They marched through the barrier, guarded on the right and left, led by Milkau.

It had worked. Ten of the July 20 resisters had escaped certain death.

It was not the first transport that Milkau had accompanied to Torgau, but he had never before risked what he risked that day.

The very name Torgau struck terror into all German soldiers. Its Fort Zinna was the notorious Wehrmacht central prison. Here thousands of soldiers, after sentence, were imprisoned under inhuman conditions in so-called preventive detention. Fort Zinna was also a transit station for soldiers who had been expelled from the Wehrmacht and were to be delivered up to concentration camps and the mercies of the S.S. Torgau's most horrid function, however, was the execution of condemned Wehrmacht servicemen.

Each soldier sentenced to hard labour—and under that draconian system it could easily happen for the most trivial offence—lost his "military honour" and was transferred to a penal camp, usually Fort Zinna. Apart from Fort Zinna there were field detention camps I-III, based in Norway and Lapland, and penal prison camps Esterwegen and Alta, under the jurisdiction of the Reich Ministry of Justice.

A decree issued on November 17, 1939, left little doubt regarding the treatment of Wehrmacht prisoners. It read:

"According to experience, during the World War dishonourable and cowardly elements often commit petty crimes in the hope of safeguarding their lives behind the front line for the duration of the sentence.

"To discourage such desires, in future prison sentences will not, as a rule, be carried out immediately, insofar as they are not, for other reasons, deferred to the end of the war. Those sentenced will instead be confined to a penal camp, under the most severe living conditions, for the duration of the war. The time served in a penal camp will not be deducted from the sentence; the sentence will only be carried out after the war.

"To achieve a lasting deterrent effect on the unreliable elements among the troops, the following principles are to be observed, among others, for the treatment of penal camp inmates:

1. Prisoners will wear uniforms without marks of rank, cockades or epaulettes.

2. As regards food, prisoners are to receive a maximum of 70% of the small ration quota. Additional foodstuffs are forbidden.

3. The working day will consist of 10-14 hours. Prisoners will be utilised for the hardest labour, if possible directly or indirectly serving the defence of the Reich.

4. In addition to work, daily drill (without weapons) is compulsory.

5. Any breach of order and discipline will be met with the utmost severity, with immediate force of arms if need be. Special disciplinary measures of the severest kind are permissible.

6. Prisoners are to receive no wages or service pay.

7. Private visits are forbidden. It is vital that correspondence is to be confined to the barest minimum. None of the usual remissions of sentence is permissible.

One of the prisoners in Torgau, Professor Werner Krauss, wrote a restrained, but thereby all the more impressive, eyewitness report on the conditions there and in the Departments of Field Penal Prisoners (*Feldstrafgefangenenabteilungen, F.G.A.*). Günther Weisenborn quotes it in his book on the German Resistance movement, *Der Lautlose Aufstand* (The Silent Insurrection):

"For a while I was employed as clerk in the company, whereby I got the opportunity of looking up the legal files and getting to know, in detail, the glaring miscarriages of justice in our courts. One had the impression that the ever-recurring statements under the heading 'Subversion of the Armed Forces' (e.g., doubt of final victory, scepticism about the success of secret weapons, regret about the failure of July 20, imprecations against Dr. Goebbels and Dr. Leys) were crimes with set penalties. Such statements were punishable by 2-8 years' hard labour, whereas often the sentence for persistent theft was just a few months in prison, and even then the offender was usually sent to a probation company or to his own unit after a few weeks.

The more serious cases came to the Department of Field Penal Prisoners. There, treatment varied; in some cases men were systematically starved, and when someone collapsed over his work he was sentenced to death, after a summary trial, for 'malingering' and shot or hanged on the spot.

In the secret reports (which I read in my office) about the behaviour of the F.G.A., the usual complaint was that prisoners had no inclination or talent for anything except eating, that their military department was utterly unsatisfactory and that unfortunately the staff often tended to be infected by the defeatism of the prisoners. Actually entire F.G.A.s (F.G.A. 19, for example) went over wholesale to the enemy, staff and all; I don't know of a single one of the countless soldiers attached to the F.G.A. in Torgau who didn't go to battle with the express intention of deserting to the enemy at the first opportunity.

The treatment of inmates in penal camps was even worse.

They were just systematically decimated through malnutrition and brutal treatment. On a transport back from Finland such a camp 'lost' over 75% of its complement. We had a man from one of those camps in the sick bay, his face lacerated with bloodstained weals. He was still much too intimidated to confess to the army doctor, when questioned, the origin of this ill-treatment; he attributed his wounds to 'an accident.'

About once a week condemned civilians were transported in a closed truck to Halle to be executed—soldiers were shot at Torgau. A favourite punishment consisted of taking a soldier, who had been condemned to death but reprieved, along to the sand-heap with the other doomed men; it was only when everyone else had been shot before his very eyes that his pardon was handed to him.

Birching constituted a new departure in military methods of punishment; this was to be administered in certain cases (e.g., cowardice in the face of the enemy) as a supplementary punishment by express order of the chief of the home forces. It was difficult, at first, to find anyone to undertake the task. It was supposed to take place in public, but the commandant of Fort Zinna did not adhere to this section of the rules. The birching was carried out in his presence and that of a small circle of people but under the supervision of a doctor, who had to ascertain that the offender's fighting capacity would not be adversely affected in the process."

This was the place where the ten men saved by Corporal Robert Milkau would have been condemned to die—men who had rebelled against the Nazi régime in the hope, perhaps, of delivering Germany at the eleventh hour from her irrevocable plunge into the abyss.

I looked more closely at ex-corporal Milkau as he sat before me. He was still a powerful man, and the material of his white Sunday shirt stretched taut across broad shoulders. He was still blond, with a few streaks of grey at the temples.

He had a benevolent face and his eyes, as he talked, gleamed astutely behind his glasses. He had fewer wrinkles than you would expect for a man of 64.

The table at which we sat, in the living-room, was covered with documents—Milkau's papers, reports on the war period,

139

when he served as warder in the Wehrmacht prison in Lehrter Strasse 61, Berlin. Letters of thanks from men whom, in that critical time, he helped to overcome their despair, and to contact, from their cells, their relatives in the world outside ; whom he even helped to gain life and liberty, like the doomed men travelling to Torgau.

"Why not ? " Milkau asked, when I asked him for a Saturday afternoon interview. It turned out to be one of many.

" He was always a bit mad," said his wife, who sat beside him.

"Oh, belt up," said Milkau, winking.

" Quite mad," she repeated. " If they'd got something on you. . . ."

" They didn't, though."

Milkau had received orders to accompany a transport of thirty-six prisoners to Torgau ; at five in the afternoon one day in August, 1944. He had to get his escort together, then he took himself at about six to the station, where they handed over the prisoners to him, plus a transport list.

He sorted the prisoners out. The ten condemned men, who were consigned to him with the express order that he was to keep a particularly watchful eye on them, he put into carriage two—i.e., the last on the train—with eight other prisoners ; the rest were in number one.

Milkau himself undertook the check-up in carriage two. The prisoners squatted on the floor, looking apathetically or defiantly in front of them. All of them had their hands manacled behind their backs. The condemned men wore civilian clothes—they were officers expelled from the Wehrmacht because of their part in the July 20 conspiracy.

During the " check-up " Milkau pulled out his handkerchief near one of the doomed men and blew his nose. In the process, by accident as it were, a handcuffs key fell out of his pocket. Because of the position in which he was standing at that moment, only this particular man could see what happened. Milkau saw his eyes light up. He went out, pushed the carriage door shut, positioned the steel bar and secured it with the padlock. Now it was up to them.

" I'd had that second key for some time," Milkau said.

"I fixed it during an air raid, when bombs were falling in the Lehrter Strasse and everything was in a state of chaos.

They couldn't accuse me of anything. The guards had taken their places in the passenger coach, according to regulations; the doors of the two transport carriages had been locked from the outside; I myself had checked the handcuffs of all prisoners before moving off.

The officer on duty at Fort Zinna interrogated me and my escort at once, of course. But no one had a clue how the ten of them had come by the key.

The officer sent me back to Berlin immediately, where I had to report to Lieutenant-Colonel Maass, our chief. I made a statement."

"And they didn't take the matter further?"

"Yes, but then they let it slide. The prisoners from carriage two stuck to their story. We were asleep, we heard nothing, we saw nothing, most of them said. And those who'd heard or seen something assumed that the ten must have got the key from some orderly in prison. Of course they interrogated the orderlies, too, but none of them wanted to own up."

Milkau grinned again, and flashed his lively, cunning eyes at me.

Sometimes I got the impression that Milkau did not quite realise, at the time, how he was playing with fire.

I asked him straight: "Mr. Milkau, did you actually think of the possible consequences to yourself of doing what you did?"

"No, he didn't," said his wife, pouring out another cup of tea.

"Quiet, mum," said Milkau, laying his hand on her arm.

"It wasn't easy for me, I can tell you," continued Mrs. Milkau, not put off. "In the morning he'd go to work with a rucksack crammed with bread and potatoes. Herbert, I said, Herbert, surely you don't eat all that up by yourself. No, I don't eat it all myself, he said, and then he added, what the eye doesn't see the heart doesn't grieve over. But then one night I asked him, Herbert, who is all that food for? and he said, that is for my prisoners. He was always risking his neck."

"What about you ?" he asked. "You did just as much."
He turned to me. "She was chasing all over town with the
prisoners' letters, that they weren't supposed to write, running from one post office to another so that they wouldn't
notice."

"Awful, it was," said his wife.

"No. It wasn't awful. It was good that we had a chance
to help." He looked at me, took off his glasses and wiped
his eyes.

"I was wounded in the fighting in France ; when I got
over that I was sent to my company's offices in Strausberg
and then notified that I was to be transferred to the Wehrmacht prison in Lehrter Street, Berlin, as an overseer. This
promotion seemed like a punishment to me at first ; but
when I'd been there four weeks I thanked my God for it.
Suddenly, I felt that my life had some meaning. . . ." Milkau
spoke quietly, as if he were ashamed of talking that way.
But they weren't just big words ; he wasn't shooting a line ;
it was the truth.

The prison at Lehrter Strasse 61 was mainly for Wehrmacht men remanded in custody. The institution consisted
of an administrative building and the actual blocks of cells
—both connected by a vaulted corridor. In the administrative section, where the offices, the kitchen and the warders'
rest rooms were, there were also two special cells for V.I.P.
prisoners. In the actual prison building there were four
blocks of cells.

"After a probationary period on the first floor I took over
the ground floor division as a block senior. Five guards were
allocated to me as warders. The ground floor was reserved
for officers who faced the death sentence because of the
seriousness of their crimes. Any contact with the outside
world was forbidden to them. They could not write or
receive letters and were not even allowed legal aid during
the hearings. They sat in their cells, for the most part hope-
lessly, all help denied them. Most of them were in a desperate
psychological state. On admission they had to surrender
their honours and decorations, and for some of them—

especially the younger officers—that was very hard ; some of them had the *Ritterkreuz*.

The admission of an officer was conducted this way : Usually the prisoner was driven in a closed car to the prison's main entrance. As escort he had an officer of equal rank from the Greater German Guard Battalion. The officer being admitted often wore an ordinary private's uniform as camouflage.

The prisoner was immediately taken before Lieutenant-Colonel Maass, the prison commandant. Maass had, as I discovered later, some connections with the anti-Hitler resistance movement centred round General Beck. One of his friends was the Town Commandant of the City of Berlin, Lieutenant-General Paul von Hase, who was arrested in connection with the July 20 plot and executed in August, 1944. Incidentally, there was a direct hit on our prison eight days before the surrender, and Maass was killed.

After the prisoner had been introduced to Lieutenant-Colonel Maass I would be summoned by 'phone to the admin. section to get the prisoner. I would lead him through the various barred doors to the prisoners' wing. In the guard-room in my block the prisoner had to surrender his personal effects and his money against receipt—also his decorations. He was allowed to go on wearing his uniform with his insignia of rank. Then I would take him to one of the cells. There were nineteen cells in my ground-floor block, secured with thick, wooden doors with tiny peepholes. Anyway, we overseers just carried one single key to the cells which fitted all locks. The cell furniture consisted of iron bedsteads, chairs, small tables and presses for the officers' clothes. As for crockery—all ranks except generals had the usual tin bowls. Generals got china.

As for our guardroom, it wasn't any more luxuriously furnished than the cells. There was a cupboard for the officers' confiscated belongings, a table and six chairs, then a telephone connecting us with the commandant's office and the secretariat.

Work began for me and my five underlings at six a.m. At ten to seven we had to be on the main floor of the admin. building to receive orders. Then, the guards were allocated to prisoners' transports and other duties. For block and cell duty there were usually only the senior and another man left.

All the prisoners were woken at seven a.m. Shaving tackle and washing water in aluminium basins were handed out by two orderlies who were common soldiers. They also had to empty the dirty water and chamber pots and sweep out the cells. The prisoners could now eat up the bread ration they'd been given the afternoon before for supper and breakfast; they got nothing extra in the mornings apart from some thin ersatz coffee. Lunch practically always consisted of a one-course stew. Then I'd go with my two orderlies to the kitchen in the basement of the admin. building, and supervise the filling of the food containers. Then the prisoners' eating bowls were collected together and filled in a little wash-room in our block, and taken by the orderlies to the cells which an overseer—I, usually—unlocked.

There was half an hour's exercise daily in the prison yard. Officers did not have to participate. Many took advantage of this concession, particularly if they had no civilian clothes at their disposal—they were ashamed of being prisoners in officers' uniforms.

If a prisoner reported sick he was brought before Professor Hess, the medical officer, in the admin. building. If he was seriously ill he was sent to the prison sick bay in Berlin.

The summons for his first hearing before the Reich Military Tribunal usually came shortly after a prisoner's admission. They were issued by the Reich Military Justice, Jürgens, and were handed over to the block senior when we received our orders in the mornings.

Before the hearings I had to hand his decorations back to the prisoner—all except the *Ritterkreuz*. Apparently they thought it would look rather peculiar if a prisoner awaiting trial ran around with that. Probably, too, they wanted to avoid too much unwelcome publicity; passers-by could not help noticing the comings and goings between the prison and the military tribunal.

I would deposit the prisoner in the governor's office where he was received by his escort, an officer of the same rank, who would then accompany him to the hearing. He was made to swear on oath that he would not escape. It was

only in particularly serious cases that officers were hand-
cuffed during transit; other ranks, on the contrary, had to
appear before the judge in handcuffs. However, whenever
I escorted such transports myself, I dispensed with the handcuffs. A closed truck was used for the transport itself. Behind
the driver's cabin was a box-like construction in which the
prisoner sat with his guard; the driver locked them both in
during the journey.

As I said at the beginning: at first the detainees had no
kind of contact with the outside world. It was only when
the hearings were wound up by the Military Justice—and
that usually took months, or even as much as a year and a
half in individual cases—that they were allowed to get in
touch with their families. Then, they were allowed letters
occasionally, or even an opportunity to meet. Only then were
they allowed an advocate, who had to be licensed to practise
at the military court."

After a pause, Milkau continued his story:
"It all began quite innocently. One of the youngsters on
the first floor, where I worked at the beginning, asked me
for a cigarette one morning. He wasn't allowed to smoke. I
led him to the toilet, gave him a cigarette and ordered:
'Smoke!' Two minutes later I fetched him out and took
him back to his cell. I slipped him another two cigarettes
and a few matches.

Next day a young corporal, recently married, asked me
on the way to the toilet if I could get a message to his
parents. They knew nothing of his predicament and were
sure to be worried to death. I had been sizing him up for
days and knew he was a decent young man, whom I could
trust. He was there for making a silly political crack. I told
him: 'I'll do it, but if you don't keep your mouth shut
you'll regret it.'

When I came off duty that day I went to the address he'd
given, near the Alexanderplatz. A woman in her mid-fifties
opened the door. When I told her where I came from and
where her son was she was naturally scared stiff. I calmed
her down and told her that if she wanted to send her son
something she'd better get it ready. She prepared a little

145

parcel of food, cigarettes and matches, scribbled a hasty letter, packed it all up together and gave it to me. I took the things home. Next morning I stuck the letter in my sock and the parcel in my briefcase. When the shaving tackle was distributed I whispered to the kid that he should report at the toilet entrance within the hour. I couldn't hand him the things then and there because he shared his cell with others ; so later, in the toilet, I gave him the package and the letter. He had to read the letter in my presence, tear it up and flush it away. He hid the articles from the parcel on him, then I took him back to his cell. As I locked the door behind him I noticed my hand shaking. I had befriended my first prisoner. I was now all set for hard labour if they found out. But I'd made a start and there was no looking back."

Milkau naturally safeguarded himself as much as he could. Before he contacted anyone outside on a prisoner's behalf, or smuggled in to him some food, cigarettes or something to write with, he ascertained first from the prison office what kind of affiliations his protégé had. A lance-corporal called Rempel worked in the office and when he and Milkau were alone he let him see the personal files. Milkau could find out from these whether they were criminal or political cases, and whether the persons concerned were Nazi party members or not. Usually he wouldn't touch party members ; he couldn't be sure that they wouldn't betray him later. He only befriended the unequivocally " political " cases, or those where a young man—through stupidity, ignorance or a momentary impulse—had committed some trivial offence. He impressed on each individual that he was to keep quiet.

Nevertheless, it was no secret among the prisoners that the tall, blond sergeant-major from Block I was, so to speak, the guardian angel of Lehrter Strasse 61. Soon he was running errands for his protégés almost daily. He smuggled piles of letters out of prison. In the morning he appeared at work with briefcases crammed to bursting point with food provided by the prisoners' relatives, whom he had secretly put in the picture. The parcels were posted to his Berlin address or to Gross-Ziethen, where the Milkaus had a summer cottage on a big allotment. In 1942 so many parcels arrived there for the prisoners under surveillance in Milkau's block that Mrs. Milkau often had to go to the post office with a handcart. There she would throw an old sack over the packets, and on the way home she used to collect horse-dung from the street and shovel it on to the cart, so as to hide the packages from the other allotment residents.

At the beginning Mrs. Milkau had no idea what her husband was doing. He held the view that it was best for her not to know. But when she had to help him by running from one post office to another to post "illegal" letters, he was compelled to be honest with her.

At that time there wasn't a day when Milkau didn't risk being put behind bars himself. But the most hazardous hours of his life, when he literally gambled with death, were yet to come. They began the day when the Gestapo located Colonel Oster's core of resistance in the Counter-Intelligence Division of the Wehrmacht High Command, and consigned two of the most prominent members, Hans von Dohnanyi and the Munich lawyer, Dr. Josef Müller (known as Ochsensepp), to the military prison in Lehrter Strasse 61.

The Gestapo, by order of the Reich Security Head Office chief, Ernst Kaltenbrunner, and S.D. chief, Walter Schellenberg, had been shadowing the Wehrmacht Intelligence Division under Admiral Canaris for some time. Through carelessness on the part of some Counter-Intelligence personnel, the Reich Security Head Office, whose S.D. was in constant competition with the military intelligence service, had got wind of an anti-Hitler conspiracy within the Counter-Intelligence Bureau. However, the S.D. were very much in the dark, for a long time, about the membership aims of this circle.

However, in the autumn of 1942 the Gestapo had arrested a German businessman for smuggling currency into Switzerland. This "businessman," it transpired, was an Intelligence officer. The money he was taking over the border was from Counter-Intelligence chief, Canaris, for paying out to Jewish refugees abroad; this had been going on for some time. Intelligence also issued forged passports on Canaris's order to undercover or refugee Jews. This operation of solidarity was known to the initiated as U7.

The arrested " businessman " admitted to the Gestapo his errands for U7, and revealed the name of the man behind the project. During interrogations he recounted pretty well everything he knew (and that was more than his former colleagues had dreamed of) about what was going on in Counter-Intelligence. He incriminated, for instance, Hans von Dohnanyi, one of the master-minds of the Resistance and instigator of the aid for Jews abroad. To this day, historians describe Dohnanyi as one of the most inspiring figures of the Resistance. The officer also informed the Gestapo that Dr. Josef Müller had established contact with the Vatican in 1940, so that the German opposition could make its peace overtures to the British Government through the Holy See. And he betrayed the fact that in 1942 Pastor Dietrich Bonhöffer had travelled to Stockholm for negotiations with the British Bishop of Chichester on a false passport issued by Counter-Intelligence. Actually the man knew no details of the many plans for assassinating Hitler (the attempts were constantly being postponed) but he had heard enough about them to give the Gestapo a pointer in this direction.

Dr. Josef Müller, whom I interviewed in Munich about what happened at that time, explained to me that since that time Counter-Intelligence had expected some action from the Gestapo. However, his own arrest and that of Bonhöffer and Dohnanyi on April 5, 1943, came as a shock because the Resistance fighters were not clear about the extent of the betrayal.

" The first indication we had that something was brewing came when suddenly the S.D. began to check the applications for foreign currency by Dohnanyi and others. Just before my arrest I had a discussion in my flat with Lieutenant-Colonel Fichte, chief of Counter-Intelligence in Munich, about the possibility of my travelling to Rome again with Bonhöffer to renew our attempts at making direct contact with the British. This plan was also the subject of a memo which the Gestapo later found in Dohnanyi's desk when they arrested him. Dohnanyi had previously destroyed any documents which might be incriminating, but he overlooked this one.

Early on April 5 I telephoned Berlin Counter-Intelligence

over the so-called Adolf telephone network, through which one could get direct lines on urgent Government business. Both Canaris's secretary and Colonel Oster's secretary were pretty agitated, but I couldn't get anything out of them. Shortly afterwards I was arrested in the Munich Counter-Intelligence headquarters. They took me straight to Berlin —first to Tegel then to Wehrmacht detention prison in Lehrter Strasse 61."

Herbert Milkau recalled:
" Dr. Josef Müller was admitted to our institution one morning in April, 1943. He was an Intelligence officer but he appeared in civilian clothes, with a small suitcase. Müller was a thick-set, powerful man, radiating energy and confidence. I liked him at once. Lieutenant-Colonel Maass, our governor, sent for me and impressed on me that Dr. Müller should on no account discover that Hans von Dohnanyi was also there under investigation, and in one of the two V.I.P. cells in the admin. building."

Shortly after his admission Müller was taken to see Maass. Maass greeted him with undisguised cordiality, shook his hand and informed him that he would be given a grilling by military justice Roeder the next day—one of the most ruthless prosecutors of his day. He had, among other things, conducted the inquiry into the spy ring at the Reich Ministry of Aviation, the so-called " Rote Kapelle " (Red Orchestra). Maass told Müller he would need nerves of steel. Müller expressed his gratitude for the trust that Maass showed in him. Maass replied: " Dr. Müller, I bring you greetings from your leader—your *real* leader." Müller was taken aback for a moment ; he had no idea Maass was so well informed. By the real leader he could only mean Colonel-General Ludwig Beck, the military head of the anti-Hitler resistance.

After hearing Maass's words Müller got up and laid the photograph of Hitler which stood on the desk—Maass kept it there for appearances' sake, obviously—flat on its face. Maass said nothing ; he just smiled at the other and nodded unobtrusively. Then Müller expressed the desire to reciprocate the good wishes of his leader—his real leader.

"Maass then gave me the details of the orders he'd received

149

in connection with me. ' My dear Dr. Müller, you yourself are a State secret—not merely your file,' he said. I was not allowed to form contacts of any kind with my fellow-prisoners ; I couldn't even share their exercise period in the big yard—I'd be taken for walks by Maass himself or one of his officers in the small yard, the ' chicken run,' as he termed it. After his conversation, which was very warm and friendly and highly encouraging, I was conducted back to my cell."

At this stage Dr. Müller still did not know that his fellow-sufferer, Hans von Dohnanyi, was at Lehrter Strasse. He was ignorant of the circumstances of Dohnanyi's arrest, and of what they had found on him. However, he had to reckon with the possibility that the Gestapo may have confiscated some very incriminating material at Dohnanyi's, and naturally the uncertainty played on his nerves. After all, he was involved in a conspiracy against Hitler, and that—if they could bring the slightest proof to bear against him—meant death.

And then Corporal Herbert Milkau stepped into the picture.

" Dr. Müller was in a cell in the ground-floor section with the remand prisoners who, because of the gravity of their crimes, faced the death sentence. Shortly after his admission I pretended to carry out a check-up of his cell. He was in solitary. During my inspection I asked Dr. Müller, ' You know, I suppose, that you're not alone here ? ' He looked inquiringly at me. ' Dohnanyi is here, too,' I whispered to him. His eyes widened ; but not a muscle of his face twitched. He had great self-control. ' Who are you ? And what are you ? ' Müller asked, after a brief spell of hesitation. ' A Communist,' I replied without batting an eyelid. I wasn't, actually, but at that time it was the only way to express one's opposition to the Nazi régime plausibly, without getting long-winded, and to win the confidence of a Resistance member like Dr. Müller. ' Where's Dohnanyi ? ' he asked at last. ' Over in admin. in one of the special cells,' I replied. ' How is he ? ' I shrugged. ' As well as might be expected.' Then I put all my cards on the table : ' Wouldn't you like to get a message to him?' For a moment Dr. Müller's eyes narrowed to tiny slits. His kindly face was quite hard for a moment. Then he said: 'All right; I trust you.' It must have been a difficult decision.

Dr. Müller wrote a couple of hasty lines on a small piece of paper I pushed into his hand. I rolled up the message and stuck it in my sock. Then I concluded my "inspection," locked the cell door from the outside and went back to the guard room as if nothing had happened.

A little later I wandered over to the admin. building on some pretext or other, and looked in at the office. I had a little chat with Private Rempel in there, smoked a cigarette and just hung around. I was lucky; after a bit the control lamp linking Dohnanyi's cell with the office lit up, a sign he wanted something. I said to Rempel, who was busy finishing a report, 'Don't worry, I'll go over.' I took the key and went upstairs to the block where the two special cells were. Dohnanyi wanted to go to the toilet; I accompanied him. When the door had closed behind us I pulled the note out of my sock and handed it to him. Dohnanyi rolled it open. He turned quite white when he saw who it was from. His hands shook, and he gave me a disturbed and frightened glance. 'Read it, tear it up and throw it away,' I ordered. Then I added: 'If you want to get in touch with Dr. Müller I'm at your service.' Dohnanyi had pulled himself together. He nodded, his eyes full of tears. 'Keep your chin up,' I whispered, and left him alone. Later, when I'd taken him back to his cell, he scribbled a few quick words on a piece of paper, which I concealed and delivered to Dr. Müller that evening."

The contact which Milkau established between Dr. Müller and Dohnanyi probably saved Müller's life—quite apart from his strong nerve and indefatigable fighting spirit. The two important remand prisoners were able to keep in touch by means of the secret notes, and to discuss their conduct during the hearings—what to deny and what they could safely admit.

Milkau also saw to it, from the first day, that everything was done to mitigate Müller's conditions of imprisonment. He deliberately abandoned, for instance, the practices of burning a light in Müller's cell all night and carrying out check-ups every half hour. When Dr. Müller had been in Lehrter Strasse for some time, Milkau used to leave his cell door open at nights, to allow him complete freedom of movement. Sometimes he used to sit for hours with Milkau and his subordinate, Wagner, who supported Milkau in his errands of mercy, listening to the radio in the guard room. Soon they were even listening to foreign stations together, with Müller translating the BBC news bulletins for the benefit of the two overseers.

One day a new prisoner, a colonel, was admitted to Lehrter Strasse; he sat in his cell, cowed and apathetic. Milkau told Dr. Müller about him. "Wouldn't you like to see to the colonel, doctor?" Müller agreed at once. That evening Milkau took him to the colonel's cell and left him alone with the officer for two hours. When Dr. Müller emerged the officer had regained complete composure. Dr. Müller had briefed him about how to behave at the hearings, and what legal means he had at his disposal.

From this point onwards Milkau or Wagner always fetched Müller out of his cell to dispense comfort and courage to the new arrivals. Or they took political prisoners to Müller's cell to consult with him. Among them was Helmut Kindler, publisher of the German original of this book, whom the Wehrmacht had handed over for sentence to the People's Court—which was unusual before July 20, 1944.

"The lives of the remand prisoners," Dr. Müller says today, "often depended on their behaviour during the first hearing. Milkau and Wagner knew that; they brought me in contact with the prisoners for that reason. They saved many a prisoner from the death sentence in this way."

"Your legal and tactical advice must have played a big part, too," I told Müller, as I sat opposite him in his lawyer's office in Schwabing. This man, who fearlessly faced the interrogations of the notorious Nazi prosecuting counsel, Roeder, for a whole year—they called him the Bloodhound —brushed my remark aside. "That was just my duty," he said.

Müller, during his term at Lehrter Strasse, helped a large number of prisoners, but his own fate often hung on a very tenuous thread.

"The worst day for me was April 30, 1943," he recalled. "I was cross-examined by the Nazi military tribunal the whole day. I had managed to destroy, or get out of the way, all evidence about my participation in the anti-Hitler Resistance and my secret mission to the Vatican to make contact with the English, so they had nothing foolproof on me, apart from the statement of the Intelligence agent arrested in 1942 for a currency offence and a sketch map of Pullach, with the position of the Führer's bunker marked on it. I had obtained this plan a short while previously, from the Jesuits, who had a seminary in Pullach. It was meant for Colonel Oster in Counter-Intelligence, for passing on to the officers who were to assassinate Hitler. I hadn't been able to hide this sketch map. You can imagine that this suspicious bit of paper made them apply the pressure pretty hard. 'We'll just have your family shot if you don't talk,' the officer in charge of the proceedings, Möller, said to me. I replied ' Here we are in the building of the highest German court ; surely I have the right to demand that I be treated according to the rules of law and justice!' Möller replied: ' I'll tell you one thing—any cheek from you and you'd better think of saving your skin, not your rights.' Then he moved his hand across his throat."

Müller answered coolly that a clairvoyant from Hamburg had foretold that he would live to be at least sixty. A bizarre thing happened : the officer allowed himself to be drawn into a discussion on clairvoyants, and whether one could believe them or not!

"He worried me for six whole hours about the sketch plan of the Führer's bunker, and even alleged that I might know something about an assassination plan. But I went on repeating that it was absolutely private ; I had the plan for professional and official reasons. Möller went on threatening and warning me. I got nothing to eat or drink the whole time ; he tried to browbeat me in every possible way."

He refused to be browbeaten, however.

Dr. Müller succeeded in contacting the Pullach Jesuits from his cell. Kreuzberg, the prison chaplain—according to Dr. Müller he was of tremendous help to the prisoners—travelled to Munich for him and spoke to the Jesuits. They agreed to testify, if called to a hearing, that Dr. Müller was their adviser on matters of finance and real estate, and had received the map from them. Since the Luftwaffe had often asked the Jesuits for arable land for ack-ack purposes, this explanation was plausible. The Jesuit fathers, when interrogated in Munich, were honourable enough to testify on Müller's behalf in the manner agreed. Therefore, the point of suspicion which had arisen from this sketch map was dropped.

However, they still regarded Müller's journeys to the Vatican and his Resistance contacts as suspicious. But they could prove nothing. In the trial that followed he was, therefore, acquitted.

However, he was not out of the wood. After the decisive proceedings were over Lieutenant-Colonel Maass sent for Müller and informed him that he was going to take him into protective custody, because the Gestapo was tailing him and wanted to pack him off to a concentration camp. Müller stayed in Lehrter Street prison for the time, for his own safety.

His fellow-sufferer, Hans von Dohnanyi, was not so lucky. He became ill in prison and incapable of facing trial. As the main proceedings against him were constantly being deferred, Maass could not prevent him being taken into custody by the Reich Security Head Office and transferred to a special bunker in Sachsenhausen concentration camp. We lose trace of him here. His friends all agree that he died in Sachsenhausen in April, 1945.

Dr. Josef Müller was imprisoned at Lehrter Strasse for 18 months altogether. After the abortive attempt on Hitler's life on July 20, when the Gestapo were hounding everyone who, because of their opposition to the régime, were even remotely suspect, the guards Milkau and Wagner forged an escape plan for Müller. They were pretty certain that Lieutenant-Colonel Maass would not be able to keep Müller in custody in Lehrter Strasse much longer, and after that he would be vulnerable to arrest by the Gestapo. Maass himself was under suspicion because he was friendly with the City Commandant of Berlin, Lieutenant-General Paul von Hase, who was arrested after the attempt. Müller had to disappear, without anyone seeing him or having the slightest idea *how* he had disappeared.

There was a food store in the prison basement, to which Milkau possessed a key. The window was secured with removable crossbars. Milkau made an impression of the lock of this grating with soap. He went to a locksmith and got a key which more or less fitted, then filed it down to size. In a certain place in the vicinity Corporal Wagner had a motor-cycle hidden to take Müller to Milkau's allotment in Gross-Ziethen. In the meantime, Milkau had ascertained that Müller's Counter-Intelligence identity card was kept in the iron safe in the prison office. It was one of the so-called " green cards " which bore no name but assured the bearer a safe conduct everywhere, even through S.S., Gestapo or police cordons ; and all officials were obliged to give the holder every possible assistance.

Milkau and Wagner had soon spied out the hiding place where Private Rempel, who was responsible for locking the safe, kept the key.

The final preparations were made. When the time was ripe Milkau or Wagner would take Dr. Müller by night into the cellar, let him into the larder, help him through the window and then lock window and larder after him—and Müller, complete with green card, would jump on Wagner's motor-bike and drive to Gross-Ziethen, where he could lie low for a bit till he got the opportunity to continue his flight —or till the end of the war, which seemed to be in sight.

But it was not to be.

" Dr. Müller hesitated too long," Milkau said later. " He was worried—quite rightly—about his wife and child. He was afraid that if he escaped the Gestapo would arrest them. Nevertheless, we begged him to beat it—before it was too late. One afternoon in August, 1944, just after lunch, Lieutenant-Colonel Maass telephoned me. I had to produce Dr. Müller immediately, all packed and ready to go. I knew what that meant. He was to be transferred to another prison! I ran to his cell and for the first time he lost control. ' This is it,' he whispered, white as chalk. 'The Gestapo!' He clutched my arm. ' Milkau—have I still a chance ? '

It was broad daylight. We could not risk letting him escape through the cellar because the store window looked directly out on to the street. He wouldn't have gone ten yards—the guard at the main entrance would have seen him and shot him down on the spot.

'Milkau, old boy,' said Dr. Müller, 'I've missed the boat!' But he regained composure immediately. He pressed both my hands. 'You've done a lot for me,' he said, 'you and Wagner. I'll never forget that, never.'

I was pretty miserable as I took him over to admin. I knew that he'd need a lot of courage, and even more luck, to get through what was coming to him."

Müller was transferred to the Gestapo prison in the Prinz-Albrecht-Strasse. Most of the July 20 conspirators were in custody there already, among them the former Chief Mayor of Leipzig, Carl Goerdeler, who after the intended revolution was to form a new government as Reich Chancellor; and numerous prominent politicians, generals and professors. They were nearly all executed in the months that followed. Only Müller escaped this fate. One of the highest army judges, who had himself been arrested after July 20 and was now imprisoned in Prinz-Albrecht-Strasse, managed to whisper to Müller when they met that he had destroyed his —Müller's—trial files. From then on Müller knew he was safe. Actually he passed through a couple of concentration camps, but he was eventually liberated by the Americans.

Milkau and Wagner had risked their lives by helping Müller. But they never slipped up. Milkau knew, however, that they could never have done all this without the tacit tolerance, and even support, of the prison governor, Lieutenant-Colonel Maass.

Needless to say, it was not only Dr. Müller that Milkau helped in those critical months. There was Major Kastner, who had been arrested on an alleged sabotage charge. Milkau established contact between him and his wife, who up till then had been completely ignorant of her husband's fate. Mrs. Kastner came from Ullerring, near Munich, where she lived, to Berlin, and for weeks Milkau smuggled letters and food parcels from her to the Major in his cell. Seven months later Kastner was exonerated without demotion. Then there was Lieutenant-Colonel Schenck from Berlin, who was on remand for subversion among the fighting forces. He had a young, very pretty wife living in the Alexander-platz, Berlin. Milkau asked her to the prison and bribed his colleagues with cigarettes to get them to turn a blind eye to her presence. In one of the visitors' rooms he was able to discuss her husband's case with Mrs. Schenck undisturbed. She was thereby in the position to get herself a good lawyer, who actually managed to procure Schenck's release after four months' imprisonment.

In 1941 there was a sensation in prison; Stalin's son, Jacob, who had been taken prisoner by German troops on the eastern front, was admitted. Milkau took him on. When he wanted to take the young Russian officer to the shower he refused to go, because Milkau was carrying an automatic. He thought he was being taken down there just to get shot in the back of the neck. It was only when Milkau laid the regulation weapon on one side that Stalin's son agreed to go with him. After a while he was transferred to another prison. Milkau lost sight of him. He does not know what happened to him; presumably he died in a German camp.

One day a quixotic figure appeared in Lehrter Strasse: an Englishman, Dick Jones, swathed in Beduin robes. He was a British agent, captured behind the German lines in North Africa and flown immediately to Berlin, because he was regarded as one of England's star agents. Milkau was sorry for Jones, because it was winter in Berlin and the English-man was freezing miserably in his burnous, despite his exaggerated air of typical British nonchalance. Milkau encouraged him to write to the Swiss Ambassador. In the evening, when no one was looking, he threw the letter into the Embassy's front garden. Within four weeks an inter-national Red Cross parcel, with food and a suit for Dick Jones, arrived at Lehrter Strasse. Milkau thinks that the English-man was later bartered for a German agent in British hands.

Mrs. Milkau was a match for her husband. Near the allot-ment colony in Gross-Ziethen, French and Russian prisoners-of-war worked as well as concentration camp inmates. Every morning and evening they passed the Milkaus' fence. Mrs.

Milkau used to stand behind the fence with fresh fruit and vegetables from the garden, occasional bread, and always a container with some refreshing drink for the emaciated and exhausted prisoners. She was particularly sorry for an old man, a Jew ; you could see how severely his hardships had affected him. She would hand him sandwiches furtively over the fence ; he would devour them on the spot, without a word, with an intensity which was almost animal, while his eyes wandered fearfully in all directions.

The Milkaus were pretty daring. All their escapades met with success. But luck is not eternal. The Gestapo came on September 15, 1943.

A Luftwaffe Lieutenant-Colonel was imprisoned in Lehrter Strasse at the time. One evening a food package from a Miss Tiessen, his secretary, was delivered at Milkau's flat. He took it with him next morning to Lehrter Strasse. That morning the officer asked him to deliver a letter for him—to Friedenau, to an actress niece of his. This young woman, whose name Milkau had forgotten, lived in an elegant villa. Milkau went that evening—it was September 14—to her home, but got no answer. He put the letter in the box and returned home.

Next morning Mrs. Milkau, looking out of her window, noticed a couple of men hanging around in a manner which was too obviously nonchalant on the other side of the street. Something was up ; she felt it intuitively. To be on the safe side she immediately burned in the kitchen stove all the addresses and documents her husband had brought from prison, which she used to keep in a tin box. She had barely finished when the bell rang. The two men from the other side of the road demanded access. They were Gestapo officials.

" Hand over the letter ! " That was the first thing they said.

"I've got no letter. I don't know what you're talking about."

The Gestapo ransacked the whole flat and threatened Mrs. Milkau. But she stuck to her story ; she knew nothing about a letter.

" You got a parcel, didn't you ? "

Yes—she'd been ill and a friend had brought her a food parcel.

Mrs. Milkau was taken in a closed transport car to Luft-gaukommando II in Florastrasse. She was interrogated and asked again about the parcel; Mrs. Milkau said it was a present. The woman had been sorry for her because she was just recovering from a serious illness.

That day, shortly before finishing his duties, Milkau was interrogated by a Luftwaffe High Court judge.

" You smuggled a letter out."

" I don't remember doing that."

" And yesterday you delivered another letter. We have it in our possession. In the files here."

" Maybe someone threw the letter out of the lavatory window on to the street."

" You don't believe that yourself, surely ? "

" I certainly do!"

" All right. What about the parcels ? "

" My wife ate what was meant for her. The Lieutenant-Colonel got everything which was meant for him. He was always hungry."

Milkau looked innocently at the judge. " Foodstuffs for a remand prisoner are not against the rules, and if a man is hungry. . . ."

" Quiet!" The Luftwaffe officer was brought in. He looked pale but composed.

" Colonel, who delivered the letter to your niece ?"

" I threw it on to the street through the bars of the toilet window."

" I see. And what did you do with the food ? "

" I shared it with the other three in my cell and we ate it."

Milkau was suspended from duty for six weeks. Then came the trial. To all tricky questions he replied with a stubborn: " I can't remember!"

The prosecutor shouted at him: " Nonsense! You must remember!"

" I suffer from loss of memory," Milkau explained. " I was bombed twice in the war. It's in my papers. Then again, I had an accident a short while ago."

" Then how can you fill a responsible post, like that of a guard in a remand prison ? " shouted the prosecutor.

The presiding magistrate and his assessors whispered

together. Then the magistrate yelled at him: "Get out!"

Mrs. Milkau was called to the stand. She maintained that she had received a parcel as a present, the contents of which she had "eaten up." She knew nothing of letters. The trial was very brief. Then came Miss Tiessen's turn. After half an hour the court announced its verdict: Not guilty! They had fallen for Milkau's "loss of memory." The prosecutor had to grit his teeth and turn him loose.

Milkau had orders to report to Lieutenant-Colonel Maass immediately after the close of the proceedings. In order to keep up appearances, presumably, he took disciplinary action against him for "smuggling comestibles." He got 14 days in Spandau.

The improbable had happened: Milkau, who had already forwarded hundreds of letters against the rules, established contact between prisoners who were conspirators against the régime, saved men doomed to certain death by contacting lawyers or influential people—this man had fallen into Gestapo hands—and got away with it! Fourteen days in Spandau: hardly worth mentioning compared with what would have happened to him had he been found out.

When Milkau was released from Spandau he had to report to Maass at Lehrter Strasse. He could stay if he liked, Maass said. He had interceded for him "in high places."

"There was no doubt that he knew how I stood with the prisoners; how I tried to help Dr. Josef Müller, who was still with us then. Shortly before the war ended I ventured to say to him: 'Sir, the war is over, we've had it, and if we don't beat it pretty quick we'll be buried under the ruins of our own prison!' He just nodded and said: 'You're right, Milkau, but we've got to stay; what will happen to the prisoners otherwise?'

He was right. We couldn't let the prisoners go because the machine of justice was still operating at top gear, although the Russians were at the door. And we had to see to it that the S.S. did not suddenly appear, as had happened in other prisons, and just stand the prisoners up against the wall. At that time I didn't go home at all; I slept at the prison. A large number of the prison officers had been conscripted to the front, or had discharged themselves. Many prisoners had been moved. We still had 34 men. One night First Lieutenant Gehrke and a private in my block broke out and escaped. I should have made a cell check-up, but didn't. They'd got themselves a file and sawn through the bars. Of course I knew what they were up to. I just went on sleeping peacefully, though the sawing sound shook the whole block. Maass just brushed it aside when I reported it next morning. Have a scout around, Milkau, he ordered ; see where the Russians are.

The Russians were less than a mile away, actually. That evening a bomb hit our admin. building. When I had struggled through the debris to the governor's room I found him lying half under a beam. He was dead.

Next morning some officers appeared at Lehrter Strasse 61, appointed the remaining 32 prisoners members of a commando unit, armed them and sent them to the front. I'm quite convinced they took to their heels in the next street.

For us, the last of the overseers, that was the last of Lehrter Strasse 61. We had been relieved of the responsibility for our prisoners. We could go home."

Milkau took six and a half hours to get home from Lehrter Strasse to Neukölln. Most of them he spent crawling on his belly on the ground or crouching in shell craters to protect himself from machine-gun fire and bombs.

At home Milkau discarded his uniform, put on civilian garb and waited for the Russians, who two days later were standing before the basement door of his flat in the Kienitzerstrasse. He lives there today. It was there that he told me his story.

Berlin, 1942. Gestapo Headquarters, Prinz-Albrecht-Strasse.

A Gestapo official: "*Surely, Dr. Baeck, not even you can deny that the whole German nation is behind the Führer's measures, and therefore behind his policy regarding the Jews.*"

Dr. Baeck, President of the Representative Council of German Jews: "*I wouldn't like to be dogmatic on this question, but I would like to say just one thing. When I go home from here, now . . . with my yellow star, nothing bad will happen to me. . . . On the other hand, here and there someone will try and push his way over to me, a stranger; he will look nervously around him and press my hand. Perhaps he will even push an apple into my hand, a bar of chocolate or a cigarette. Apart from that, nothing will happen to me. I don't know whether the Führer, in my place, would have the same experience.*"

Ina Prowe-Isenbörger, "Deutsche Juden" (German Jews), H. Warecke, Hangelar, 1962.

8

" ' So far so good,' my father had written from England. 'I've found you jobs and got a work permit. Your application for an exit visa will now be supported by the authorities at this end. It can't be more than fourteen days before the British Consulate-General in Berlin grants you your visa. Keep your chins up—we'll soon be united again.'

The city buzzed with a thousand rumours. We knew that nothing would come of our emigration plans to England if war broke out.

And how had Hitler's right-hand man, Hermann Göring, put it, after that notorious *Kristallnacht* ('Night of the Broken Glass') a year ago, when the S.A. had burned down Jewish synagogues and business premises and dragged thousands of Jews to concentration camps overnight ?

' If the German Reich, in the foreseeable future, becomes involved in disputes with foreign powers, it goes without saying that we in Germany must think, first and foremost, of settling our account with the Jews—and in no uncertain fashion.'

After that night my father had taken all the necessary steps for emigration. But it was not until April, 1939, that he succeeded in getting to England—alone. He promised to send for us as soon as possible. But this " soon as possible " became weeks and months. We simply did not understand why my father was no longer putting the pressure on. We did not know that the British authorities then made things extremely difficult for Jewish immigrants. But now this letter arrived, which plunged us simultaneously into hope and even deeper despair, because time was slipping through our fingers. Even tomorrow might be too late.

' Mummy ? ' I said one night when I couldn't sleep.

' What ? '

'You're going to the consulate again tomorrow, aren't you ?'

'Of course, child.'

The red tip of her cigarette glowed in the dark. My mother's voice sounded calm and controlled. But I knew she was just as scared as I was ; the same problems troubled her, the same doubts tormented her.

'But if. . . .'

'If what ?'

'If war breaks out. . . .'

'We're sure to manage it before then, Inge. We need only pack a couple of cases. Everything else is at Hamburg Free Port ready for shipment. All we need is the British consul to stamp. . . .'

Yes, the vital stamp.

'Sleep well, child,' my mother said, and stubbed out her cigarette. She opened the window. A cool breath of wind wafted in and fanned my burning forehead.

I closed my eyes.

I could see my father's letter before me, the letters dancing in front of my eyes.

'Soon we'll be together . . . so far, so good. . . . Chin up . . . soon, soon, soon. . . .'

Next morning we were awakened by a persistent, stubborn knocking on the front door.

My mother got up, throwing a bathrobe over her shoulders. She went to the door and opened.

There was Mr. Blumenthal, a neighbour in the same house. Behind him I recognised the pretty, resigned countenance of his blonde wife.

Blumenthal looked at my mother. It was some time before he spoke.

'It's happened,' he said at last.

'What's happened ?' my mother asked.

'It was just announced on the wireless. It's war, Mrs. Deutschkron.'

'War ?' my mother said, and something like a sob escaped her throat. 'War ? It's too late, then. . . .'

Mr. Blumenthal nodded. 'It's too late for us all,' he said softly.

With her last words Inge Deutschkron's voice dropped. She lowered her gaze. Then she raised her dark eyes and I saw that memories were crowding in on her again ; memories of that time almost 25 years ago, when she was still a child and fear was her constant companion.

Inge Deutschkron survived those years. One of the few who survived of the numerous Jewish girls who were in Berlin when the trap snapped shut. Thousands of girls of her age perished in the Nazi extermination camps. She was saved. By the help of someone she loved. By her own fantastic courage. And by the helping hand of a few courageous Germans. But first and foremost by Otto Weidt.

"Without him, I wouldn't be alive today," said Inge Deutschkron, when I visited her in her flat on the Bonn-Tannenbusch estate. Inge Deutschkron had been working as a journalist in Bonn for some years. The era of persecution lay far behind.

"The Berliners—so many Berliners helped us. The little people ; the shopkeeper round the corner, the guard in the underground, the policeman in our district. Naturally there were a lot of fanatics, but without the aid of all those anonymous Berliners we would never have been able to stay underground for two years."

Inge Deutschkron smoothed her thick, dark hair with her hand. "Two years," she said. "Only two years—but they seemed like two decades to us."

It cannot with accuracy be established how many German Jews lived "illegally" in Berlin during the war. Certainly there were quite a number. Gerald Reitlinger, in his book on Hitler's attempt to exterminate European Jewry, "The Final Solution," calculated on the basis of statistics from the Reich Security Head Office and other Nazi organisations, that about 10,000 Jews must have been living underground in Berlin in the middle of 1943. He writes :

"During the day they roamed the streets without ration books or identity cards and were precariously sheltered at night by Aryan friends."

Many of these fugitives were discovered and deported in the months that followed. Others died in air raids or in the battles round Berlin. When war broke out 95,000 Jews lived in Berlin. About 85,000 suffered deportation and death in extermination camps. There is almost nothing left today in the old Reich capital of the once flourishing Jewish community which helped to give Berlin its character from the middle of the nineteenth century ; for only 5,600 Jews live in West Berlin today. Many of them are elderly people who do not want to leave their home town, in spite of all that happened. They live with the memory of an era, over thirty years ago, when Berlin was one of the most liberal cities in the world, where each man could follow his own spiritual inclinations and where you would have been thought insane if you had maintained that, one day, the German " Christians " would go forth and murder the German Jews.

" It took us some time to get over the shock of hearing of the outbreak of war," Inge Deutschkron told me. " For the first few days we wandered around in a trance, then we had to adapt ourselves to the harsh facts of the times."

Göring's words of a year ago became reality overnight. The " settlement " with the Jews began.

It began with the issuing of food cards : Jewish cards were stamped with a J, so as to prevent Jews from the outset from buying unrationed foodstuffs, which you could only obtain by producing the card. The rations themselves were considerably smaller than those of other Germans. Full-cream milk, coffee, fruit and confectionery were no longer available to Jews. So as to cut them off from the outside world completely, their radio sets were confiscated and, finally, their telephones disconnected. Indignities increased month by month. Laundries were not allowed to accept washing from Jews ; hairdressers had to deny them their services. We had to give up our furs, cameras, binoculars and electrical equipment of all kinds. We could not visit theatres, cinemas and concert halls or, eventually, public parks. But this was a mere pinprick compared with what was to follow.

Very soon Jews had to give up their apartments in houses owned by non-Jews, and were crammed together in so-called " Jewish houses." My mother and I had to move to the Bayerischen Platz, where we had to share a five-room flat with eleven other people. Usually Jews only had a day's warning to move house; sometimes they only had a few hours for the removal. So as to be ready for all eventualities, therefore, many Jews began to sell their furniture—and they practically had to *give* it away.

Of course, all Jews were conscripted for war work immediately—the hardest kind of manual labour, and mostly very dirty work, too. Jewish men were put on refuse collecting and street sweeping; or they worked as navvies, or in factories, where they were made to carry heavy loads like mere drudges. My mother was a factory hand in munitions; I was at a silk-spinning factory. The working day was ten or twelve hours and the wages miserable. Under the existing laws firms were not allowed to pay Jews more than sixty pfennigs an hour. Fifteen per cent of this went to the State, a so-called "Jews' duty," quite apart from income tax and social insurance. Our monthly salary did not even cover the rent of our flat. In spite of the heavy physical labour, rations for Jews were constantly being cut, and eventually consisted only of potatoes, bread, a tiny portion of fat, turnips, sugar and a little skimmed milk. Then they thought up another way of humiliating us: Jews had to do their shopping between four and five p.m., and only in certain shops. Most of us were still at work then, and, of course, it was too late to do any legal shopping after hours.

But the real degradation of the Jews began with the introduction of the "Jewish star" in the autumn of 1941."

The wearing of the yellow Jewish star, with which they had already tried to brand the Jews in the Middle Ages, was ordered by a police regulation of September 1, 1941. Now they wanted to outlaw the Jews, to expose them to the scorn of the German *Volksgenossen,* and render them so conspicuous that a check could easily be kept on whether or not they adhered to the limitations imposed on them.

Here is a quotation from the regulation:

"Jews over six years of age are not allowed to appear in public without showing the Jewish star. This consists of a six-pointed star about the size of a small plate, in yellow material on black background, with the word " Jew " in black lettering. It must be securely sewn on the left breast of the outer garment and must be visible."

This regulation came into force on September 16. It was the brain child of the Reich Propaganda Minister, Josef Goebbels, who was also the " inventor " of separate park benches for Jews, of the cinema and theatre prohibitions and most of the other humiliations which were forerunners of the deportations and thereby of the " final solution " in the death camps.

Inge Deutschkron told me of her experiences on the day the Jewish star was introduced.

" Alice Licht was my friend. She was a very pretty girl of my own age. She had jet black hair with a centre parting, and was slim and dainty with the face of a spoilt doll. Her big, black eyes could bewitch any man who came near her —and did she know it!

On that morning—September 16—she came to call for me. We had decided to travel to work together. We were going to support each other ; for on this particular day, for the first time, we were wearing the Magen David on the left side of our coats, above the heart, sewn on with fine stitches, all according to regulations.

' How do you feel ? ' I asked Alice.

' Just like you do.' She tried to laugh, but her charming child's face was a rigid mask behind which she endeavoured to hide her pain and humiliation.

' It's best for us just to make nothing of it,' I said. ' We'll pretend it's a decoration.'

' A decoration!' Alice laughed, but it was a grim laugh.

We went arm-in-arm from the Bayerischen Platz towards the underground station. My heart contracted, because I knew that on the train I'd see a young man who, every morning during the journey to work, used to give me appreciative glances. How would this fair-haired young man behave today ? How would he react to the Jewish star ?

' Better keep a stiff upper lip,' I said, and laughed. But it wasn't a natural laugh.

The train roared into the station and came to a halt ; the doors opened with a hiss of compressed air and we got on.

Everyone looked at us; like every morning. Their gaze moved over our faces, our coats. Not an eye fixed itself on the star of David. It was as if we weren't wearing it at all.

There was my young man, too. He stood a couple of paces away from me; and smiled, as always.

I looked around me. I saw dozens of people also wearing the star of David—people one would never have taken for Jews; blond men, red-haired women, a white-haired old gentleman with the boldly etched features of a Viking.

All of them Jews; all wearing the yellow badge of shame which was to stamp them as pariahs.

But we were not pariahs.

Today, more than twenty years later and in the perspective of time, I can swear as I could have sworn then:

A secret, intangible, and yet immediately perceptible wave of sympathy flowed towards us from our non-Jewish fellow-citizens of Berlin.

One of the passengers made no bones about this sympathy. A middle-aged man, who got up from his seat.

'Please, young lady,' he said, pointing to his place.

'I'm not allowed to sit,' I said, and remained standing.

'But I insist,' he said, in the same polite tone.

I was not allowed to sit; Jews were not allowed to sit. But I could not draw attention to myself, either.

'Please,' said the gentleman, who had taken off his hat and now stood before me. 'Please sit down. Nothing will happen to you; I'll guarantee that. I offer you my protection.'

He said that so confidently that I could do nothing but sit down.

The young man who stood a short distance away smiled again. His smile said: All right, don't be afraid. It won't be all that bad. But we deceived ourselves, all of us; we Jews and those sympathetic Berliners in the underground that morning. It was going to be very bad for many millions of my co-religionists in Europe, and for millions of Germans, too.

The great massacre was just beginning.

In the period immediately after September 16 we experienced many instances of humanity on the part of non-Jewish Berliners. Now we realised, for the first time, that there was another Germany, not just that of the brown oppressors. Shopkeepers sneaked us food for free—vegetables, fruit, bread; and sometimes I found in my pocket cigarettes that someone had pushed in there furtively, in the underground crush. For a time I even received meat tokens regularly from some anonymous benefactor by post. I never found out who this friend in need was.

I was very young then, and despite the sympathy many people showed us, wearing the Jewish star got me into such a state of nervous hysteria that I simply couldn't bear it any more. Before we had to wear the yellow star we could still get round the curfew, which prevented Jews going out in the evening, now and again. That was over now. But fourteen days after the star was introduced I decided that I'd disguise myself at every favourable opportunity, no matter how severe the penalty. So from then onwards I always used to carry a second item of clothing in my briefcase, without the yellow star sewn on—a sweater, a blouse or a jacket, which I'd pull quickly over me in some doorway when no one was looking. In this way I could go to the theatre or cinema occasionally, or attend a concert or lecture from time to time. If I had been found out I'd have been deported to a concentration camp at once.

As I said, we lived in the Bayerischen Platz at the time. The journey to and from work took about an hour and a half. Not being able to sit in the tube added a lot to the burden of the hard work—ten hours of it—which I had to perform standing up. As for working conditions, they were particularly bad for Jews. In our factory (A.C.E.T.A.) the yellow star for Jews during working hours had already been introduced in 1940. Our rest-rooms with their rough wooden benches, and the toilets—naturally segregated from the 'Aryan' toilets—were extremely primitive. Any contact with 'Aryan' workers, male or female, was strictly forbidden, of course. For some unknown reason, too, we Jewish girls were subjected to regular gynæcological examinations by the factory doctor. I was just eighteen then!

I was constantly racking my brain for a means of escaping these humiliating surroundings, and the hard work which I just wasn't up to. I turned in my trouble to Mrs. Gertrud

Prochownik, a former director of the Jewish Labour Information Bureau. She sent me to a Mr. Weidt, who ran a workshop for the blind in Rosenthaler Strasse. He employed, exclusively, Jewish blind people and deaf mutes."

Otto Weidt was a small man with a creased-up face; he was slim and fragile, but had a lion heart. He employed in his workshop, over the years, 165 physically handicapped Jews; he financed 56 Jews living "underground" and procured food and board and lodging for them. The Gestapo came to search his house fifty-two times and he was arrested eleven times. Twenty-seven of "his" Jews survived the war. Inge Deutschkron was one of them.

Weidt did everything for "his" Jews. He employed far more of them than his little business could support financially; he negotiated, on behalf of others, with sympathetic firms ready to employ Jews on the quiet. Also, though Inge did not know it at the time, he hid a number of hunted Jews in a place behind the workshop.

The day Inge went to Weidt her right knee was swollen up through being on her feet constantly, and even the Nazi doctor at A.C.E.T.A. had to issue her with a certificate to the effect that she was no longer fit for standing work. Weidt, who was himself half blind, put on his blind armband and went with Inge to the Jewish labour office. He managed to convince the staff there that the young girl, since she was " of no earthly use to anyone else," would be best taken care of at his firm with the other physically handicapped. In the end Weidt got permission to engage her. At the time he didn't have a single vacancy she could fill; but he knew of a way out. He came to an arrangement with a firm in the same line—i.e., brush manufacture—that they should employ Inge, though Weidt would still carry her on his books. This job with the Meyer firm was, of course, illegal. When Inge Deutschkron commenced work there she was glad it was a general holiday. At the time there was no one at all in the office apart from the proprietors, Meyer senior and his son; this was to have obvious consequences.

" One day I was just sitting there typing. I was alone in the office, as always.

The door behind me opened. I carried on typing.

The door closed. I didn't turn round. I knew who it was. I heard his panting breath as he came up behind me. His hand rested on my shoulder, slid up to my neck and stroked my skin.

I made a defensive movement with my shoulder and shook off the hand.

'Not finished work yet?'

'No, Mr. Meyer.'

'How do you like it here?'

I stared at my machine.

'Fine, thanks.'

'I should think so. As a Jewess you won't get such an easy job in a hurry.'

'I know that.'

'I only took you on—because I like you.'

I said nothing. What could I say?

'Do you understand?'

He was still standing close behind me, and I could feel him getting still nearer. I leaned forward to evade his touch.

'Yes, I understand you, Mr. Meyer.'

'Well, I like you. A lot.'

'I'm wearing a Jewish star, Mr. Meyer.'

'I don't care.'

'There are such things as Nuremberg laws, in case you've forgotten.'

'So what?'

'I only meant. . . .'

'Quite a temper! Just like a little pussy cat! But that's what I like.'

He laid his hand on my shoulder again. His other hand glided round my waist. I froze.

At that moment the door opened again. Meyer let me go.

'Father! There you are! I've been looking for you all over the place!' It was junior. You could tell from his voice that he was furious. 'Mr. Arnold is here—he wants to speak to you urgently.'

'All right—I'm coming.'

He made his exit, growling to himself. His footsteps faded away down the corridor outside.

174

Young Meyer came round the desk and grinned at me.
'The old man been pawing you again?'

'I don't know what you mean.'

'Well, well, quite a little innocent.' He propped himself
with both elbows on the desk and stared at me with his pale,
widely-set popeyes.

'He's much too old for you,' he said.

'I have to get on with my work, Mr. Meyer.'

'Now, don't get on your high horse.' His eyes became
crafty. 'You've no call to, you know. You should be glad—'

The telephone rang at that point.

Meyer junior answered. 'Yes, I'm coming,' he snarled
into the receiver, and hung up.

'See you, sweetie.' He vanished.

It was just like a farce; Box goes out and Cox comes in.
Two minutes after junior's departure the old man came back
again. He shut the door behind him, and when he'd made
sure there was no one out in the corridor he came quickly
up to the desk and produced an envelope from his breast
pocket.

'Put that away quick,' he said. I took the envelope and
pushed it into my handbag.

'It's meat and bread tokens,' he said.

'Thanks very much, Mr. Meyer. I'll give them to my
mother.'

'Blow your mother—they're for you! So you get big and
strong!' He grinned and managed to look just as oafish and
artful as his son.

I got up and walked over to the roll-top bureau to get
a card index.

Suddenly he was standing behind me. I avoided him and
fled into the furthest corner of the office.

'How old are you?' he asked.

'I'm—please, leave me alone, Mr. Meyer!'

'You're only nineteen, aren't you?'

'I'd like to work in peace, Mr. Meyer.'

'Now don't make such a fuss!'

He made a grab at me. I fended him off.

'Quick—a kiss!' he ordered.

I ducked and tried to escape under his raised arms. He

got hold of my blouse.

'There—got you!'

I felt the blood rushing to my head.

'Let go of me at once, or I'll scream!'

It was just like a bad comedy. At that moment the door was thrown open ; enter junior again. He stared at me, stared at his dad.

'Hee,' was all he said.

'What the hell do you want now?' The old man was fuming.

The son began to smirk. Without a word he closed the door and sat on the desk.

'Shall we toss up for her?' he asked his father.

'You oaf! You've got no shame!' The old boy began to yell.

'Hush,' whispered the son. 'Don't forget she's a Jewess.'

'That's just what I don't forget! She's a person who should be pitied . . . but you wouldn't understand that.'

'I know your kind of pity.'

'Shut up!'

I took the card index and sat at my typewriter.

'Come on,' the old man commanded his offspring. Together they left the office. I could hear them arguing at the top of their voices, but it died away gradually.

I stared at my hands. Of course it was all quite ludicrous ; but I felt more like crying than laughing."

At last she had found a job with light work, where she wasn't victimised—and now this! She couldn't remain with the Meyers, that was certain. Both of them got more persistent every day. All she could do was to approach Mr. Weidt again.

Weidt was absolutely wild when, after a good deal of hesitation, she told him what indignities she had been subjected to at the Meyers'. "You don't go there again!" he said at last. True, he still had no vacancy for her in the workshop, but from then on he employed her in his office where Alice Licht, Inge's friend, had already got a job. Since Jews were only allowed to undertake manual labour, Inge and Alice, as well as the Jewish bookkeeper, Werner Basch, had to disappear immediately from the office into the workshop when a checkup was in the offing—no rare occurrence.

" Weidt had severe heart trouble and the perpetual worry and agitation which his Jews—without meaning to, of course—caused him, set him back a lot. But he didn't spare himself ; he was always at our disposal. He was perpetually having to reclaim his workers, because every morning someone or other would appear looking desperate and saying that he'd got his lists. Weidt then had to go to the Gestapo and reclaim the person concerned as 'indispensable.' He described his business as absolutely vital to the war effort, which, of course, it wasn't, but he usually got away with it. Naturally, he had to bribe the Gestapo officials involved with food, schnapps and cigarettes. He found a very good supporter in Hans Rosenthal, supplies administrator for the Jewish community, who procured from kindly non-Jews all sorts of goods for us persecuted Jews. It was Rosenthal's job to get goods for the Jews, and he obtained more from firms and factories in Berlin than many an " Aryan " supplier. Naturally the Gestapo knew that, too, and were quite willing to accept bribes from Rosenthal. In this way he could delay some of the deportations, protect many people from arrest and give others—who were threatened with arrest—the tip-off to go ' underground.'

I met Hans Rosenthal in Weidt's workshop one evening after work. He was a handsome man in his late thirties. It was not just a meeting for me. I was a young girl, full of fear and despair, but full of dreams, too, however unjustified they may have been in that grim era.

I still remember the day when I first became conscious that I had such dreams. It was Otto Weidt's birthday. He had invited his 'favourites,' Alice Licht, Basch and myself, to a little celebration in the office. Hans Rosenthal had been invited as an outside guest.

We'd stood the desks together in Basch's office and thrown a white tablecloth over them. The woman caretaker had cooked an excellent meal—goulash with mushrooms. The aroma permeated the whole house.

Weidt and Alice sat at one end of the ' table,' Hans and

I at the other. Basch had made himself as comfortable as circumstances allowed at the tail end of the desks.

The goulash was demolished practically before it reached the table. Alice and I ate with the ravenous hunger of young people who never got enough to eat.

Our good appetite pleased Weidt.

'Eat, children, there's plenty left.'

We didn't need a second reminder.

Weidt stood up and went over to the coat-stand where his briefcase lay on the floor. He picked it up, opened it and came back, strutting before us with a broad grin.

'Have a guess what's in here,' he said.

How could we guess?

He produced two bottles of brandy and stood them in the middle of the table.

'Good God!' Hans Rosenthal gasped.

'Let's forget all our troubles for today,' said Weidt. 'Let's not think of our problems.'

I felt the tears rush into my eyes. Not think of them! How could we possibly forget the peril of being taken away, suddenly, unexpectedly, to be dragged off, perhaps within the next hour, and end up in a concentration camp? How could we stop thinking of the trifling annoyances and great sorrows that beset us daily? How could we forget that we were third-class citizens, without rights, without protection and always at the mercy of our persecutors?

Alice seemed to share my thoughts. She looked up at Otto Weidt. 'Do you think it's easier to be a Jew with a glass of cognac in your belly?'

'Please,' said Otto, almost entreating, 'don't let's discuss it today.'

Hans Rosenthal was on his side. 'He's right. Today let's just be human beings. Not Jews, not Germans, not Christians, or what have you—just human beings.'

He was answering Alice, but he looked at me as he did it. It was then I really saw him for the first time.

A middle-aged man around forty, tall, slim, with well-groomed dark hair, intense brown eyes and a smooth but powerful face, which reminded me involuntarily of my father's. He attracted me. I felt it rise in me like a hot wave.

Rosenthal looked at me, and suddenly he grasped my hand and pressed it tightly. Then he stood up.

'Where's the bottle opener?' he asked.

Otto Weidt produced his penknife and handed it over. Skilfully Rosenthal drew the corks; Alice fetched the glasses meanwhile.

'Go on, you pour the drinks,' said Weidt to Rosenthal. Rosenthal did so.

We raised our glasses.

Rosenthal looked at me again in that particular way. I felt a strange excitement within me, the awakening of an emotion I had never experienced before. I knew I was blushing. I drank quickly and put the glass down.

We had become unused to alcohol and it soon went to our heads. We sat and argued; we all talked at the same time; we bewailed our sufferings and comforted each other; we laughed, and sometimes there were tears in our eyes; but it was the loveliest evening of my young life.

'It will all pass,' Weidt prophesied. 'One day it will all be all over—the Nazis, the war, all that! It will melt away like a ghost!'

'We won't be here to see it,' Alice replied.

'Yes, yes,' he insisted, 'you will; I won't perhaps, but you. . . .'

We protested loudly.

'You'll live to a ripe old age, Mr. Weidt,' I assured him.

'We'll all see the end of this war,' Hans Rosenthal assured us—he was still looking at me, like that—'all of us, you, too, Mr. Weidt.'

Weidt shook his head sadly. Alice sat next to him stroking his hand.

Basch, the Jewish bookkeeper, said: 'Some day it will be all over; all the horror will be over. That's for sure. But it's not so sure that we'll be here to see it.'

All at once I had a terrible hunger for life. I lusted for it, longed to grasp it and enjoy it with every part of me, for a long, long time yet. . . . Suddenly I wanted to live, not to die —not to die before I had lived.

I glanced up at Hans Rosenthal, and I knew I wanted to

live because I had never yet been in love. Because I did not know yet what love was.

A poor, persecuted, hounded Jewish girl in the middle of the war, in Berlin, who thinks of love.

Suddenly I found myself crying. I couldn't suppress my sobs any longer. I laid my head on the table and howled.

I felt his hand on my shoulder, on my hair.

'Don't cry,' he said, 'you mustn't cry.'

I could only shake my head dumbly.

'Everything will be fine, everything!'

'I heard Alice's voice: 'Pull yourself together, Inge.'

I thought of my mother, of my father in England; I thought of myself, of all of us who were persecuted, and I had to cry.

'Baby, don't cry,' Weidt urged.

Hans Rosenthal's soothing hand slid over my hair. I sat up and wiped away the tears, blowing my nose into the handkerchief he gave me.

'Sorry,' I said. 'It just came over me.'

Hans Rosenthal nodded quietly. 'I'll take you home,' he said.

Outside, in the cool air of the Berlin night, he took my arm, as if it were the most natural thing in the world.

We walked through the deserted, darkened streets. Sometimes a car passed us, the headlights covered with masks so that only a little light fell on to the street through a narrow, horizontal slit. Individual pedestrians hastened by. Some wore luminous badges on their coat lapels which danced like glow-worms in the dark.

'What's going to happen?' I asked Rosenthal. 'You must know—you're in touch with *them*!'

'I don't know, either,' said Hans. 'And I'm not really " in touch with them." But I know one thing; they can do what they like to us, but they can't destroy our will to survive. Even if you and I have to die, others will survive. They won't manage to murder us all. A few will come through, and from them a new people will arise: the new State of Israel!'

I stopped and looked at him. I could not see his eyes properly in the dark.

'You really believe that?'

'I believe it,' said Hans Rosenthal simply.

It was a long way to our house. We covered it in silence.

Before the front door Hans laid both his hands on my shoulders and looked at me. His face was very near to mine.

'You must always be brave,' he said.

I just nodded.

'You must always have faith.'

I nodded again.

'Goodnight!'

'Goodnight. . . .'

I wanted him to kiss me. But he only turned round and paced away through the darkness ; a tall, slim shadow which blended swiftly into the grey twilight."

One must have had the courage of despair to believe, as Hans Rosenthal did, in the survival of the Jews at that time. The Jewish community's "removal van," under Gestapo orders, was driving through the streets of Berlin every day to take the Jews away ; and every day their numbers diminished.

The organised deportation of Berlin Jews began in October, 1940.

"It was then that the notorious 'lists' were sent, for the first time, to about a thousand Jews," Inge Deutschkron explained. "We did not quite grasp their true significance then. On October 17, 1940, all those who had received their lists were taken away by two Gestapo officials. Their flats were locked up. The possessions entered in the lists were declared State property and later sold by auction through the Gestapo.

Those first thousand people were then taken to a detention centre in the Levetzowstrasse synagogue and sent a few days later to an "unknown" destination in the east. The first transport consisted mainly of people between 65 and 70, who were sent to Litzmannstadt, the former Lodz. From there they sent home postcards with printed messages on them saying, "I'm quite well." After that they were not heard of again. People over 65 were later deported to Theresienstadt. But even of these the majority suffered further deportation to Auschwitz. As time went by the lists were discontinued. The Jewish community itself had to pick out people to deport ; the community's vehicle usually appeared at night and drove the victims away without giving them time to get ready. Conditions governing deportations varied constantly. One day a person would be spared because he did important war work ; next day the work of the firm concerned would no longer be regarded as vital to the war effort. Some firms did their utmost to keep their Jewish employees on, but in the last analysis it was in vain.

At first the transports departed from ordinary stations, but later from certain suburban stations, Grunewald for example, in the middle of the night, so that there would be no spectators. Because of the transport of troops railway equipment was becoming more and more scarce in Germany ; but there were always engines and trucks available for deportations. I remember a transport in that icy winter of 1942 when people were loaded on to open railway trucks.

But the Gauleiter of Berlin, Propaganda Minister Goebbels, still did not feel that the Reich capital was becoming " Jew-free " fast enough.

In December, 1942, therefore, the S.S. Major Brunner, of the Viennese Gestapo, was ordered to Berlin with an escort to achieve this aim more swiftly and ruthlessly ; for the Vienna Gestapo had proved itself superior in brutality to the Germans. Brunner made short shrift of the job ; he simply snapped up Jews who crossed the road at the wrong point by mistake or hadn't sewn on the Jewish star tightly enough for his liking. His cars would suddenly pull up somewhere, no matter whether they found a family all complete or not ; Brunner just took what was available.

A man called Robert Gerö had arrived with the Gestapo from Vienna. He was a Jew who had helped the Viennese Gestapo with the deportation of Jews from that city. Alice Licht knew Gerö from the time when she had worked in the Jewish Assistance Bureau and had to travel frequently to Vienna. Gerö had come with Brunner because he had done his job well there, and the same was expected of him in Berlin.

'We must get in touch with Gerö,' said Alice Licht when she heard of his arrival. 'Surely a man with those contacts can help us.' At that time we were constantly expecting to be deported, and clung desperately to every straw, even when the protection offered was illusory. But the thought of getting in touch with a Nazi stooge, a Gestapo collaborator, which was what Gerö was for me, was extremely repugnant. However, I eventually gave in to Alice for my mother's sake. We contacted Gerö and from then onwards he would warn us and our friends when an action was pending. He was extremely well informed. He never let the " removal van ", stop directly in front of the house where we lived, cooped up with several dozen other Jewish families, when he had to fetch someone from there. Usually he made the driver park about fifty yards ahead. It was only on one occasion, when my mother was on the way home from work, that the van was standing right outside the front door. My mother was half crazy with fright. She wouldn't venture into the flat for fear of being taken away herself ; on the other hand, she could not be certain that I was not already there. It was not until the van drove away at last, after several hours, and she could establish that I hadn't been at home, that she gradually calmed down.

Our landlady was taken away that day. She had opened every gas point but was eventually dragged downstairs by force. A few days later the bell rang furiously : ' Open up ! Gestapo !' As it happened my mother was at home, since she was on night shift. She opened up ; they had come about the deported landlady's property. Then a Gestapo official appeared in my mother's room and said, ' Well, what are you doing here ? By rights we should be taking you with us.' My mother kept her head and didn't answer his threats ; she just carried on with her work. I think that her calm— though it was only external—saved her from the worst.

We were at the end of our tether, and this incident forced us to a decision.

That evening we were sitting together in our room. We were so disturbed that we hardly exchanged a word.

' We can't go on like this,' said my mother at last. She sat motionless in her chair, her hands folded in her lap, and looked past me at the light of the lamp which glowed on the table.

' No, mother, we can't go on like this, we must. . . .' I broke off.

'Yes—'

I took a deep breath. 'We'll have to go into hiding,' I said, 'or we'll get deported, too. And we know what that means.'

Did we really know? Could we really envisage the horror of the camps, the hell of the gas chambers?

No—we knew only that death awaited us there. But the tortures we would be subjected to beforehand—we had no idea of those. No one who had not been in a Third Reich concentration camp could possibly assess that.

'If they catch us. . . .' my mother interposed.

'Well, it couldn't be worse than being taken away—like Mrs. Lichtenfels.'

'But maybe. . . .'

'No, mother, let's not deceive ourselves. One day they'll knock at the door and order us to go with them. One day it will happen: the van will be downstairs outside the door, waiting for *us*, not for someone else, but for *us*.'

My mother passed her hand over her forehead. 'Where shall we go, then?'

'I've already discussed it with some friends. Several people are willing to take us in. It would be best to go to Mr. and Mrs. Gums.'

They were Aryans, proprietors of a small laundry who still took in washing for Jews, against the rules. They had offered to let me and my mother move in with them for a bit, just in case we had to 'go underground.'

'We mustn't endanger others,' said my mother.

I shrugged it off. I was twenty then and could only see the immediate demands of the situation, the constant danger we faced here in this house. I had no thought for the far distant future and I didn't want to have any.

'We'll have to risk that, mother.'

We both lay awake that night. Our thoughts centred on the days to follow, on the dark future.

Next morning, just before going to work, my mother said: 'I'll get everything ready—for tonight.'

Tonight! I glanced at the calendar. It was January 15, 1943.

At the office I confided in Weidt. He patted me on the

shoulder. 'You're right, both of you. You can't run the risk of deportation any longer. You can go on working for me.'

'But—I'm registered here under my own name. They'll look for me here, surely.'

He smiled. 'They won't, you know. I reported a fortnight ago that you'd left.'

I looked at him uncomprehending.

'I've engaged a new girl in your place. Someone called Gertrud Dereczewsky.'

He fumbled in his pocket and produced a work permit in the name of Dereczewsky.

'I hope it doesn't worry you,' said Weidt, 'but I bought it off a prostitute. You're now employed by me as a secretary, quite legally.'

I couldn't help it ; I pressed a quick kiss on his cheek. I knew he'd help us whenever he could. He'd built an "emergency camp" in an old workroom, where he was hiding Alice and her parents who had also "gone underground" recently. I told Weidt about the Gums's laundry, and he agreed with me that for the time being it was best to move in there.

When I got home my mother had our cases already packed. Everything else—bedding, crockery, books, things we didn't want to lose—were ready to be collected next morning. Weidt had offered to come with his goods van and remove them when all the inmates of the house were at work.

That night was the worst we had spent yet. We conjured up all the perils of life underground, but at the same time consoled ourselves that the whole business could not last more than a couple of weeks or so. The battle of Stalingrad was just nearing its end. The feeling was spreading in Berlin that something like the end of the world was approaching. Everyone expected something spectacular to happen, like a sudden, abrupt turning point in the war, an armistice, peace, the collapse of the Nazi régime—all illusions, empty dreams, hallucinations, but that is what we thought then. We certainly did not think that we would be living underground for nearly two years, moving from one place to another, never knowing peace, hunted and persecuted, always on the run, always in danger, always in fear of policemen.

We made a start next morning at seven.

On the way downstairs we met Mrs. Wachsmann, another Jewish woman who lived in the house.

' Going to work so early ? ' she asked, astonished.

' Yes,' I replied unhesitatingly.

She stared at the cases we were carrying and her eyes narrowed. But she said nothing, just stared after us as we descended the staircase and went out into the street.

' God,' my mother exclaimed suddenly, ' I've left my watch behind.'

Her gold wristwatch—a present from my father.

' I'll have to go back,' she said, putting her bags down. ' What a bad omen,' she added fearfully.

I waited a few agonising minutes till she appeared again. Then we walked quickly down the street."

The Deutschkrons, after going underground, found shelter at the Gums's in the first instance. They were evangelists, and their kindness knew no bounds.

Inge Deutschkron went on working—as Gertrud Dereczewsky—in Weidt's workshop. But the arrangement was not to last long. One day Miss Dereczewsky was caught in a police raid while plying her trade. The criminal police telephoned Weidt about her. Inge Deutschkron, who happened to answer the 'phone, was terrified when the police announced themselves and said they wanted to speak to Weidt about the Dereczewsky case. She reacted with presence of mind, however. " I'll put you through to personnel," she said.

Of course there was no personnel department. It was Alice who went to the telephone and explained to the police that Weidt was away on business and would ring them next day. This gave them time to decide what to tell the criminal police. Weidt himself telephoned, and explained that it was true that he had Dereczewsky's papers ; she had worked for him for some time, then skipped it. He'd be glad to get rid of her, the lazy bitch.

To everyone's relief the criminal police didn't follow this hot trail to the Jews' secret refuge in the Rosenthaler Strasse. Of course Weidt had to send back Dereczewsky's work permit, so Inge's semi-legal status was over.

One day in January, 1943, the Gestapo fetched from their apartments all the Jews who worked for Otto Weidt. When he arrived at the workshop that morning none of the blind and deaf mutes appeared. When ten o'clock came Weidt got on the telephone. He knew after the first couple of minutes what had happened; S.S. Major Brunner had carried out one of his dreaded raids again. Weidt's employees were all in the temporary camp in the Grosse Hamburger Strasse.

"I was already underground then, living with friends, and so I wasn't arrested," Inge Deutschkron said. "I arrived rather late that morning, and Weidt was running around in a panic. Alice Licht, who was also living 'illegally,' was trying to soothe him.

'I won't put up with it!' Weidt shrieked. 'I'm going over there! I'll get them out!'

'Otto—don't do anything silly!' Alice implored. She was white as chalk and stared at Weidt with wide eyes. At that moment I knew that Alice felt more for him than the friendship of a young girl for a man who has saved her life.

Weidt said nothing. He fixed his blind armband on his left arm, patted our cheeks and left the building.

And he actually went to the Grosse Hamburger Strasse, to the temporary camp for Jews ready for deportation. How he managed it, I don't know, but early in the afternoon he came up the street—and behind him a group of about fifty Jews, blind men and deaf mutes with Jewish stars and blind armbands, and men with sticks, helping each other to walk. It was both a terrible and heart-stirring picture, like a scene from some ancient tragedy. People stood on the street as if turned to stone, gazing dumbly after the procession. Everyone made way for them. Even the police dared not interfere."

This time Weidt succeeded in saving "his" Jews. But then came February 27, 1943—the black day for all Jews who remained in Berlin.

That night the Gestapo and Security Service (S.D.) occupied all houses where Jews lived; heavily armed units of the "Adolf Hitler Bodyguard" surrounded all factories and workshops where Jews were employed. The Jews were then

confined to their dwellings or places of work until such time
as the transports to the extermination camps were ready for
departure. That night and the following morning, 9,000 Jews
were taken away from Berlin. Before this date 27,000 had
lived in the Reich capital, 10,000 of them illegally. The
remaining 8,000 were so-called " privileged " Jews who had
contracted mixed marriages with Aryan partners.

With the deportation of this last group, the yellow star
disappeared from the Berlin street scene. The capital was,
as Goebbels jubilantly announced, " Jew-free." Nevertheless, he noted in his diary that as far as the " illegal " Jews
were concerned, the raid had not been particularly successful. " The élite circles—particularly the intellectuals—again
warned the Jews." But they'd get these underground Jews
yet, he consoled himself.

Just before this action Inge Deutschkron got a telephone
warning from Hans Rosenthal, who had heard about it at
the last minute. She therefore stayed with her mother in
their hideout in the Gums' laundry, and so escaped deportation. Also Rosenthal, as Supplies Manager for the Jewish
community, was not deported ; not because there would
have been any Jews left for him to look after, but because
the Gestapo needed him and his good contacts with Berlin
factory owners, so as to go on procuring all kinds of goods
without dockets and permits.

Even the Weidt firm, which had been a refuge for blind
and deaf-mute Jews from Berlin for years, now had to cease
employing Jews legally. Weidt got " Aryan " workers. He
now devoted himself entirely to helping those underground.
At that time he was hiding at his house a family called Horn
—a father, mother and two children. There was a great
cupboard standing against the wall in the Rosenthaler
Strasse workshop, filled to bursting with brushes and brooms.
The cupboard had a sliding back panel. At the back was a
small room, and there the four fugitives lived. For the time
being the Horns—just like the Licht family in the "emergency camp," could feel safe here.

" To find a new job—that was my most urgent task. We
were entirely without means and needed every penny. Since

we had no food tokens we had to buy dockets or provisions on the black market, and that was terribly expensive. The occasional docket handouts which came our way through kind friends were hardly enough to ward off starvation. It was, therefore, a relief to find work at a stationers'; the owner was a friend, Dr. Ostrowsky. He had strongly urged my mother and me to ' go underground ' and was now only too glad to offer me a means of subsistence.

The accommodation problem was difficult. It was soon clear that we could not stay with our friends at the laundry for long. For one thing, there was a danger that the woman who did the ironing—she wasn't in the picture—might find us out. The air raids constituted another danger. Naturally we could not register ourselves as ' visitors ' in the air-raid shelter because we had no papers. So we had to stay in the house during an attack ; this would have had the most serious consequences for our hosts had we been found wounded or dead as bomb casualties in her flat. And so we started leading a completely unprotected, haphazard vaga-bond existence. I still shudder at the thought of it.

Our friends, the Ostrowskys, only had a one-room flat and could not put us up, so my mother and I slept for a time on the floor, in a little room behind the shop. Whenever there was a raid we tried—so as not to endanger the Ostrowskys—to go to one of the public air-raid shelters, which were only used by passers-by, and then to slink back to the shop unobserved. For a week we lived on an allotment on the verge of the city, and then with some nice people in Friedrichshain for a few days.

At long last we were taken in by a Mrs. Holländer in the Sächsische Strasse. She was related to Mr. Rieck, an old acquaintance of ours, and her husband, a Jew, had perished in Mauthausen. She was very willing to have us. Her house, the Rosenhof, was so rambling, with so many entrances and staircases, that one could wander in and out without being seen ; during raids we ran to the nearby shelter in the Fehrbelliner Platz, from where we could reach the house later without attracting attention. So we were safe for a time.

I was really happy in my work at the stationers'. No one knew my name ; they just called me ' Inge.' With the increasing paper shortage I gradually became an important person, to whom people gave food on the sly, and who insisted on being paid in kind by butchers, milkmen and greengrocers ; I was able to save enough to keep my mother and me going.

All this was very nice, but then an incendiary hit our hideout in the Sächsische Strasse. The Rosenhof was burned down, and we had to look for somewhere else to stay.

The Riecks were bombed out, too, and had taken a room in Potsdam, where many Berliners sought shelter at the time. Since the Riecks were constantly travelling between Bavaria and Potsdam, we were able to use their room for a time, but then we had to look for our own place for the duration of the war. After wandering around vainly for ages we eventually found, on the Potsdam-Eigenheim estate, an empty cowshed, which was normally uninhabitable. It was built of cement, with one miserable little window and a wooden door leading directly outside. It was marvellous there in summer, but soaking wet in autumn and full of icicles in winter. The stall was connected to a little washhouse where we were able to cook ; but unfortunately the brick stove gave out no heat whatsoever. Now, procuring fuel constituted a new problem.

We settled in as best we could, and various neighbours, who had heard that we'd been bombed out in Berlin, helped. So we soon acquired a bed, a table, a cooking pot, plates, knives and forks.

We spent all our free time looking for wood and mushrooms in the near-by copse ; apart from this, I collected coal from the cellars of the bombed houses in Berlin, with the feeling—not so pleasant!—that the ruins could collapse any moment and bury me underneath them.

Meanwhile, I had become sole boss of the stationers'. The Ostrowskys had left Berlin ; he just came to town at regular intervals to settle up with me. In the shop, the barter business flourished. I did big business, exchanging butter for coffee, schnapps for coal, cigarettes for bread. I was constantly travelling backwards and forwards with a rucksack and two heavy cases. It was dangerous, of course, but during the big raids thousands of Berliners were wandering around with their bags and baggage, so no one took any notice.

My mother had now found work again, too, with Rosenthal's help, with a printer at 26 Rosenthaler Strasse—the manager was a Mr. Theodor Görner. Every week Görner surreptitiously pressed into my mother's hand a food token for the printing works canteen. He bought the tokens on the black market.

Meanwhile, the Gestapo had noted our disappearance and appeared one day at the house of our friends, the Riecks, to inquire about our whereabouts. The Riecks informed them that they'd heard nothing from us for ages ; they thought we'd either been deported or committed suicide. We were therefore declared 'dead' by the police, and Hans Rosenthal, who because of his 'business dealings' with the Gestapo had an easy entry there, removed our cards one day from the 'moonlight flitters' index' when no one was looking and destroyed them. So our 'death' was legalised. Anyway, since we'd lived underground we'd been calling ourselves "Richter"; Mrs. Richter and her daughter.

More and more people were leaving Berlin. One day a customer, a Mrs. Schwarz, took me to one side. She had a confession to make. The Schwarz family, who had been bombed out, were about to move to Ingolstadt. Dr. Schwarz was a university lecturer. Mrs. Schwarz informed me that she had been hiding a Jewess and she now had to bequeath her to me. I couldn't help it ; I burst out laughing in her face. At first she was rather annoyed, but when she heard that I was Jewish myself she stared at me, quite beside herself. ' No—that can't be true,' she whispered. I just nodded. ' And all this time ; aren't you afraid, then ? ' I shrugged. ' Obviously you didn't notice anything,' I said. She shook her head, bewildered. Then she gave me a radiant smile, pressed my hands and murmured : ' All the best, good luck ! '

Her protégée, a Jewess called Lotte Eifert, found accommodation all right—as domestic help in the house of a Nazi district leader ! At that time, when only work vital to the war effort was recognised and even Nazi bigwigs could not get servant girls any more, the district leader was only too glad to take Lotte, without papers and without an interview. From that time we received food cards regularly from

191

Ingolstadt ; Mrs. Schwarz divided them equally between my mother, Lotte and myself.

My mother and I existed from one day to the next, and gradually became used to leading the lives of adventurers, tricksters and hypocrites. But then something happened that really terrified me, and really brought home to us the terrible danger in which we lived."

At that time, in Berlin, a dreaded Gestapo stooge was at her evil business—the blonde Jewess, Stella Kübler-Gold-schlag. She was the daughter of the composer, Goldschlag, whom the Nazis had put in a concentration camp, together with his wife. The Nazis had promised Stella that her parents would be kept alive if she would help the Gestapo to root out Jews in hiding. Stella sold herself to them, not dreaming that her parents had been gassed long since.

In January, 1943, she and her husband, a man called Isaakson, were brought from Vienna to Berlin by S.S. Major Brunner, to help detect " illegals."

Stella was hated and feared by all persecuted Jews. Every-where the beautiful, but ice-cold blonde appeared, she left fear and despair behind her. " She must have had a sixth sense for anything concerning Jews," said Inge Deutschkron. " She simply smelt them out. She sent dozens of illegals to the slaughter—hundreds perhaps."

Horn, who was living illegally with his family in Weidt's business premises, happened to meet Isaakson, Stella's husband, during one of his evening walks. The two got talking. Horn did not know Isaakson, but soon found out he was a Jew. It was not long before Horn confided his secret to his " fellow sufferer."

The inevitable happened. On October 15, 1943, the Gestapo turned up at Rosenthaler Strasse. Isaakson had betrayed the Horns' hiding place. The whole family was arrested—also Alice Licht, who had just been visiting Weidt's office and had fled into the room behind the broom cupboard when she heard the alarm which Weidt invariably set off when danger threatened. Weidt himself was imme-diately taken to the Prinz Albert Strasse for interrogation. It looked as if his fate was sealed.

But this man, so frail in outward appearance, achieved something which no one would have dreamed possible: he was free again that very evening! He even managed to get Alice's parents, and the girl herself, sent to the "privileged" ghetto of Theresienstadt. That was quite unheard of; young people like Alice were usually sent immediately to extermination camps if they were caught living underground. Weidt's method was simple. He just shamelessly bribed the appropriate Gestapo officials in the Prinz Albert Strasse. On one occasion after the war he himself described as quite considerable the number of food parcels and bottles of schnapps with which he plied hungry and boozy Gestapo men.

But even Weidt could not stop Alice Licht from being suddenly transferred, in 1944, from Theresienstadt to Birkenau, the actual extermination camp in the Auschwitz setup.

What happened then sounds fantastic, but everyone concerned has testified to the unadulterated truth of it.

Alice Licht managed, during the journey from Theresienstadt in Czechoslovakia to Auschwitz in Upper Silesia, to throw a postcard addressed to Otto Weidt out of the train. Someone found the card and stuck it in a pillar box, and Weidt was informed of Alice's fate before she even got to Auschwitz. This postcard, a horrifying document of contemporary history, is today among the files of the Yad Vashem Institute in Jerusalem.

Weidt responded immediately. On June 9, 1944, he wrote to the administrative section of the Birkenau labour camp, offering his services as brushmaker. He offered, as "supplier to various labour camps and the Berlin Gestapo," brooms for barracks and yards, scrubbing brushes, scouring brushes, street brooms, office brooms, dustpan brushes; and added, "In anticipation of your agreement, I will personally present the above-mentioned collection during the period between June 12 and 20, 1944."

On June 15 the *Kommandantur* of Auschwitz Concentration Camp II, Waffen S.S., acknowledged receipt of Weidt's letter and gave him permission to present his assortment of brushes to the camp administration. Weidt packed his display case, filled a second case with tinned food, cigarettes and schnapps and set off. On July 20 he was in Auschwitz. He presented his paraphernalia to the camp authorities, looked around him furtively but conscientiously and made overtures to a Polish foreman. Within half an hour he had actually succeeded in persuading the man to take an interest in Alice Licht and see that nothing happened to her. In collaboration with this same foreman he also thought up a secret way of smuggling food packets and letters to Alice Licht.

Weidt is probably one of the few people who managed to enter a concentration camp under false pretences. " It was terrible—the long columns of prisoners, the grey, worn-out figures, the gigantic stretches of barracks, heavily armed S.S. running around everywhere—in fact, the whole setup, planned with such military exactitude ; partly a macabre barrack of death, partly an enormous, monstrous factory. It was frightful . . ." Weidt narrated after the war. But while he was in Auschwitz Weidt must have assumed a façade of extraordinary fearlessness and cold calculation. It is true that he exaggerated his usual eye trouble to accentuate his disguise, and always wore a pair of dark glasses, which actually he didn't need, during his more important rounds ; nevertheless, his sight was genuinely very faulty and he was handicapped accordingly. But he achieved what was practically impossible in Auschwitz ; he made contact with the prisoner Alice Licht.

Weidt took advantage of the fact that in Auschwitz, as in all camps, there was a secret organisation, founded by the political prisoners. This organisation was sometimes able—because of its contacts with the camp leadership—to protect some prisoner or other from liquidation and even, in certain circumstances, to ensure him a fairly secure existence. Alice Licht was lucky ; Weidt succeeded, through the Polish foreman, in winning over the Auschwitz " camp committee."

What was more, he rented a furnished room near Auschwitz where he deposited underclothes, top clothes and money, in case Alice should manage to escape from camp. After all, this possibility could not be completely disregarded, because any sensible person could see, in this critical summer of 1944, that the German front in the East could not hold out much longer. At this time the central army group was engaged in heavy defensive battles on the former Russian-Polish border ; Russian troops had broken through in the south, and the position in the Balkans was becoming more dangerous all the time. One could assume that Auschwitz would be evacuated, sooner or later. A spirited young woman like Alice Licht might well have thought of escaping, then. Weidt wanted to provide for this contingency.

His foresight was certainly justified. As early as September, several thousand women from Auschwitz were transferred to Ravensbrück. In October, about 8,000 able-bodied men followed, who were to be marshalled for work in German armaments factories.

When the German Eastern front collapsed in January, 1945, 64,000 prisoners still remained in Auschwitz. The camp was evacuated. Since there was transport available for only a limited number of prisoners the majority were driven westwards on foot. These death marches were the frightful culmination point of the "Final Solution." Thousands of people, starving and frozen, marched through snow and ice, perpetually harassed by the S.S., who used their weapons unscrupulously whenever they encountered the slightest resistance, or whenever the last energies of the wandering skeletons threatened to flag.

Eighteen thousand prisoners from Auschwitz perished in the death marches. Forty-six thousand were distributed among other camps. Many of them were still to die there before liberation by the Allies. Only a few thousand escaped with their lives.

One of them was Alice Licht, who shortly after leaving Auschwitz managed to jump from an open cattle truck and make her way to the place where Weidt had rented her a room. There she was able to discard her camp clothing and furnish herself with money and forged papers. After a few days' rest she started on her way. She was caught up in a refugee column and taken with them to Berlin.

For Inge Deutschkron the discovery of the hiding place

in the Rosenthaler Strasse meant that in future she had to be more careful still.

" For us, the dangerous situations and moments of sudden terror multiplied. Once, when we were sitting in a tram, two officials entered at the Zoological Gardens station and called: ' Identity cards please!' Thank God, they began the check-up at the other end, and as the tram drove into the Tiergarten station we jumped out. Another time, an acquaintance in Wehrmacht uniform sat opposite me, looking at me inquiringly, and asked: ' Aren't you Miss Deutschkron ? ' For a minute I didn't know what to answer. I pulled myself together. ' You must be mistaken,' I said. ' My name is Richter.' He shook his head in consternation. ' I could have sworn. . . .'

I got out at the next stop. My knees were shaking.

Shortly after that I had to give up my post at the Ostrowskys' business. I found out, just in time, that the Ministry of Labour were carrying out another check-up, so I had no choice but to leave off work. And, as bad luck would have it, my mother became unemployed at the same time. Görner, the head of the printing works which had employed her, was a bit of an obsessionist. He had adopted a child, half Jewish, whom he loved very much, and now insisted that the child be accepted at a grammar school. A flaming row broke out between him and the authorities, and one day the Gestapo turned up to close the firm down.

Rosenthal, who had heard about the action taken against Görner, telephoned me that afternoon at the stationers'—it was during my last few days there.

' Have you heard from your mother ? ' he asked.

My heart almost stopped. ' My mother ? What's the matter ? I don't know a thing.'

' The Gestapo is at Görner's. They've taken over the business.'

I had to sit down. I pressed the receiver against my ear, but Hans said nothing more.

' Say something, for God's sake!' I yelled into the 'phone. ' I've heard nothing from mummy, I don't know a thing, and that's the plain. . . .'

' I'll make inquiries at once.' Rosenthal tried to calm

me down, but his voice didn't sound very reassuring.
'Something has happened to her,' I whispered.
'I'll call you again,' Rosenthal promised, and hung up.

I sat there and simply could not move. I glanced at the
clock ; it was half past eleven. I had to stay in the shop till
seven ; I couldn't just run off, possibly right into the arms of
the Gestapo.

We lived in Potsdam then, in the Riecks' flat. I wouldn't
be home till eight.

Till then every hour was a torment. I have never been so
terrified in all my life as I was during those eight hours. I
heard nothing more from Rosenthal. At last it was seven.
I shut up shop and ran to the underground. Oh God, don't
let it have happened, I thought all the time. I pushed my
way through the crowd and eventually got a train ; waited
impatiently as one station followed another ; then I was on
the street again, racing home like a madwoman. I stormed up
the stairs. The door was not locked. I flung it open. Inside,
everything was dark. I almost stopped breathing. But then
came my mother's voice from the blackness : ' Is that you,
Inge ? '

My bag fell from my hand with relief.

'Why—why don't you put the light on ? ' Suddenly I
was angry as well as relieved.

'It's fused,' said my mother, and I heard her groping
around in the dark. I ran to her and fell round her neck. We
cried and cried, and meanwhile she told me what had
happened.

When she got to work the Gestapo were already there.
However, Görner found time to whisper to her to behave
quite naturally. In her first moment of panic she wanted to
escape the back way. But then she decided to mingle with
her colleagues, and to leave the building by the main
entrance with the others, as the Gestapo ordered. That was
what saved her. S.S. guards were lying in wait round the
back waiting for someone with a bad conscience to beat it
from Görner's firm.

For a few weeks we ran around jobless. We had to pretend
to our neighbours in Potsdam who, of course, took us for
' Aryans,' that we were regularly travelling to town to

work, because everyone in Germany was doing war service then and anyone loafing around unemployed become conspicuous at once.

Eventually I managed to get a job in a little dairy. My mother found work as a tutor—to the children of a high-up Nazi official, of all things! She said she was a schoolmaster's widow. The Nazis were so delighted with my mother that in no time she had a whole circle of children to give lessons to. Just like myself, she let herself be paid in kind—in foodstuffs—and we were soon over the worst hurdle again.

Then, a new horror. In the anarchic period of the Berlin air raids, breaking and entering was the order of the day. One night our dairy got its turn. Thieves had broken the window panes and made a clean sweep of the small amount of butter, cheese and milk in stock. When I turned up, all unsuspecting, to work in the morning, the criminal police were just arriving.

It's all up now, I thought. Naturally they'll take down particulars, ask for your identity card, and then the cat's out of the bag. I dared not run away; I dared not stay either, but I had to stay, otherwise I'd give myself away. Two ghastly hours followed. The officials, two elderly men, took down the facts of the case quite cheerfully and then disappeared with the proprietress into the back room. Apparently they were more interested in scrounging a pound of butter than in investigating the robbery.

Having got safely over this experience, further complications arose. New travel passes came into force, which were only handed out to employees at the request of their firms. How were we going to continue using public transport?

Once again we were lucky. The Nazi official whose children my mother taught even got us priority travel passes—green and orange in colour. The green voucher with U—Underground—printed on it was for clerks and workers in works of lesser importance; the other orange one, with S.T. on it —*Strassenbahn* and *Stadtbahn*—was only issued to armaments workers. Apart from these there were red vouchers for workers in water and electrical installations. These differences in colour made it possible to prohibit the respective categories from travelling, at short notice, for rolling stock had become scarce because of the bombing. That is why non-workers, old people, children and invalids were not able to travel at all.

Soon afterwards we lost our lodgings ; the Riecks decided to get a divorce and we had to quit their flat. We were afraid that Mrs. Rieck, who was all agitated about the divorce proceedings, might start blabbing about us, so we couldn't go back to our cowshed which the Riecks knew about. Where to, then ? One night we slept with friends in the Konstanzer Strasse ; next morning we found, to our horror, a yellow paper star glued to the door. We had been recognised ! Now what ?

It was now February, 1945 ; the Russians were approaching. Chaos increased daily, and Berlin was overflowing with refugees from the East. Mr. Görner, whom my mother used still to visit sometimes, and to whom she turned for advice in her despair, said : ' Why don't you travel to the nearest border, mix with the refugees there, travel back with them to Berlin and legalise yourself that way ? ' This idea was obviously a good one, but at first we were afraid of taking this final step.

In the Ostrowsky stationers' shop, shortly before my ' resignation,' I had found clothing and food vouchers in the name of Amanda Heubaum, whose details corresponded roughly to those of my mother. These cards were a great help to us, particularly the clothing card, because we as Jews, even before becoming ' illegal,' had never possessed one ; and now, for the first time for over five years, we were in the position of being able to buy a pair of stockings, sewing tackle and such like. But the real blessing of this find was that it gave us the means of procuring the necessary travel tickets to Lübben, a railway junction for refugees from the east ; because at that time you could only get railway tickets if you produced your clothing card. Naturally we ran the risk of stumbling into a checkpoint, but luckily there was such unholy chaos in the direction of the front line—the direction we were going—that this was almost out of the question. First we made a careful study of the way these refugees dressed ; for instance, nearly all the women wore big headscarves and carried cases tied round with string.

Then we listened to some of their experiences and set off.

Actually it all passed off very quickly. We were terribly excited, and at the same time so relieved, as we sat in the Lübben train ; now the die was cast!

In Lübben a droning loudspeaker directed the 'refugees from our east German homeland' to the other platform. We only needed to turn round and we were no longer "illegals" without identity cards, terrified of a glance from any person in uniform, but refugees who had lost everything —including, of course, their papers. A mere five minutes after our arrival in Lübben we were pushed into a packed train to Berlin. As it drew into the Görlitzer station the sirens were beginning to howl. The train raced out of the station, fast as the wind. In the confusion many people, poor things, lost what belongings they still had left. We, of course, also took the opportunity of 'losing all our baggage' and reported this to the railway authorities immediately. After that they sent us to the N.S.V. (Nazi Public Welfare Department). The office was adorned with a garlanded portrait of Hitler and everybody there, male and female, was rushing about in uniform. We described our misfortunes so convincingly that they were all extremely helpful to us. My mother became so hoarse with excitement that soon she couldn't get another word out. I pretended we wanted to go to relatives in Berlin. We had fled from Guben. But first we simply had to have a good meal. And I must say we hadn't had such a meal in years! Then they presented us with two Hitler Youths to show us the way to the hostel for Guben refugees. I'm convinced that I'd have succeeded in getting rid of them on the way somehow, but then the preliminary alarm for the second air raid sounded. 'You won't get there tonight now. You'll have to spend the night here,' we were told. Then we had to sleep in a mass shelter in the cellar of a school in the Glogauer Strasse, and camp with the masses on bunk-beds in the cellar. It was filthy, and full of bugs. We hardly closed an eye, and our main thought was—to get out!

Next morning at crack of dawn I approached the camp organiser. I told him that we wanted to get to our relations in Charlottenburg. They went out to work so we had to arrive there before they left that morning. He gave us a certificate to the effect that the widow, Paula Richter, and her daughter, Inge, from Guben, Am Markt 4, had lost all their papers in their flight from the Russians.

There was a special reason for the Guben address. My father had once received a prize for stenography, a picture showing the market place at Guben. This made a great impression on me as a child. I suddenly remembered the picture as I was giving the organiser our ' exact ' particulars. He referred us to the local depot in Charlottenburg which would concern itself with our future welfare.

So we travelled at an unearthly hour in the morning by tram to Charlottenburg. Now we had to find someone who would ' adopt ' us for the time being—i.e., someone to sign our applications for residence permits. We had a good friend in Droyenstrasse 10a, a Mrs. Grüger, who owned a baker's shop. She knew us and knew who we were ; but we could trust her implicitly and now the problem was to establish a new ' legal ' existence with the help of the substitute documents.

At our request Mrs. Grüger signed our applications without a moment's hesitation and forged the name of the female caretaker. Thus armed, we went to the appropriate Nazi welfare office. Something extremely amusing happened there. The lady official who dealt with us explained that we could not remain in Berlin. First, it was ' much too dangerous,' and secondly we'd have to go to Osthavelland anyway, the reception centre for Guben refugees. Then the following dialogue ensued : ' But we'd like to work here ; we've got relatives here who'd put us up.' ' Yes, but don't you realise it could come to a siege here in Berlin ? ' To which my mother replied with conviction : ' Certainly not! Our Führer would never allow it!'

The woman behind the desk turned grey with terror. Had she let slip such a defeatist remark in the presence of a dyed-in-the-wool Nazi ? She gave us our residence stamp without further ado.

Our next move was to the foodstuffs and clothing depot, where we got our ration cards, which were meted out very generously to refugees.

Now, all at once, we were ' legal !' It was like a miracle
—possessing all the necessary documents, moving around
freely, being able to use the same air-raid shelters as the
other house occupants. But I had a shattering experience in
the Ludwigkirchstrasse, where we had rented a furnished
room ; we saw a man with the Jewish star, probably
' privileged' because he had contracted a mixed marriage,
without children or with children brought up as Christians—
he was sitting segregated from everyone else.

The last weeks passed quickly. We knew hope again. The
Russians were outside the city ; our liberation was near.

When the bombardment of Berlin began we moved back
to our cowshed in Potsdam on April 20, 1945, to await the
arrival of the Russians.

On the evening of April 22 ten Hitler Youths and a labour
corps leader were stationed near us for the defence of the
Drewitz-Potsdam road. Next morning they set off their anti-
tank rockets and made themselves scarce. And so the defence
of our road section came to an end.

I shall probably never forget the clanking of the first
Russian caterpillar tanks. However, what followed was quite
different from what we had been dreaming of."

Although the war was over now, Inge did not manage to
contact her father. The last she had heard from him was
shortly before the war broke out in 1939, when he was living
in England.

In August, 1945, she happened to meet an English soldier
who had been assigned to the Potsdam conference. This man,
Edward Matthews, offered to send a letter for Inge by
military post to England.

" This was against the rules and, since we didn't know
my father's address, an almost hopeless undertaking. But
the letter went off. Then Edward came late one Saturday
evening to say goodbye ; he had to leave Potsdam and
return to the Western zone. Since no reply at all had been
received from my father so far, and there was no postal
service for civilians even inside Germany, the one solitary
hope of contacting my father vanished with him.

You can imagine our surprise when, on Sunday morning,

a motor-cycle with two English soldiers pulled up in front of our cowshed. One of them, Eddie, rushed in, terribly excited. He was brandishing a letter in his hand—a letter from my father, which had arrived that morning!"

Inge Deutschkron smiled at the memory of that morning. "You can't imagine what that meant to us! My father was alive! We had survived the war, the three of us! We were saved!"

Otto Weidt died a few years ago. He went on caring for his Jewish fellow-citizens, even after the war. Through his initiative the Jewish children's and old people's home in Niederschönhausen was rebuilt in 1947. In the same year he approached German and overseas organisations with the suggestion that a monument be erected to the victims of Nazism in every town! They just shrugged their shoulders.

It was dark outside when Inge Deutschkron left our house. We had got together on two occasions, once at her place in Bonn and the second time in our home in Donrath.

"If everyone had behaved like Otto Weidt," she said as she shook hands with us in farewell, "the world would be a totally different place today."

" If England is going to intervene in the Polish campaign we must make a lightning attack on Holland. . . . We can't rely on protestations of neutrality."

Hitler to his generals in Berlin, May 23, 1939.

9

If he listened carefully he could hear the tramping of hobnailed boots along the road leading to the bridge. There were invariably five paces ; five forward and five back. And in between, a pause.

Once he heard the shrill, distant whistle of a steam engine. Otherwise there was no sound, save for the moaning of the wind sweeping across the flat, icy landscape.

Hendrik raised his head, listening attentively. The guard's footsteps had suddenly ceased.

He pressed his ear against the freezing sheet of metal that covered up his hiding place. Silence.

" Hell," he murmured. He groped along the walls with his hands, feeling the dampness trickling down, measuring the space inside that disused shaft where he had been crouching for three days now, hiding from the men out there who had been guarding the bridge since yesterday.

He had no idea what had happened to cause them to place this bridge, which they had ignored for years, under guard just now—just now when he was on the run and hiding from them, down here.

He heard a long, drawn-out whistle. Someone shouted something Hendrik could not make out. Then there was a sudden roar of engines and again the tramp of the boots along the road.

Swiftly, the footsteps drew nearer, right up to the mouth of the shaft.

Hendrik squeezed himself into the furthest corner. He suddenly felt a tight band encircle his throat ; a smooth, cold noose which gradually increased its strangling grip.

He could scarcely breathe. He stared up into the darkness, at the metal sheet across the mouth of the shaft.

" Very well, sir," someone called out, directly above him.

Then, an unintelligible yell ; another " Very well, sir," and the footsteps above him halted.

His hand was convulsively gripping his pocket knife ; his only weapon, and a pathetic one. Those men up there had automatics and rifles ; he had his knife.

If they get you, you've had it.

Easy, easy now.

" Get moving!" cried someone. The shuffling of feet, the noise of engines ; a clattering of metal ; another abrupt command. Engines roared again, with a rumbling which soon grew fainter. Then—nothing.

The boy's hands were still clutching the knife.

Hendrik inclined his head backwards and raised himself gradually, pressing his ear to the metal.

Not a thing. They had gone.

He waited a while, then cautiously lifted the cover a little. His eyes, which had become used to the darkness of the shaft, soon took in the evening scene : the arch of the bridge over the railway track, the trees in the background, the slope near which the shaft was sunk ; and the deserted, snow-shrouded landscape.

He lifted the cover a little higher.

Nothing ; just snow, the pallid darkness of a winter's night, and a washed-out moon behind tenuous clouds which drifted speedily past.

Not a soul. No guards. No Germans.

Hendrik lifted the cover off completely, rested his hands on the shaft's edge and, standing upright, swung himself out of the hole.

At first his legs nearly gave way. For three whole days he had squatted in a cramped position down in the shaft. He stretched himself, drawing a deep breath. Faintness overcame him. He fumbled around for the nearest tree and leaned against the trunk, his pulse hammering in his ears.

Three days, shut up in that hole. Enough to knock anyone out cold, even a strong, sixteen-year-old. And now, out in the open, he suddenly felt ravenously hungry.

The first evening his father had been able to smuggle through to him a packet of sandwiches and a thermos flask of warm broth ; but the next day the guard was mounted and he had had nothing to eat since.

He drew a few deep breaths. Gradually the blood began to circulate through his limbs again with a healthy, youthful surge.

He looked around him. A long way behind, and barely visible—though actually it could only have been about a mile and a half away—lay Kerkrade, the Dutch border town where he lived with his family. Farther to the left were the coalmines where his father worked. Even here, not a single light was burning ; even here, he could no longer see the luminous reds, yellows and greens he had once found so comforting. Darkness everywhere. War had put all the lights out. It could be a very long time before they shone again. It was the winter of 1942 ; the Germans still occupied most of Europe and there was no sign of the liberating armies. The Americans were only too glad to be able to keep the Japs off in the Pacific. Would they never get to Europe ?

Hendrick clenched his fists, rubbing his nose with his right one. This bloody cold!

If his father had heard that the guard had been withdrawn he would come soon. It was only half an hour's walk to Ham Street, where they lived ; half an hour's walk through the icebound countryside.

Hendrik walked over to the bridge. He was careful to choose a bit of slope where the wind had blown the snow away. He mustn't leave any tracks.

He walked to the middle of the bridge and looked down at the railway lines. No trains had passed through since yesterday. Probably the lads had been sabotaging the tracks again, farther up the line.

They must have had explosives. And weapons, guns. With those one could soon show those Germans. . . .

But what could a few sixteen-year-olds do ? They could loosen a few rivets somewhere, sprinkle a few handfuls of sand in the axle-boxes of the trucks ; they could chuck a few jagged man-traps, made of bent barbed wire, on to the street ; they could tear down some Nazi placards somewhere else and chalk up Resistance slogans on the walls.

And—they could run errands. Errands for people they

didn't know. There were mysterious journeys at night, on foot or by bicycle ; those who gave the orders were strangers to them, known only by their code names—Buzzard, Eagle, Lion or Tiger. And the people they delivered the messages to—they, too, had similar names, or were just simply Wellem, Jan, Hubert. There were modest acts of sabotage ; young lads couldn't do more. It was still almost a game, but one which the Nazis played in deadly earnest. From month to month raids against Dutchmen suspected of Resistance activities increased ; people were arrested, dragged off to concentration camps. And the notices pasted on the display pillars, announcing the shooting of hostages as a " reprisal," appeared more frequently.

From the very first the opposition of the Dutch Resistance to the German's occupation measures was determined and well organised. The first Resistance groups were formed in the summer of 1940, only a few weeks after the Nazis marched in. By the autumn the Germans were making mass arrests. The most famous Resistance groups were the " Orde-Dienst," the " Organisation der Geuzen " and the terrorist Black Hand. Over 21,000 Dutch Resistance fighters were killed. Many of them died trying to help their Jewish fellow-citizens, who were almost without exception deported and murdered by the Germans. Over 140,000 Jews lived in Holland before the war ; 104,000 of these died in the holocaust.

As time went on 2,000 Dutch hostages were shot or hanged by the Nazis ; 10,000 Dutch forced labourers died in Germany of malnutrition or diseases for which they received inadequate treatment, or in air raids. Altogether about 300,000 Dutchmen were deported to the Reich. But despite these terrorist methods, the first deportations of the Jews evoked an act of protest which had no parallel in any other Nazi-occupied territory—the courageous general strike of Amsterdam in February, 1941. Then there was the Dutch railway strike of September, 1944, which paralysed the transportation of German supplies ; this lasted till the end of the war.

Hendrik Meijers was one of those tough, determined

Resistance fighters, one of the youth group. He was sixteen that winter, 1942. He had been forced to hide from a raiding party which was covering the whole of the southern border territory.

Over the fields in the distance, in the direction of Kerkrade, a figure was approaching.

Hendrik escaped into the darkness under the trees. He squatted among the bushes, waiting.

The figure drew nearer and walked along the road towards the bridge.

" Hein," a muffled voice called, " Hein!"

Hendrik jumped up and ran to him.

" Dad!"

" Hush!" his father whispered. He grabbed his son's arm and pulled him back to the shadow of the trees.

" Have they gone ? " he asked.

Hendrik nodded. " Dad, it's so cold there, hell, am I hungry, and I'm frozen stiff—oh heavens it's cold. . . ."

" They've got Hubert and Mennes," his father replied, softly.

Hendrik's gesturing hand fell to his side.

" Hubert," he murmured. " And Mennes. . . ."

His father nodded.

Hendrik gulped. They were his best friends.

His father looked at him. " You've got to beat it, Hein," he said. His voice trembled ; but he was determined. " You've got to! You'll have to make for Switzerland."

Hendrik nodded.

" You know I'm in their black books. Ever since I made that daft remark about Hitler when I was working in Germany. Since then they've been keeping an eye on me. They probably won't touch me, but they'll try to take it out on my eldest son, I know that. I know them, the gangsters! They'll drag you off to a concentration camp. . . ." This man, usually so strong, stood there with bowed shoulders, now enervated and helpless himself. He could not protect his own son.

" Here," he said, passing Hendrik a package. " From your mother. Something to eat." Then he took off his thick winter overcoat. He had a light summer one on underneath it.

"Put this on."

"But that's your coat, dad."

"Shut up and get it on. Yours is too light for this weather." Dumbly, he did as he was told.

"O.K. then." His father rested his hand on Hendrik's shoulder for a whole minute. Then he turned round and walked off. Hendrik wanted to say something, to shout something after him, but not a word came out. He could only look at that human shape gradually becoming smaller till it vanished altogether.

The man who sat opposite me at the small boulevard café, " Select Latin," near the Sorbonne, had a narrow face, tanned by wind and weather, and piercing eyes. He was 37, but looked older.

Hendrik Meijers had gone through a lot since that winter of 1942 when he ran away from the Germans. He had done time in German prisons ; joined the Dutch partisans who liberated his homeland ; fought in the Foreign Legion at Dien Bien Phu ; seen the break-up of French rule in Algeria. He had been a mechanic, a long-distance driver, a hotel porter and a chucker-out, a garage attendant and a tourist guide. But he had never quite landed on his feet again ; not since the Nazis dragged him out of school in 1941, put him on hard labour and threw his whole life out of joint.

I arranged to meet Hendrik Meijers, who now lives in Bordeaux, in Paris. He had written to me ; he wanted to tell me about his experiences, and particularly about " that night on Lake Constance, in a little boat, when we were making for Switzerland."

He had aroused my curiosity. And now, I still didn't know what he had to tell me. He ordered a lager and lit a gauloise. He laid all his papers on the table before me : Legion documents, testifying to a long list of honours and decorations ; letters from friends in the Dutch Resistance ; photos of women and girls, of his father, of Indo-China ; and one of a little Annamite he has a child by.

" I tried to settle down in Holland again, but it didn't work," he said. " Since that night in 1942 I've been a bird of passage."

He didn't think that had anything to do with the Germans; it was "just fate." But it began with them. With those who persecuted him and those who helped him. And that is what he wanted to tell me. For one of them sacrificed his life to help Hendrik Meijers.

"That very night—when my father came to the bridge where I was hiding—I got going," Hendrik recalled. "I knew that border territory like the inside of my coat pocket. After all, I'd grown up there. It wasn't far to Aachen. I had relations there, but I couldn't go to them because if they were after me it would be the first place they'd try.

Around midnight I managed to creeep over the border through the barbed wire, near Locht. I was in the lions' den now, but if I wanted to escape to Switzerland I'd have to do it through Germany; it was my only hope. I didn't know French then but I spoke German like my mother-tongue. Besides, I had my German work permit, from the works where the Nazis made me do my labour service. At a pinch —once I had the border territory behind me—I might get by with this. Maybe.

I got to Aachen around three in the morning. There was an air-raid warning. I wanted to hide away somewhere in the bombed-out buildings, but a patrol sent me to a shelter. I was lucky they didn't ask for my identity card, but they were pretty keen to find shelter themselves because the bombs had started dropping. The place was shaking with the shocks from the high explosives. The people just sat there, eyes big and staring, gazing in front of them. The women tried to calm their children down.

Someone next to me offered me a swig of schnapps. I got talking to him. He was a middle-aged man; his wife sat next to him. They'd had two sons at the front and one had been killed. The youngest daughter had been conscripted for labour service just a few weeks before, and the letters she sent home were enough to make you weep, as the woman said. In the very first 'political training' lesson—so called —they'd told that innocent eighteen-year-old girl that it was her duty to present a child to her Führer. One of the young servicewomen objected, rather naïvely, that they weren't married yet; the supervisor who was doing the 'enlightening' just gave a suggestive laugh.

'One day,' muttered the man, looking at me, 'one day we'll all pay for this.' His wife was terrified and shushed him. 'Don't worry, mother,' I said, 'I'm not one of *them*.' The word 'mother' just slipped off my tongue; I couldn't have addressed that woman any other way, somehow.

After the all-clear they took me home with them. I didn't tell them anything definite, but they were soon in the picture; they knew I was on the run. His wife called the man Frank and outside on the door I'd seen the name 'Kuckelhorn' under the bell—well, Frank brought his youngest son's school atlas out and sat next to me without saying a word, while I studied the map.

'Where d'you want to get to?' he asked. I indicated Switzerland.

'Don't try the Basle route,' he warned me 'They'll pinch you there. I know that area. My firm sent me down there on a service job a year ago. About that time they pinched three Germans who were trying to get across. You'll have to try to make it over Lake Constance—that's your only chance.'

I spent the rest of the night with them. In the morning I got a first-class breakfast—marmalade, butter, fresh, white bread, things we'd forgotten about in Holland long ago. Frank went to work early. The woman advised me to stay till evening, but I felt as if there were hot cinders under my feet.

I said a warm goodbye to the kind woman and went to the station.

I had to behave as normally as possible. I bought a rail ticket to Cologne. Of the German money I'd had on me I now had about twenty marks left. The Wehrmacht guard at the barrier, who was inspecting the papers of soldiers on leave, took hardly any notice of me. I was a powerful type, but one look at my fresh, young face was enough to indicate that I wasn't of military age yet.

The journey to Cologne passed without incident. Once a patrol walked through the train, but they didn't ask to see passes, either.

Maybe all this sounds very natural now, but in retro-spect it seems pretty odd to me that everything went off so well. I was naïve and full of bounce, throwing myself into an escapade that could have cost my neck. But you must realise that I was little more than a kid.

Things got a bit dodgy at Cologne. Down in the station hall I saw a Hitler Youth patrol checking on youngsters. I went into the men's toilet. I locked myself in and heard some-one retching in the closet next to mine. Somebody was being sick ; a drunk, probably. Possibilities here—perhaps.

The partitions between each individual closet didn't quite reach to the floor ; there was a gap, about a hand's width. I bent down and saw a jacket lying on the floor in the next compartment. Part of the material was within reach ; I gave it a careful tug. The jacket glided nicely over the floor ; the racket next door was still going on. I went over it quickly and found a slim wallet. I left the money inside ; I took only the identification card, issued in Mayence for a young man of eighteen. The photo wasn't much like my mug but with a bit of imagination and bad light it might pass. I pocketed the card, pushed the jacket with the wallet back again and left the toilet. I made tracks out of the station."

Actually, he had more luck than sense. During the night he managed to snatch a lift on a goods train heading for southern Germany. He hid in an open truck piled high with strongly aromatic barrels ; they contained dyestuffs, probably. He didn't dare go into a closed truck because he knew that these were usually locked and barred from the outside.

He arrived at the Black Forest next morning, practically frozen stiff. During a steep gradient he jumped off, landing on all fours in the snow ; he turned a couple of somersaults but didn't hurt himself. The train puffed and groaned round the bend and disappeared.

Hendrik made a cross-country trek through the knee-deep snow. Soon the pale arms of the wintry forest embraced him. Peace and silence reigned everywhere. The world was a quiet, lonely, white heaven.

Hendrik was still a lad and was soon caught up in the

H   215 aura of that day. He ran through the wood like a child, not looking where he was going ; he saw wild deer grazing, and birds of prey, and wished he were the forester's son.

But he was not the forester's son. He was a young Dutchman who had run errands for the Resistance and committed acts of sabotage. He was someone the concentration camp was waiting for ; perhaps even the noose.

The sun set quickly. During the day he had skirted round the villages, but now it was time to think of food. He had had nothing to eat for two days and his stomach ached with hunger ; his head felt light and glassy. As he struggled up and down hill his legs seemed to carry him reluctantly now ; the snow had made his progress doubly tiring.

When darkness fell he crept up to the houses of a village on the edge of the forest. He made sure that the wind was against him, so as not to bring the dogs out on him.

One of the houses right on the edge of the wood looked deserted. Having walked round it a few times he went to the door. He knocked. No answer. He looked round him ; no one was watching. Radio music blared from a neighbouring house ; in another, children prattled.

But the house just in front of him stood mute in the darkness.

Hendrik pressed down the latch. The door was locked, naturally.

He made a tour of the house. One window was slightly open. He stretched up and pushed against the window frames ; the two wings opened with a creak.

His behaviour was quite calculating. After all, he was now a wanted man ; that evening he had turned into a hunted beast that had to exploit every opportunity. He says now that the dominating impulse was hunger. But it was much more than that. It was the urge to survive—to hell with how.

He jumped into the room and his feet hit the floor with a thud. For a moment he lost his balance and lurched against a piece of furniture ; then he regained his balance.

When his eyes had become accustomed to the blackness he saw that he was in a bedroom. High, old-fashioned beds with mountains of bolsters occupied one end of the room ; there was a large wardrobe at the other end.

He went over and opened the door.

There was a row of shoes at the bottom. He cursed gently ; they were all women's. But then he found a pair of high-laced boots behind them.

He slipped off his wet shoes and tried the boots on. Not too bad.

He rifled the linen drawer and stuffed two pairs of men's socks into his coat pocket. Nobody would notice—the thing was crammed with hosiery. He shut the wardrobe and pushed his wet shoes right underneath it where they wouldn't be noticed for some time. Then he left the bedroom, groped his way along a dark passage to a row of doors and eventually found the kitchen.

Next to the kitchen was a small larder. He had to restrain himself from grabbing the bread and butter off the shelf and tearing the wurst off the hook.

He cut a chunk off both loaves—one white, one of brown farm bread, carved himself off a slice of sausage and stuck an apple and a handful of nuts in his pocket. He took as little as possible ; it wouldn't do for them to notice right away that they'd had an uninvited guest. One temptation he just couldn't resist ; on the larder floor stood over a dozen pots of jam. He put one of these in his pocket. Then he closed the larder door, slunk back into the bedroom, left it again by the same window and drew it carefully to.

The snow had been swept away, up to about a yard from the wall of the house ; so he left no tracks there.

He found the road, followed it awhile, then made for the wood. It was only when he was among the trees that he dared to breathe again, deeply and freely.

"Of course, I was lucky," he admits now. "Apparently nobody noticed I'd been on the scrounge, because I didn't hear any unusual commotion in the village, although I hung around for quite a bit because I had to wait for the moon to come up. Naturally this stroke of luck cheered me up. I trudged through the woods, towards the south ;I kept under cover during the day and made a few round tours at night— that is, I'd break into a deserted house somewhere and help myself. Now and again I'd steal a chicken or a rabbit ; I'd hide myself in the wood during the day and roast it on a spit. Usually the thing tasted awful because I'd no idea how to do things like that. But at least I didn't starve. This went on for nearly a fortnight. No one ever bothered me. As soon as I saw anyone I took cover. And so I got to Lake Constance. The last stage was hard going. There were no woods there, just open fields ; sometimes a bush or two and lots of orchards and vineyards. I took shelter in the little stone huts one sometimes finds in the vineyards. The cold—that was the worst.

I 'celebrated' Christmas in a barn in a place near Meersburg, on Lake Constance. The sound of carols wafted from the farmhouse ; children were singing ; I heard merry laughter and a dull, booming bass voice—that must have been the farmer, who was obviously on Christmas leave, because I once saw him in the yard with his grey military jacket on.

I lay up in the hay and swallowed three fresh raw eggs I'd pinched from the hens down below.

I must have fallen asleep then, because after a bit I heard somebody talking. Soft voices, right beneath me. The hay rustled. It sounded as if two people were wrestling. 'Now don't be like that,' said a man's voice, then a woman's: 'Now, Max, don't, stop it, I don't want. . . .' And he said, 'But today's very special, Clara,' and the girl laughed at that. It was a saucy laugh, and suddenly I felt hot all over. Then I just heard some mumbling and muttering and then a groaning, as if someone were a bit sick.

I was sixteen and hadn't a clue about such things, but that night, on Holy Night, 1942, I got my initiation.

I couldn't see, only hear. At first I stopped my ears up, but then I listened. I wasn't disappointed either. I tell you, it was a gala performance those two put on down there in the hay."

Hendrik Meijers regarded me with a huge grin. He rubbed his hands together, as if he'd cracked a big joke. The inhibitions, the scepticism and the slight distrust with which he had first greeted me had all evaporated.

But his face hardened again, very quickly.

"Well," he said, "that was Christmas night for you—a

pleasant one, for those two down in the hay, at least. But soon it was to become pretty serious.

I spent Christmas up there in the barn. In the night, when everybody was asleep, I'd climbed down and slunk up to the kitchen door, but those suspicious farmers had locked everything up. So I had to go hungry the whole day. But I consoled myself with thoughts of the evening. Surely I'd be able to forage something.

I was all strung up, the whole time. Through the cracks between the boards of my barn I could see far over the landscape—and far over Lake Constance in the night. I couldn't make out the water—it was too dark for that—but on the far horizon I saw bright, winking lights ; a most unusual sight. Switzerland, that was. The first glimpse of those lights made my heart beat like thunder.

At nightfall I crept down the ladder and into the open. Loud voices boomed from the farmhouse and children laughed happily in between.

This time the dog joined in. But I was already on the road. I was undecided and turned this way, then that. Finally I set off downhill towards the lake.

I passed through the village. Thin streaks of light gleamed through the chinks in the blackout blinds. In one house a harsh voice was droning over the radio—a Christmas message. I could catch bits of the speech. German soldiers . . . a wartime Christmas . . . stand steadfastly together . . . victory . . . Germany for ever . . . 1918, never again. . . .

I kept going till I came to a little hill with houses at the foot. Then I saw the water, too, glimmering faintly in the moonlight.

I left the road and climbed down the hill to the lake. In the dark I ran up against some barbed wire and tore my coat.

I cursed and pulled myself free. The path led to a house. I made a detour and came to some gardens with high hedges on either side.

Suddenly I was standing near a clump of trees ; there was another house there.

I simply had to find something to eat.

The house was surrounded by trees. Further along to the

right was a kind of elongated shed; behind it I heard the rippling of the lake.

The building seemed silent and deserted in the pale glow of the moon; a dark ruin, an obsolescence, shrouded in creeping ivy.

The first storey had a balcony; the French windows leading on to it were half open.

I made a circular tour of the house. It was a small villa in the 1930s style, two storeys high. A flight of stone steps with a Grecian pillar on either side led to the front door.

I crept up to the wall and ran my hand over the luxuriant ivy. It rustled. But the twigs were rooted pretty fast to the wall. They'd hold.

I gripped the foliage tight, used the branches as leverage and swung myself up.

There was a crackling. One foot slipped and knocked against the wall.

I dragged myself up with my hands; the ivy was trembling and creaking. But I managed to get up to the balcony. I started clambering over the iron rail.

'Where d'you think you're going?' a voice greeted me.

For a minute I lost my balance. I had to cling with both hands to the parapet so as not to topple off.

A man came out on to the balcony. From the darkness inside the room I meant to break into. His hands hung down by his sides; he wasn't armed, but he didn't look exactly helpless.

'I—I'm hungry,' I whispered.

'Hungry?' He began to laugh.

Then: 'Come on in, my little friend,' he said, stepping aside.

I just stayed there.

'Well, come on!' he snapped.

I made lightning calculations. Should I jump down? A sprained ankle—then what?

I went into the room and got a thump in the back. 'Just look smart about it,' he grunted.

I stumbled against a chair.

I heard the french windows close behind me, the curtains being drawn.

It was a large room; the walls were lined with book-shelves. A desk stood against one wall; there was a couch, covered with a woollen tartan rug, at the other side of the room.

Near the desk, a radio. The green light was on but I couldn't hear any music.

The man turned the radio off, then he looked me in the face.

He was twenty-eight or thirty; a head taller than I, over six foot. He had cropped, blond hair and an angular face with big, thoughtful eyes. He didn't look like a bloke you could try any funny business with.

He stood there, hands on hips. The grey pullover stretched taut across his muscular chest.

'Well, start talking before I get the police. What do you want here?'

'I'm hungry. I ran away from home and I've got nothing to eat.'

'Where d'you come from?'

'Cologne.'

He stared at me unbelieving. 'Cologne, huh?'

I nodded.

'How old are you?'

'Fifteen.'

'You're older than that.' I denied it.

'What rank d'you hold in the Hitler Youth?'

'Lieutenant.'

Suddenly a smile lit up his face. 'Well, well—Lieutenant.' He walked up to me. 'Lieutenant!' He made as if to hit me. I backed away. 'Lieutenant,' he said yet again, and began to roar with laughter.

He sat on the chair by the desk, crossing his legs.

'Look,' he said, 'I'll give you one chance. The truth and be quick about it.'

'And if I don't?'

He shrugged. 'I'll tell you one thing: any lies and I'll get the police for sure. If you tell the truth, we'll see what we can do. It depends on what kind of record you've got. O.K.?'

'I'm hungry,' I said.

'Afterwards, if I like your story,' he nodded.

I glanced quickly round the room. No Nazi pictures any-where; no photographs of Hitler, no maps with flags on; just sports certificates, trophies, pennants, pictures of boats. I had to risk it.

'I'm Dutch,' I said.

He didn't answer. He leaned back, eyes half closed.

I was silent.

'Carry on!'

'I had trouble with the Germans. They put me on forced labour in Germany. Aachen.'

I got my work permit out and held it before him.

'Put it on the table!' he ordered. I did so.

'There was a raid ten days ago. The greenies rounded up all the Dutch kids. I beat it.'

'Greenies?'

'The German uniformed police.'

He nodded. 'And now, you want to get to Switzerland?' he asked.

I looked at him without speaking.

'Why do you want to risk your neck just because you don't fancy working in Germany?'

'You don't know what the Germans do to us Dutch! You don't know what it means being under the Nazis—.'

The word had slipped out; I bit my lip.

He brushed it aside 'Not exactly a bed of roses, I suppose?'

We were silent a moment.

I felt my hands getting damp. 'Why don't you hand me over to the police?' I burst out.

'Take it easy. One thing at a time. So you aren't altogether pleased with the situation?' He gave me a penetrating look. 'Don't try to kid me.'

'We—sabotaged transports. We pulled up railway lines —we—' and then it just poured out, it burst out from me like a waterfall, everything I'd kept bottled up broke loose.

I was sixteen years old. I was finished. My nerves had given way. My escape, the loneliness, the game of hide-and-seek, my shattered hopes—being suddenly caught within the sight of the lake, within reach of Switzerland, where I would have been safe—all these played their part. I told him every-thing; about the young couriers, the secret act of resistance, the cutting of telephone wires, the mantraps on the streets, the hastily scrawled slogans; about the hunger, and the Nazis, and those bloody swine the Gestapo. I told him about the shooting of hostages, people being dragged away in the fog and dark; about the camps in the north of Holland and the mass deportations of Jews; about the children who got no milk and all the tragedies and vexations of life under totalitarian rule.

I wept, cursed, swore at everything and everybody.

When I'd finished, all I could get out was: 'Leave me alone! Leave me alone!'

The man got up and came over to me. Grabbing my arm, he led me to the door.

We went downstairs. I knew now that he would get the police.

He guided me to the kitchen.

'Sit down!' he ordered.

I sat.

He laid a place for me: a plate, a cup, a basket of bread. On the plate he put some wurst, butter, cheese and apples. 'Go on, eat.' In the corner, on the sideboard, stood a pot of steaming coffee under cover. He poured me out a cup.

'You interrupted my supper preparations just now,' he said, smiling. And when I hesitated—'Well, eat.'

'What are you going to do with me?'

He replied with a question. 'You want to go to Switzer-land?'

I nodded.

'Well, then!' No more.

I couldn't breathe. 'You mean. . . .'

He looked at me, eyebrows raised. 'Nothing. Just go on eating.'

Eat! I fairly shovelled it down. I chewed and stared at him and he nodded back at me. He had lit a pipe and was pacing up and down the kitchen, obviously overcome by a sudden restlessness.

When I'd finished he looked at the clock over the kitchen cabinet. It was half past seven.

He muttered something to himself that I didn't understand.

Then he said: 'Come on.'

I followed him outside. The corridor was dark, apart from the faint glow of light coming from the open kitchen door. He asked me: 'Do you know where you are, actually?'

I shook my head. 'The day before yesterday I came from Meersburg. But this place—I don't know. . . .' I shrugged. I honestly didn't know where I was.

He nodded. 'All the better. Wait here.'

I waited in the corridor while he disappeared into one of the rooms. Five minutes later he reappeared wearing a green mackintosh like the German despatch riders have. He'd slung a thick, woollen muffler round his neck, and his fur hat, set square on his head, was pulled down slightly over his eyes.

'Wait.' He switched out the light in the kitchen.

'What are you going to do?'

He didn't answer.

When we got outside he shut the front door carefully and took me over a gravelled path to a hut on the lake. It was a boathouse.

Suddenly my heart began to beat madly.

Without speaking he lifted up the sash door.

'Here, help me.'

I helped him and two minutes later we had the boat in the water.

'Come on.'

I jumped into the boat; it rocked. I sat down.

'Mr. . . .' I said hoarsely, 'Mr. . . .'

'Just call me Bert,' he replied curtly.

'Where are we going?'

He jerked his thumb towards the far shore.

I said nothing.

He got busy with the boat's outboard motor. Then took the oars and rowed against the current without cutting-in the motor. In a jiffy we were out in the open water.

His strokes were steady and even ; and the dark silhouette of the shore soon mingled with the blackness of the water. I turned my head and had eyes for only one thing: the lights of Switzerland, gleaming with promise.

If it had come off—maybe my life would have turned out differently!"

His brow was furrowed now. He had stopped talking. It was as if he listened to the sounds of that night ; the water lapping and the hoarse cry of the gulls disturbed from sleep.

After a while Bert started up the engine ; from then on she gained speed steadily. Hendrik tried to get out of Bert who he was, but found out nothing. Bert dropped a hint, just once, when the boy asked him why he wasn't in the army. "That's all over," he said, "that's nothing to do with me any more." Then he explained to Hendrik that it was almost hopeless to cross the lake unobserved. But on this particular night—Christmas night—there might be a chance, the only chance. He knew the customs people and the lake police, and knew when they made their patrol inspections.

Hendrik didn't dare ask him why he went out of his way— why, in short, he risked his life to save a young Dutchman who might easily have been taking him in.

" He must have believed me. Something in what I told him must have made him do what he did. Once, when I talked about the Nazis he said, ' those swine,' but that was the only time he let slip such an expression. Otherwise he accepted all I told him without comment.

Apparently he didn't want me to find out anything at all about him. No doubt he was making sure that if we were caught I couldn't give any concrete evidence. Then, perhaps, he wanted to prevent me from saying over in Switzerland: ' So and so helped me.' There were Gestapo and S.D. spies everywhere then, even outside Germany. And maybe he didn't want me to come thanking him when it was all over. I think he did it because it was, to him, the obvious thing to do—to help someone in trouble. If people ask me why he helped me and not others, I can only say: ' I don't know.' Maybe he'd already helped others ? If so, why hadn't they caught him a long time ago ? They're all questions without answers ; things I asked myself during the long nights in prison, in Indo-China, in Algeria. But I never found an answer."

They were within a few hundred yards of the Swiss shore. Then, suddenly, a patrol boat loomed up out of the night.

It was upon them before they could do anything to avoid it. They were caught in a blaze of searchlights ; it was as if the boat had been lying in wait for them.

' Down!' Bert yelled.

Hendrik ducked, shutting his eyes in terror. But he soon opened them as a resounding voice, which seemed to waft high over the water, commanded: " Heave to! Halt! German police!"

Bert's boat doubled over to the right, rocked, jerked over the waves. The outboard engine roared and spray drizzled over the starboard side.

The searchlight moved away from them ; for a few seconds they were in the dark again. They raced for the Swiss shore ; those lights shone nearer and clearer than ever, now.

" Stop!" cried a voice over the megaphone. " Heave to!" The same moment the searchlight had enveloped them again.

Hendrik turned to Bert.

It was then the hammering of the machine-gun began. A solitary, abrupt burst of fire, whipping over the waves.

" Can you make it over there ? " cried Bert.

Hendrik pulled himself together. " I'll make it!" he called.

" Go on, then—jump !"

Before he realised what he was doing Hendrik had sprung overboard. Icy water splashed into his face.

He sank and came up spluttering. Tore his coat off while swimming.

A second burst of machine-gun fire crackled over the lake. In the same instant Hendrik saw the powerful, squatting figure in the motor-boat—which was still making frantically for the Swiss shore—slouch and lurch forward.

Hendrik submerged. He swam under water till his lungs nearly burst.

He surfaced again, swimming right into the centre of the searchlight's chalky cone. Bert's boat drifted in front of him, directionless. The engine was silent.

A rope cracked into the water near Hendrik. He grabbed it. What else could he do ?

" They pulled me up. One of them pushed me along the narrow gang plank into the cabin. Another shone a torch into my face. They didn't say anything. They stood me with my face to the wall and searched me. Then they left me standing like that.

I heard voices outside and heavy footsteps. They carried something in ; I turned to look. It was Bert. His head was streaming blood. It gave me a horrible shock. He's wounded, I thought, hell, I hope nothing serious. . . .

' Well ? ' said one policeman.

' He's dead,' said the other. ' Shot in the head. Must have driven right into the path of our second warning shot."

I felt it coming up. It was the lake water. I vomited as I stood there against the wall, and the police said nothing."

They brought Hendrik ashore. A closed van, which the lake police had summoned over the radio, was waiting for him. An S.D. man in grey uniform and a Gestapo officer in civvies accompanied them ; he does not know where they took him. In a brightly-lit office he was given an old suit to wear while his things were drying on a big iron stove. In that office he was questioned for the first time.

" It was quite a normal interrogation. They didn't threaten me or beat me up. They were obviously more interested in the man who'd helped me. But he was dead. He couldn't say anything, and I didn't want to. What could I have said, anyway ? That I'd only met him a few hours before ? Of course I said that, and in the end they had to believe me."

During the cross-examination, which lasted three days, the Gestapo apparently came to the conclusion that this couldn't be a " political " case. Hendrik had given them his proper name and address, since lying would only have made his position worse. He was lucky ; a check-up in Kerkrade, in Holland, brought nothing incriminating to light, except that he had shirked his labour conscription in Germany. There was no mention of his connections with the Resistance or of his participation in acts of sabotage.

A few days later, Hendrik was transferred to Lörrach.

"Why Lörrach exactly, I still don't know," he said. There, in February, 1943, he was sentenced to a year in prison for attempting to cross the border illegally, theft and refusing to work. They took him from there to Landsberg to serve his time. A Gestapo man in civvies accompanied him, warning him not to do anything silly on the way. "He wasn't a bad bloke. He had the usual leather coat on and a black hat with feathers. We had to change a few times. In Munich he took me to a restaurant and ordered me some wurst and sauerkraut, and even stood me a beer. When he handed me over in Landsberg he must have spoken well of me, too ; later on I heard that he'd said they mustn't be too harsh with me. I was a decent boy, 'a crazy young Dutch kid who'd been taken in by the Communists.'"

In prison Hendrik had plenty of opportunity to think of his unsuccessful attempt to escape and of the people who had helped him. He regarded it as a miracle that he'd come out of it alive, that terrible night.

But he wasn't out of the wood yet. His gaolers made it clear to him that after he'd served his sentence he'd be transferred to a concentration camp. He knew what that meant.

However, luck was on his side. After serving half a year he fell ill. He had a high fever, swollen feet and dizziness, and was sent to the sick bay for observation. The fever didn't abate. Eventually he developed boils on the left foot, which had to be lanced several times. He was suffering from an acute inflammation, the cause of which even the doctors coudn't ascertain. He was in hospital for six months; the day of his release came and went. Eventually he could walk again. But he was so weak that even the S.S. had no further interest in putting him on forced labour ; so they gave him a ticket from Landsberg to Aachen, where he had to report to the Gestapo. Having done that, he got a permit to cross the border, and within six hours he was at home.

"The Gestapo visited us a couple of times, but they left me alone. The authorities seemed to be quite satisfied that I'd done a year's stretch in Germany. They grinned at me and said : 'Well, what was it like in clink ?' That was all ; then the Yanks came. Nobody ever guessed I was one of the boys that had sabotaged coal transports from our mines to

Germany. I could have saved myself that getaway in that icy cold winter of 1942-43—if I'd known. But I wasn't a clairvoyant, and to take a risk then could have proved a deadly mistake. One of my pals, whom they actually could prove something against, was caught on the run in the Pyrenees and shot. He'd left it too late."

After the war Hendrik Meijers made two vain attempts to get some more detailed information about Bert. He wrote to the Mayor's office in Meersburg and to the local police, but his letters were either ignored or came back undelivered. So his researches were quite unsuccessful ; probably because there had been a number of such escape attempts over Lake Constance during 1942 and 1943, usually with the same tragic end. Later on it became gradually more difficult to get to Switzerland via Constance ; by the beginning of 1945 it was quite impossible.

Hendrik and other Resistance fighters joined the Americans when the Dutch southern provinces were liberated by the Allies, and went with them to Germany. He lived a mercenary's life ; it was a time of chaos and he was young. He never really adapted himself to peacetime. He had known only violence, resistance, war. When he should have looked for a regular job in Holland he absconded, joined the Foreign Legion and served in the Algerian and Indo-Chinese campaigns. During the last few years he had lived in the south of France doing casual work.

When he said goodbye he jumped on a passing bus and waved to me from the platform. The last I saw of him was his narrow, hard face, the eyes bright, alert and somehow sad. I felt as if I were looking at the face of a whole generation.

According to the wishes of the Reichs-führer S.S., Auschwitz became the greatest human extermination factory of all time. When, in the summer of 1941, he gave me personal orders to prepare a mass extermination site in Auschwitz, and to carry out this extermination, I could not in the slightest degree imagine its extent and consequences. . . . I didn't waste time thinking it over then—I had received the order—and had to carry it out. Whether the mass extermination of the Jews was necessary or not, I could not allow myself to judge. As the Führer himself had ordered the 'Final solution of the Jewish problem' there was nothing for an old Nazi to 'think' about.

Rudolf Höss, Auschwitz Commandant, Autobiographical Notes.

10

It was snowing. The wind drifted over the fields and drove the snowflakes obliquely before it. It was an east wind, heralding colder weather. Everyone who did not have urgent business in town was hurrying home.

Evening set in swiftly in the little village. With it came the darkness, the "blackout" which people could never get used to, though it was the sixth year of war.

Clara Greulich pulled the blackout curtains down over her living-room window, after she had cast a last glance down the street. The pavement was deserted. There was snow lying there again, though she had swept it away an hour before.

She turned and went over to the table where the children's exercise books lay. A few of the exercises were teeming with errors. But how could children learn anything at a time like this? It was a miracle that one could keep the schools going at all, what with air raids, evacuation schemes, adults having to serve in the home defence corps and the premilitary training courses of the Hitler Youth.

Even the quiet little Westphalian town of Borken had been touched by the war. Every day you were frightened to open the newspapers, because there could be a death announcement there again—a black-bordered obituary notice for a young man who had been sacrificed so that Germany might live, as they so touchingly described it.

How long would it last? It was the winter of 1944; the Americans and British were dropping bombs over German cities every single day. In many places the railway network was so severely damaged that transport facilities threatened to break down altogether. Supplies were diminishing; production was coming gradually to a standstill. And people were still dying. How much longer?

Clara Greulich opened the first book and dipped her pen in red ink.

At that moment the doorbell rang. It was a brief, furtive kind of sound, as if a child had just pressed the bell in passing, but it shook her so badly that her heart began to hammer loudly.

She went hesitantly outside, groped her way through the dark passage and switched on the light. Then she opened the front door.

Clara's first reaction was a desire to bang it shut again; for the person standing outside looked as if his intentions toward her might be pretty sinister.

"Please," the stranger burst out. His voice sounded harassed and pained.

"Who are you?" Clara whispered. Her eyes had just got used to the gloomy twilight of the blackout. The face of the old man who stood before her was lined with deep wrinkles and encrusted with dirt. A sticky tangle of hair stood up on his head. It was not much longer than the hair of a freshly razored recruit. A knitted jacket, much too big for him, covered the upper part of his body; the sleeves hung down over his hands. A pair of light-coloured, thin khaki trousers dangled limply over his legs; they were torn at the knees.

The stranger's eyes flickered, with an expression of mingled fear and hope.

"Don't you recognise me, then?" the apparition whispered. "It's me, Erich. Your nephew Erich from Amsterdam."

A couple of seconds passed before she grasped the full significance of his words.

"I'm on the run," he stammered. "From. . . ."

But then she understood. She got hold of his arm and pulled him into the house.

"My God," she whispered as she looked at the man, with different eyes this time. "Erich—but this is terrible!"

This old man was supposed to be Erich Blomberg, her twenty-year-old nephew from Amsterdam, the son of her sister who'd married a Dutch Jew.

"Where have you come from?" she asked in a whisper.

He answered, in the same conspiratorial tone, "From Auschwitz."

" Auschwitz—where's that ? "

" In Poland."

" And from there you. . . ."

He just nodded. " Please, could I sit down somewhere, just to rest a bit ? " he begged. He was exhausted.

" Of course!" She bit her lip.

" I ran away," he muttered. " I'm tired." His eyes flickered again. " Are you alone ? "

" Yes, I'm alone," Clara answered. Suddenly she became feverishly active.

" Come on," she urged, and pushed Erich into the kitchen. She ran to the stove and put the kettle on ; hurried to the kitchen cabinet and fetched out plates and cups.

Erich sank into a chair. He looked at the coffee pot and reached for a cup.

"I'll make you fresh coffee at once," she said. "That's cold."

" Please," he whispered, " please, just a drink." He poured out with trembling hands and drank in frenzied gulps. The coffee ran down over his chin.

Clara ran to the larder and fetched out some bread, put a dish of margarine on the table and cut some slices off, without a word ; and as fast as she sliced the bread and spread the margarine it all disappeared into that greedily chewing mouth. The starving boy gulped down ravenously everything she gave him.

It was a heartrending sight. Clara felt the tears well into her eyes. Then his hand stole over the table and reached for hers.

The fingers were cold and clammy. She couldn't help it ; she grasped that ravaged hand with both of hers and pressed it, rubbed it in her palms, till it was warm.

" I can't go any further," Erich whispered. " I can't go on. I've fled through the whole of Germany in order to come to you—please, don't send me away."

" I won't send you away," she promised.

Her heart contracted at the thought of sending this boy out again into the cold, into the night, into the arms of his tormentors.

" No, I won't send you away."

She placed a washbasin full of hot water on the dresser near the sink and laid out two clean towels and a bar of soap ; then she went over to the bedroom and fetched a set of her husband's winter underwear out of the chest-of-drawers. She dug out an old coat which her husband hadn't worn for ages. Erich watched everything she did with his alert brown eyes—still on guard, still scared.

" There," she said. " Now just have a wash and take those rags off. Put this coat on. Take it for the time being—it's the warmest thing I can give you."

" And after that ? "

" You can hide up in the loft for the time being. Nobody will find you there. My husband only comes home weekends."

Erich stood up. He had to support himself on the back of the chair. " Thank you," he whispered.

" Don't thank me," she said. " We don't know what's ahead of us yet."

A flight of stairs led from the Greulich flat up to the attic of the house. Owing to air-raid precautions it had been cleared of all lumber and nobody used it. No one who lived in the house had been up there for months. While Erich was changing Clara Greulich climbed upstairs. She had trouble in forcing open the heavy trap-door. The light of her candle flickered in the wind whistling through the fissures in the roof ; it was eerie up there, in the darkness of that winter's night.

In a far corner between the chimney and a piece of slanting roof there was a likely place. Here, she could hide Erich for a little while. She dragged a couple of stools over there, tied them with string and laid two woollen rugs on top. It was a hard bed, but it was a resting place which to Erich, after his escape, seemed like heaven. Clara built a hiding place of thin board, behind which Erich could shelter. Both of them worked half the night ; and by the early hours they had finished the job. A proper " room " had emerged, where Erich could feel relatively safe. A cursory inspection of the loft would hardly reveal it, for viewed from the trap-door it lay right behind the wide stone frontage of the chimney.

"Will you be able to sleep here, though ? " Clara asked Erich. For the first time she saw him smile.

"I'll sleep as I haven't slept for a whole year," he said.

"Remember—don't let anyone see the light."

The candle stood on a chair near the bed. She had masked its glow with a piece of tin.

"I'll put it out immediately," Erich promised. He accompanied Clara to the trap door.

"Thanks," he whispered. "Thanks a lot, auntie."

"Don't thank me, Erich—we don't know how things will turn out," she replied. "This place is crawling with dyed-in-the-wool Nazis. If one of them finds out something. . . ."

Erich nodded. "I understand," he said. But his face remained calm, this old-young face of his.

In the hours since his arrival, when he had knocked at her door, a hunted man, a change had taken place in him. It had been a wild animal standing at her door, trembling, that evening. It was a human being standing before her now —in her husband's coat which was much too big for him and old, down at heel slippers.

She climbed downstairs quickly, shutting the trap-door behind her. For a whole minute she listened for any sounds from the floor below, but nothing stirred. Apparently her neighbours had not noticed a thing. She went to own bedroom, put the light out, crawled into bed and tried to sleep.

Am I doing the right thing? she thought. Won't I be placing myself in deadly danger ? Now, alone in her bedroom, she imagined the terrors of arrest, saw herself appear before the courts, heard the verdict—death, death, death!

Fear gripped her.

My God, I'm only a weak female, a little teacher, a poor creature. I haven't much strength really. Danger lurks everywhere ; even the walls have ears ; and I want to hide a Jew, a refugee from a concentration camp. My nephew. But he isn't even my proper nephew—not even my sister's natural child.

Oh God, give me strength.

This war, this ghastly war. Tomorrow I must go to school again. Tomorrow it'll be daylight, tomorrow they'll come and search for Erich.

I'm terribly frightened.

But then she became quite calm. Once in a lifetime you have to prove you're a human being.

With that thought she fell asleep.

Erich slept for sixteen hours on end. He did not wake till the following evening at six. Clara heard his light footsteps above her in the attic. She ran at once to the stairs, scrambled up to the loft and opened the trap-door.

"You mustn't leave your hideout under any circumstances," she whispered. "The man living below us is an arch-Nazi. If he notices anything. . . ."

"I'll remember," Erich answered.

She carried a bowl of steaming soup to his little room; he fell on it greedily, swallowing soup and bread within a few minutes. Then he contentedly wiped his mouth with the back of his hand. It was only when he saw Clara's gaze that he hid his hand in embarrassment behind his back.

"Er—I got used to doing that in the concentration camp," he said. "I don't think I can ever eat with a knife and fork again."

"Don't worry, you will," said Clara. He caught the reassuring note in her voice and looked gratefully at her.

"Do you want to tell me about it?"

He nodded. "But perhaps I can have something else to eat first?" he murmured.

Afterwards, when he'd eaten another two great slices of bread, he told his story.

Shortly after the Germans marched into Holland they had been arrested: his father, his mother, his two brothers, Kurt and Helmut, and himself. Probably his mother was in their black books because she had married a Dutch Jew. They were sent to Auschwitz. Very soon the parents were separated from the sons. In 1942 they were picked out for the gas chambers in one of the infamous "selections." They died together, on the same day.

The sons had to work. The standards demanded were so high that they could only have been achieved—and hardly then—under the most favourable living and working conditions with the most nourishing kind of food. But the Nazis, needless to say, did not see it that way. The young, strong Jews were exploited with the hardest physical labour and insufficient rations until they died.

The commandant of Auschwitz, Rudolf Höss, wrote in his diary: "At the wish of the Reichsführer, S.S., the concentration camps were geared to armaments production. Everything else was to be subordinated to that. All scruples had to be dispensed with. He therefore glossed over, consciously and unequivocally, the general conditions in the camps, which had become intolerable. Arms production came first; every obstacle had to be removed.

"I had to be harder, colder, more pitiless still in the face of the prisoners' hardships. . . . I could not be held up in my task by weakness and infirmity. This had to be disregarded in the pursuit of the ultimate object: that of winning the war."

In 1943 Kurt Blomberg died in Auschwitz. Helmut Blomberg disappeared without trace. Erich never found out what became of him. He himself was at the end of his tether when he decided—with the last spark of his instinct for self-preservation—to escape.

It was pretty hopeless. He knew that. But he only had these alternatives—freedom or death.

"It was on October 29. On that day we were taken by truck to an out-door working party; we had to work in a quarry. Towards noon, one of the overseers shot a comrade who couldn't go on working and who had dropped down to rest, completely exhausted, on a piece of rock. The guard shot him from the front, in the face, right between the eyes. It was terrible. We all knew that sooner or later the same end was in store for us. A shot from a rifle, or death in the gas chamber.

On the way home our truck got mixed up in a Wehrmacht convoy. Heavy lorries with troops drove in front of us. We tried to overtake, but got wedged in between the army lorries. This distracted the attention of the guards, who were standing at the back of our truck with guns at the ready.

It was a split-second decision.

The guards were staring down at the army vehicles, not looking over at us at all.

I pushed forward, shoved one of the guards to one side and jumped.

I tumbled on to the road right in front of the next truck; the driver had no time to brake and the vehicle just rolled over me and past.

I scrambled up and ran—into the wood!

Behind me I heard yelling, the scream of brakes, hooters blaring.

I ran through the wood; twigs struck me in the face, thorns tore my flesh. I scratched my hands on branches; I stumbled over a tree stump and fell. Then I dragged myself to my feet again and ran on. I jumped over a stream and sank into a sea of soft mud up to my ankles.

Silence behind me. But I kept running. My feet would hardly carry me now; but I was running for my life.

Soon evening set in. It was dark under the trees. I had to grope my way forwards from one tree to another. Eventually I came upon a nursery, thickly planted with young firs. I made a pathway through the mass of branches and crawled on all fours, till at last I reached a little clearing where I lay down for a bit.

I didn't know whether they were looking for me. I only knew one thing: I mustn't let them get me. I knew what they did with people who tried to escape, before they killed them. I'd seen one of them once, before they strung him up as a " deterrent " to the rest.

I slept till dawn, woken spasmodically by cold and hunger and the sounds of the woodland animals. But no one came.

At dawn I set off again. My prison clothes were stiff with mud and cold. I could hardly feel my feet any more, but I went on running, always in a westerly direction. I only had one aim; I knew only one person who could help me—you."

" You needn't be afraid any more," she said.

His smile faded.

" It's all wrong, what I'm doing," he said softly. " I'm putting you in danger, too."

" Let me worry about that," Clara said.

On the evening of the second day of his escape Erich

reached a lonely farmyard. He looked into the cattle shed through the open door; no one there but the cows devouring their feed. They turned to look at him as he entered. A pair of khaki trousers and a cardigan hung on a nail in the corner of the shed; on the other side of the partition, constructed of rough boards, a man was whistling. He took the trousers and woollen jacket from the nail and disappeared as silently as he had come.

He got rid of his camp gear in the wood and put on the clothes he had stolen.

He slept in the wood that night, too. Next day he begged something to eat in a village. Hunger had driven him to the pitch where he risked going among people without considering the danger involved. Mostly he lived on water from the streams, or turnips that he dug up. In the end he no longer knew how much time he'd spent wandering. He no longer knew how many villages he'd passed through, in the night, when people were asleep; how many sentries he'd slunk past without being noticed. He couldn't remember anything clearly any more; it was like a horrid dream. He ran and ran, and found no end to it. Once he went to sleep in an empty shed in a factory yard. There was an air-raid warning, and the first he knew was being woken by the sound of people passing by as they came out of the air-raid shelter. Another time he stumbled into a deserted signal box and threw himself, half dead with exhaustion, on a camp-bed there. Finally he ceased to worry about anything. But he did not give up. He won through. He covered the whole of Germany—and came to his destination in the end; to the only person whom he knew in that world on the other side of the barbed wire.

It was terrible. In the night Clara woke herself up with her moaning. She dreamed of what Erich had told her. Dreamed of concentration camps. She dreamed of the horrors that were enacted there; she dreamed of his escape. In the dream it was she who was the hunted one; her feet sank in clay, she couldn't move them forward; her pursuers were hot on her trail. Then she screamed and woke up, stared, drenched with sweat, into the darkness and heard in the distance the eerie howling, with its strange swelling and dying, of the siren.

Air-raid warning.

She had to go to the cellar alone ; naturally she could not take Erich along. He sat upstairs in his hideout, and none of the inmates of the house suspected his presence. Clara offered up a silent prayer ; it was for him she prayed.

She knew how terrified he was when the aircraft droned past over the neighbourhood and the ack-ack guns barked ; when the explosions shattered the night.

She tried to make his life in that gloomy den of his as comfortable as possible. She bored a hole in the ceiling through to the attic for an electric lead, so as to provide Erich with light. He used to read his Hebrew Talmud for hours on end ; he had preserved it through all the dangers of life at camp and carried it with him on his flights : a tiny book with close print, the size of a pocket diary.

Clara's husband came home at week-ends. From Friday evening onwards she could not visit Erich. She would tremble until Monday, fearing her husband might find out something. She knew she could share the secret with no one, not even with him. At week-ends, therefore, the electric light lead was taken away and Erich would be supplied with a cold buffet for two days. At such a time he could not move from the spot. During those days Clara was always listening, involuntarily, for any sounds from the attic. Her husband accused her of being nervous ; she certainly was.

The weeks passed. Erich recovered gradually. His old fear of his persecutors left him, but the fear of discovery remained, both for him and Clara. Erich's food supply, too, was gradually becoming a problem. It was the sixth year of war. Clara Greulich had to live off her ration cards, and those meant breadline rations by then. Now she had to share what little she had with Erich. What was barely enough for one person had to suffice for two. Every morning at school, after lessons, she would collect the slices of bread which the country children had left and take them furtively home in her pocket. Erich devoured them with the hunger of a man who has been starved for years.

The longer Erich remained, the more the two of them

became accustomed to the dangerous game of hide-and-seek they were forced to play. But the risk that the youth would one day be discovered increased all the time.

Clara read the Wehrmacht reports with burning eyes; followed the victorious campaign of the Allies in the west; hoped every day that the war would end. December came, and with it the German counter-offensive in the Ardennes. It was a terrible blow. Would the war go on for months yet —would the tide turn again? Would evil still prove victorious; would this great miracle, which Goebbels so mysteriously and equivocally proclaimed, still take place?

"I had the feeling that the ground was giving way beneath my feet; that I must be drowning," Clara Greulich said. "Already I could hear the knocking at the door, the command 'Open up, police!' I could see Erich being led away in handcuffs, and I could see myself, alone and abandoned, before inflexible judges. Can you imagine what it meant at that time, in a little country town, in a rented flat in a house where the landlord was a 100 per cent Nazi and had eyes and ears everywhere, to hide a Jew who had fled from a concentration camp? Can you imagine the sleepless nights, the fearful thoughts—can you understand that?"

I didn't answer. I sat opposite her, on the worn, old sofa, in the narrow farmhouse room at Bronsfeld. At the back, in the garden, was the new house, still in the process of being built. The retired teacher had built it from her savings. Not for herself—she was now sixty—but for her son's sake, a boy of eighteen. She had not much in life for herself. She was a teacher; she had tried all her life to bring education to dour country children; during the war she had risked her life for a young man she hardly knew. And after the war she had to struggle through on her own, for she had divorced her husband.

"You know how it is; you get old and then the men look around for younger women, for young girls." Her smile was resigned. "But that's neither here nor there. I'm only glad that I didn't speak to anyone about Erich, not even to my husband."

Bronfeld is in the Eifel, in the midst of deep woods of fir trees. It lies far beyond the hills, and life moves easily there.

She lives here, with a cat and a sheepdog called Rolf, who will not stir from her side. She is a simple woman and she was surprised that I should visit her; she did not want to attract attention.

She knew, however, that to act as she did then was not something to be taken for granted; she did not try to gloss it over. She did not pretend it was just nothing. It was terrible; she lived in constant fear.

"Christmas came. I'd knitted Erich a pullover on the sly. I snatched a moment when my husband, during the Christmas holidays, wasn't in the house, and crept upstairs to the attic to present Erich with the pullover and cakes I'd baked myself. He cried like a child. He was a Jew, but for him Christmas was the festival of peace just as it is for us Christians. Peace, however, still evaded us.

"I tried to talk to him and comfort him. He looked at me and said: 'Christmas next year I'll live like a free man, next year I won't need to hide myself away any more—either that or I'll be long since dead.'

The days that followed were very frightening. My husband stayed at home most of the time. Sometimes it seemed to me as if he were listening to sounds from upstairs, from the attic. He followed me suspiciously with his gaze; his eyes wandered after me round the room as I did my housework. Did he suspect anything? Didn't he trust me? I was half crazy with fear."

Shortly before Easter, 1945, German troops fleeing from the fast-approaching American forces streamed through Borken. During the night American artillery fired into the township. A few houses were set on fire. As the men hurried out to put out the fire Clara slipped upstairs to Erich and whispered to him: "They're coming!" He pressed his hands to his face and sighed gently. He whispered some words in Hebrew to himself and she knew he was praying.

Yet another agonising night passed. But next morning there were heavy blows on the front door. The Americans had arrived.

"Erich visited me a couple of years after the war," Clara Greulich said. "He got married in the meantime. He's got a wife and children. He was wearing the pullover that I'd knitted for him that Christmas. We cried a little, and we talked about the past. His wife was sitting there, listening. She knew everything ; but she didn't really understand a word we were saying. No one who has not lived like that can understand it. Such a life changes a person. Erich had become a different person and so had I."

She saw me out and I said goodbye.

As I drove along I thought of Erich, fleeing through the wood, alone, hunted, in the cold of winter.

We had become different people, said Clara Greulich. Have we changed, too, we others, who have h d no such experience ? Are we greater in generosity, st nger in heart, more defiant in courage, more inflexible in love ? And that which happened then—could it ever happen again ?

" They [the Jews] are to be treated like the tubercle bacillus which can infect a healthy body. That is not cruel when you think that even innocent creatures of nature, like hares and deer, have to be slaughtered to prevent their doing damage. Why, therefore, should we spare the beasts who want to bring Bolshevism upon us ? "

Adolf Hitler to the Hungarian Regent Horthy, April 17, 1943.

11

The weeks and months have passed. For almost two years I have been travelling around working on this report. I have spoken to 87 eye-witnesses of that time ; there are 53 reels of recording tape in my archives filled to the last centimetre, as well as 14 fully-kept diaries and 322 letters that I exchanged with people whom this report brought me into contact with—an overwhelming wealth of material.

It is winter again. I have reached the last chapter of my report ; but I could write, oh, so much more. I could still spend months, years, perhaps, pursuing the trail of the past. But I must close my report some time. I must place the results of my labours before the reader so that he may judge for himself—were there such people, the few, who remained human beings in a world of inhumanity ? I should like to end this book with the account of an action of a courageous man—an action which saved the lives of hundreds of people.

" This world of ours will improve. I am sure of that." This is what the Evangelical pastor, Rudolf Strücker, said to me when I visited him in Cologne. Towards the end of the war Strücker was a mere sergeant-major in command of a vessel in the Baltic. I have saved up this account of his experience until the very end, because it reveals how people, in spite of the hopelessness of their position, can be inspired, through brotherly love, through hope for a new day and a new future, to actions which would otherwise have been inconceivable.

They lay in the last remaining bunkers. They lay in the mine craters. They lay in the ditches shattered by gunfire.

It was night. But the night was brilliant with the glow of the burning city, with flames of yellow and blue and red, with the orange-coloured flashes of the explosions. And over all lay the ghostly, green light of flares.

The ground thundered beneath the impact of the grenades. The wretched defences were shattered by machine-gun fire. Red Army ground-to-ground rockets droned ; Russian anti-tank guns rapped out their fire, sharp and clear ; gunfire and final shock coagulated into one single sound.

Dust trickled from the top of the dugout. The wounded were moaning.

No more Evipan, no more morphia. No tetanus serum, no bandages. Nothing. The doctors looked at each other. Faces pouring with sweat, pale masks, evasive, shifting looks.

The fracas of combat was approaching the city—what was left of it, that is.

In the shelter of house walls refugees sat, pressed tightly together. Deserters scurried from one furtive hideout to another to avoid the military police.

This was Pillau, in East Prussia, the night of April 25, 1945.

In the harbour, which had been seething with life for weeks past, all was quiet now. The Navy had saved thousands of refugees and wounded from the Pillau bridge-head, which had been cut off from the rest of the front, by running a daily service across the Baltic. But now the harbour approach was commanded by Russian heavy artillery. A few ships—a couple of minesweepers, one or two little coastal steamers, an M.T.B. and a tug were caught in the trap.

The crew on the tug "Buzzard" squatted dumbly side by side and waited for the end in stunned submission. They heard the raging of the last battle around Pillau. A bottle of schnapps went the rounds. There was an atmosphere of resigned despair.

Apart from the merchant seamen among the crew there were also three officers of the German Navy, among them Sergeant-Major Rudolf Strücker.

This man was standing on the deck, staring over at the land, which gleamed with the reflected light from the explosives. His hands convulsively grasped the rail.

"Don't imagine such stupid nonsense," he was telling himself. "Don't get such ideas into your head."

But—he had heard it quite clearly.

Where he had been sitting below deck with the others, he

had heard it, unmistakably: someone had called his name. Clearly, distinctly. Not Rudi, as his mates called him, but " Rudolf," the voice had called, " Rudolf!"

It had been an order.

" Rudolf!"—A third time.

Then he had rushed out, looked around him, but there was no one there.

It was just his imagination.

He had heard his name. There was no doubt about that.

Something was going to happen! That voice, that command—yes, it was a command.

The lieutenant who was to take command of the tug had not appeared. Strücker was now the highest-ranking soldier on board. The civilian skipper of the tug was under his orders.

We must get out of here. That is what the message must mean, just that.

Out of here? To save our lives? Our petty little lives?

But maybe we're still wanted—somewhere there are human beings, perhaps, who still need our help—desperately.

He stumbled down the iron staircase.

" Get ready to put to sea!" he ordered.

They stared at him as if he had gone mad.

" How d'you think we're going to get out of the harbour? " the captain asked. " The Russians are covering it with gunfire on three sides! Do you think I want to commit suicide? "

" What does it matter whether we get shot to bits here or at the harbour mouth? Come on, get ready!"

" Not on your life!" said the captain, jutting his jaw forward.

" We have to get out—we have to!"

" No!"

" In the name of Jesus!" said Strücker, loud and clear.

The captain stared at him with distended eyeballs. Slowly his mouth closed. He gulped.

It was very quiet in the cabin. They heard only the thunder of the explosions on shore; German commando troops were blasting the last vital installations.

Suddenly the captain turned on his heel and went up on the bridge. " Full steam ahead!" he shouted down to the engine room.

They steamed ahead.

In front of them a coastal steamer was making for the harbour mouth. The Russians fired ranging shots. The third burst of fire was a direct hit in the middle of the engine room. She sank within a few minutes. A ferry, packed with soldiers, was hit. Flat, long boats, the last refugee boats, hove-to before the harbour mouth and were shot to pieces.

The "Buzzard" was under way.

Bursts of fire to bow and stern. To port and starboard. Columns of water shot to the sky and then collapsed. The deck seethed with foam. Thunder and hurricane, lightning and fireburst—then they were through. The open sea took them in its arms, the sheltering darkness. They had made it.

"In that moment I didn't know why we had even attempted this quixotic *tour de force*, much less how it was we managed it. But I had heard my name ; I had received an order ; the command of an inner voice, or of a higher being—as you will. In that terrible hour of our breakout I had no idea, as yet, that I was just a tool, destined to do something, in a decisive moment, which would save hundreds of lives."

I was sitting opposite Rudolf Strücker in his bright office on the first floor of the City Evangelical Mission in Cologne. Outside the noonday sun shone, its glow caressing the kindly face of Strücker as he spoke. He was a tall man ; he wore a well-cut, greyish-blue suit. He spoke slowly, with the somewhat lilting intonation of the Rhineland. He comes from Wuppertal.

"You can't imagine what it was like. It was terrible."

Today, Strücker is director of the Cologne Evangelical Mission. The new church built two years ago—the Mission centre—is near his place of residence.

Strücker leaned back in his armchair. "We had given up completely . . . but then a miracle happened—we were safely out on the open sea."

I glanced at the sketch map he'd got ready for me.

"And then you made for Hela ? " I asked.

He nodded. "Then we made for Hela." He was silent for a while. "It was there we took over the barge—with the concentration camp prisoners."

The Hela peninsula. Heavy bombardment. A minesweeper guided the "Buzzard" into the harbour basin by megaphone. There was a job awaiting the tug: in the harbour lay gigantic cargo boats, high sea barges, chock-a-block with people. As the tug approached the barge it was about to take over, Strücker and his men saw:

Heavily armed guards, S.S. reservists, national guard—all assembled for'ard on the deck. Further back were people in tattered clothing, with shaven heads and skeletal faces, torsos with no flesh on them.

They were concentration camp inmates, Jews and political prisoners, Norwegian Resistance fighters from the camp near Strutthoff for "Germanic" prisoners.

Strücker held his breath. What was going to happen to these people?

Then came the command from the shore: "Concentration camp prisoners to be taken to Sassnitz. They are to form a convoy."

As they got under way they could see that there were three tugs altogether, to which this gruesome freight had been entrusted. Each of the tugs was pulling a barge with about a thousand prisoners.

Once on the open sea they received an order: they were to detach themselves from the convoy. The convoy dispersed, under the attack of enemy U-boats and aircraft. The three tugs were proceeding at quite a distance from each other. Each of them was now on her own. Far behind each tug rolled the barge, with its cargo of human wretchedness, on the tow rope. Strücker stared over at his barge. But he could not see what was going on there.

Many years afterwards Dr. Olga Barnitsch was commissioned in Tel Aviv, in the interests of Israeli historical research, to question survivors of this death voyage about conditions on the cargo boats. On a hot evening in April in the Israeli seaside resort of Natanya, she reported to me as follows:

" All who were on that voyage confirm unanimously that there was incredible congestion on the barges. The barges towed by the ' Buzzard ' and ' Eagle ' had women, for the most part, on the upper deck; the men were in the cabins below where there was no daylight and no air.

The boat was absolutely crammed with people ; we were exclusively women on the upper deck. I could not see who was below because I was lying, or kneeling, in mid-deck. You couldn't stand upright "—so the witness J. Kremer reported.

Arie Maierowicz, who was seventeen then, reports : " One night we just couldn't stop in the cabin because there were so many corpses. Everyone wanted to get up on deck for some fresh air. With the help of a fellow-sufferer I eventually managed it up there."

The witness Martinowsky reports : " We were loaded on to a long barge which had various compartments, separated from each other by board partitions. They segregated the prisoners according to nationality. I was with a group of Jews below deck. Here there were plank-beds piled up, which we rested on. The Norwegians were in another compartment. We were all men ; where the women were I don't know. There was no chance of changing your place or walking around—the boat was so crammed with prisoners. I'd say there were about a thousand people."

" The barge was full of pig dung," reports the witness Chaja Ber. " We had to board her by means of a narrow plank. Many people fell into the water in the process. I didn't ; somehow I managed to keep my balance, though I hadn't been able to walk for ages. We were tightly wedged together in the barge.

The prisoners received no food during the whole voyage. A few managed to scrounge some Scandinavian rye bread from the Norwegian prisoners on the barge drawn by the 'Buzzard.' This was from the Red Cross packages they were allowed to receive in camp.

There was nothing to drink. Some people, maddened with thirst, swallowed sea water, which they drew up in tins or buckets tied with string or wire. Many died from the effects of the salt water, others from hunger and exhaustion. Some even committed suicide. Things had got to the pass where people were jumping into the water of their own accord. Two Jewish women bound themselves tightly together with towels and jumped overboard. They tied themselves together so as to increase the weight and then the sea would swallow them up quickly."

The German crew on the "Buzzard's" barge did not show itself.

"The German guards locked themselves in a separate cabin," reports the witness Kaicer Perla.

All the same, the Germans had their "representatives" on the barge, Polish kapos, who persecuted the Jews with particular ferocity. "It was dangerous to go on deck. Those who went out to relieve themselves over the rail were pushed into the sea by the Polish kapos."

It was not fear of the Jews that caused the German crew on the "Buzzard" barge to remain in hiding. As witness Martinowsky rightly stressed, they had every reason to be wary of the Norwegians. These were policemen by profession, who had fallen foul of the occupation authorities back home and had therefore got deported to concentration camps. In the circumstances they constituted a considerable danger to the Germans. The Jews, on the other hand, were —as Martinowsky goes on to say—"all absolutely finished, quite exhausted; they couldn't have done a thing to the Germans. My own example just goes to show—I was 22 then and weighed no more than four stone."

This assumption, that the Jews were much too enervated to think of resistance, is borne out by what happened on one of the other barges. According to eye-witness reports there were only Jews and Ukrainians on this one.

"On the very first evening the Germans called out for volunteers who felt like shoving people into the sea. A few Ukrainians stepped forward. They picked out some people from among us, whom they then threw overboard. Those selected were undressed, dragged up a steep iron ladder and thrown through the hatch into the sea. This was their method of relieving congestion."

Witness Josef Gar also confirms this. "Every day the S.S. killers used to hunt out people who were sick and fling them overboard. Hundreds of women were murdered this way."

This was the scene on the cargo boats during the voyage out across the Baltic—through winter storms, minefields, enemy naval blockades; but at last the transport reached the harbour it was bound for, Sassnitz, on the isle of Rügen.

"You can't imagine how relieved I was as we finally approached the harbour," Strücker went on. "I had seen the people back there on the cargo boat; I could visualise their sufferings. Sometimes visibility was impeded by mist and fog; high waves hid the barge from the tug, but we could all picture what was going on there. Let's make land quickly, so that these people get something to eat and drink; that was my first thought. But I had reckoned without the harbour commandant. A motor-boat approached us and called to us. Permission to land refused. We should proceed to Warnemünde. I was in despair; but there was nothing I could do. We had to turn course and proceed. The ghostly Odyssey continued.

Bad visibility the whole way. Then a storm came up; pitch black night with thick fog descending on us. My greatest worry was the living—and dying—freight we were towing. But I could talk to no one about it. One couldn't trust anybody then.

At one critical juncture I sighted a lighthouse for a few seconds. I assumed that was Stralsund; we anchored. That was our salvation. When dawn broke we saw the danger. Steep cliffs, towering right before our bows, on which we could have been dashed to pieces. Later in the day we hit on a minefield without knowing it. We noticed it after a while from the wrecks of shipping floating around everywhere. It was certainly a miracle that nothing happened to us.

Eventually the weather changed; the fog disappeared. All we knew of our human freight was what we saw. As the sea became calmer we let the barge approach closer and pulled in the rope. What we saw was horrible. Many of the prisoners hardly had underclothes left. They were torn and filthy. They had to relieve themselves over the rail. I just can't find the words for some of it—it was so abominable."

Strücker was silent. He had clenched his fists, involuntarily. This serene, self-possessed man was overpowered by the memory. In his eyes I saw the inner conflict of days gone by repeat itself.

"That's how it was," he whispered.
I did not answer. I waited for him to proceed.

From that moment onwards, when Strücker saw the miserable prisoners for the first time, it was clear he had to help. But every act of assistance had to be carefully thought out. After all, there were also the prisoners' guards on the cargo vessels. True, most of them were conscript guards, old men who had been haphazardly raked up in Danzig and Hela—people who would never have dreamed that they would be enlisted as concentration camp guards in the last days of the war; but there were also some S.S. firebrands among the guards, and they were capable of anything.

Strücker knew he had to land the prisoners soon. Hunger and thirst were killing the weakest. He had to fix some provisions, and he had to see that the guards were lured down from the barge by fair means or foul.

The next port was Warnemünde. Now they were approaching it; but they couldn't land there, either. They set course for Travemünde. On the flat-bottomed cargo boats death went the rounds. Strücker's despair increased.

His experiences at the ports they'd hitherto approached had taught Strücker something. He ordered the barge to ride at anchor in Travemünde. The tug steamed into the harbour, the crew landed.

Strücker reported: "Everything there was in a state of disintegration. Mad disorder everywhere.

"At the landing-stage was a derailed railway train stuffed with provisions. We confiscated sacks of potatoes, crates of pickled fish, margarine. Marines and soldiers grabbed what they could. I got a box with tins of cooked ham in it. We also dragged a few barrels of diesel oil to the 'Buzzard.' After all, there was no possibility of landing the prisoners now. Nobody wanted to take the responsibility. We proceeded to Neustadt, in Holstein."

Time was running through Strücker's fingers. Something had to happen if he was still to help the prisoners.

Shortly before Neustadt the "Buzzard" sailors suddenly heard piercing shrieks from the direction of the cargo boat. A seaman called Strücker over to the rail.

"They're chucking the prisoners overboard!"

A low mist lay over the sea. You could hardly distinguish anything. Strücker let the towrope in. What he saw made him stop breathing.

S.S. men, even prisoners—presumably the Ukrainian and Polish kapos the survivors mentioned—were helping to knock down the women with butt-ends of rifles and then pushing them over the rail into the water.

Strücker pulled the tug right up close to the barge.

For'ard on the deck of the barge stood an S.S. major, hands on hips.

Through the megaphone Strücker commanded him to step on board the tug.

The S.S. officer, obviously taken by surprise, did what he was told.

"What do you want?" he bawled at Strücker, but his voice did not sound too confident.

"We're approaching Neustadt harbour. I must ask you to go with me to the town commandant, so that we get a final decision on what is to happen to the prisoners. These people must be fed as soon as possible."

The S.S. officer's hand slid to his holster. "How dare you give me orders! I ought to shoot you down!"

Strücker: "Shoot, then!"

They stood facing each other for a whole minute, their eyes glaring. Then the S.S. officer gave in. "All right," he growled. "Quite honestly, I'll be glad to get rid of that mob."

One has to assess the situation very carefully to appreciate what Strücker did. Here—on the tug—half a dozen unarmed merchant seamen, who couldn't care less anyway, and two members of the German navy under the command of a sergeant-major. Over on the barge dozens of S.S. men armed with automatics and machine-guns. There was no question of armed combat. Only cold, clear calculation and resolute action could help Strücker along now—and save the prisoners.

In Neustadt harbour Strücker and the S.S. officer went to see the town commandant. But there they received the same orders as before: Proceed! They were told to make for Lübeck.

They had hardly left Neustadt before they heard over the radio that the English had already occupied Lübeck and were advancing on Neustadt.

Now Strücker could not hesitate any longer.

" I changed course and made for Neustadt again. It was already dark when we arrived. There was complete chaos: deserters, detachments still eager to fight, refugees, escaped convicts, soldiers, civilians, women, old men and children. Most of the privates were drunk.

" I landed and pretended I wanted to obtain fresh orders. Shortly afterwards I boarded the tug again and explained to the captain that I had received an order to get the German guards down from the barge.

Strücker was silent for a while. Then he said. " You will ask me why I didn't take the tug through to Lübeck and deliver up both tug and barge to the English. I have to confess: there weren't only prisoners and S.S. men on board but also countless members of the reserve force and national guard, elderly men who up to then hadn't harmed a hair on anybody's head, and who had never had anything to do with concentration camp prisoners. They were picked up, herded together and put under S.S. command in Danzig, over 200 of them. Now they were sitting over on the barge as ' guards,' under the watchful eyes of a couple of dozen S.S. criminals. However, the English would not differentiate ; they would hold them responsible, just like the S.S. scoundrels, for the conditions on the cargo vessels, and would probably stand them up against the wall without ceremony. I had to think of these men, too, not only of the prisoners ; fathers with families, who had got into this position quite innocently. The few S.S. fanatics would get their deserts sooner or later!

" We steamed up to the barge on the tug. I bawled through the megaphone : ' All Wehrmacht servicemen on board here at once, with weapons and ammunition!'

" They literally rushed on the tug. Their relief was obvious from their expressions.

" Towards one in the morning we had put the whole lot ashore, about 250 strong. We loosened the rope which towed the barge and steamed with the ' Buzzard' into the inner harbour basin. The prisoners were now left to themselves. I was convinced that they would realise the position and act accordingly."

His calculations were correct.

The Norwegians on the barge, tough types, whose will to survive had not been broken, even by concentration camp, soon noticed that the tide had turned when Strücker ordered the guards on to the tug.

The leaders among the Norwegians assumed command as soon as they noticed that the tug had cut its rope.

On shore, meanwhile, the guards had vanished into the darkness. The tug's crew went ashore, too. Flares illuminated the horizon, heavy gunfire rolled in the distance. Everyone was waiting for the British.

Strücker remained in the harbour to see whether the prisoners made good use of their freedom.

"When it was light I saw the invasion. The prisoners had made sails out of sacking and manoeuvred the barge ashore. As I heard later, it was the Norwegians, who were still in the best of health, who took the initiative. At crack of dawn I was able to observe how the prisoners, exhausted but free, reeled over the green landing strip towards the town."

A few hours later the English entered Neustadt. Strücker was made a prisoner-of-war but the prisoners were saved.

Strücker was most reluctant to talk of his action. He regarded it as the most natural thing in the world. He only regretted that he could not do more, that his reactions had not been swifter. But if he had betrayed his intention to help, by as much as a look or a word, what would have happened, undoubtedly, would have been what the S.S. man threatened; he would have been shot down. Not a single prisoner would have escaped alive. One of the three barges which had been taken over in Hela by the tugs " Buzzard," " Eagle " and another one (name unknown) was sunk in the Baltic, with 1,200 people on board, by the crew of the tug. As for the human freight on the second, they were shot in Neustadt by pupils of the naval military college there, just because the tug's crew dumped them ashore unprotected, thereby delivering them up to the last ditch fanatics still roaming around. Only the prisoners of Strücker's barge escaped alive, because he had enough presence of mind to let the boat ride at anchor in the first place. " To land them immediately would have meant their death warrant. Therefore, I took what seemed in the circumstances the only possible course. I found no cause to regret it."

I take a trip homewards up the Rhine. In the background a tug tows several cargo vessels. On one of the boats a woman is hanging her washing up. A little black dog runs over to her and jumps up at her. A pleasant scene ; but I can't help thinking of the boats in the grey winter days on the Baltic, eighteen years ago, and the gruesome cargo they carried ; of hunger, cold and death. And I can't help thinking of Strücker and his last farewell words : " Oh, don't make so much of it. It was the obvious thing to do—you would have done the same."

During this conversation we were standing in his mission church. The light streamed through the high windows, and it was as if the stillness could never be shattered by the screams of suffering humanity.

And yet we both knew that the stillness was deceptive. We knew that the past is not dead ; that hate, cruelty and intolerance can rise again tomorrow, albeit in another form. But we have to prevent that. Whenever and wherever inhumanity raises its head again we must simply strike it down. We must be watchful ; for the enemies of freedom are lurking everywhere. Their disguises are extremely effective.

But we must not let ourselves be deceived. We must not let up in our struggle. Struggle is the mould in which our whole lives, and this century we live in, are cast. Struggle against injustice, against inhumanity and against servitude. That is the destiny of our generation. We cannot forget it ; we do not want to forget it ; and we never will.